The Man I Thought You Were

ALSO BY LEAH MERCER

Who We Were Before

The Man I Thought You Were

LEAH MERCER

LAKE UNION
PUBLISHING

This is a work of fiction. Names, characters, organizations, places, events, and incidents are either products of the author's imagination or are used fictitiously.

Published by Lake Union Publishing, Seattle

www.apub.com

ISBN-13: 9781503943223
ISBN-10: 1503943224

Cover design by Lisa Horton

Printed in the United States of America

The Man I Thought You Were

CHAPTER ONE

Anna

The last thing I remember before my husband left me was the quiet satisfaction of caramelising onions to perfection. Even now, gazing back through the hazy filter of time, I can see myself leaning against the oven, the sharp scent of frying onions stinging my nose. I stare down at the translucent golden slivers in the pan as heat glazes my cheeks, with one ear cocked towards the door as I await my husband's return. I'd no idea of the coming blow, which would be like a sucker punch to the heart. The blow that would shatter what I thought was my flawlessly formed world.

Ten wonderful years together, and our life was like one Pinterest-perfect photo of coupledom after another: dining in flickering candle-light or cuddling up in cosy blankets, devouring books at opposite ends of the sofa with our feet entwined. I believed we could stay that way forever. Perfection can't last, though . . . and maybe it's only an illusion, anyway. It's what happens in the real world that counts. I know that now.

But on that day, the day my husband went away, I focus only on keeping the onions soft, without any black singeing their tawny edges. I stir them quickly, hurry to the bedroom to shed my work clothes, then rush back to the kitchen for more dinner prep. The familiar routine is comforting, like a book you read over and over despite already knowing the ending: home, work, home, dinner prep . . . then the creak of the door as Mark returns. The feel of his arms around me, the scrape of his stubble on my cheek and a quick pat on my bottom before darting away with a piece of whatever food I've left prepared on the counter, ready to cook. Every day is the same.

Every day but that one.

That one, Mark doesn't put his arms around me. His tie is loose and his face is pale, and his suit hangs off him like folds of sagging flesh. It strikes me that he's lost some weight – or has he? He's always been slim, and I did see him naked just a few nights ago. My cheeks go red as images scroll through my mind: his hands on my skin, his lips on my neck at the *perfect* spot . . . We've always had a great sex life. That's never changed, not from the moment we married. My sister, Sophie, says she hasn't touched her husband, Asher, in almost a year! Granted, she does have a child to contend with, whereas so far, it's just Mark and me. For the moment, anyway.

'I need to talk to you.' Mark's voice cuts into my thoughts, and I reach up and pinch his cheek – a gesture guaranteed to make him grin. But this time he flinches and moves away, and I wonder if I've hurt him.

'Oh, sorry.' I smile, trying to make his long face lift. It's rare he comes home moody. Usually he's only too happy to escape the corporate world. Mark works as the branch manager of a high-street bank, a job he doesn't particularly love, but has been doing for years, despite me telling him he's way too clever to stay put. Mine is the fun job, lecturing in the English Department at University College London. I love the students, their energy and their enthusiasm. I love their fervour when they discuss books and their total absorption in the material.

I'm really going to miss that job when I go on maternity leave – hopefully in the next year or so. We've been trying for a while now, with no result. We're not exactly ancient, and I know it *will* happen, but sometimes I wish we'd started sooner. We've been talking about a family since we first got married, but Mark wanted to ensure we had enough savings in the bank 'just in case', as well as a healthy sum in our house fund. And although I was itching to have a baby, I had to agree with his caution.

It's one of the things I love about my husband: he always puts our little family first. I suspect that's the reason he stayed at the bank for so long, despite me pressuring him to go part-time and get a degree. He loves reading, and I pretty much give my lectures twice, once at work and once at home.

'Let's go into the lounge.' Mark leaves the kitchen and sinks into the armchair, leaving me no choice but to follow. His movements are stiff and jerky, like his muscles have forgotten how to bend. I'll give him a good back rub after we finish dinner, then stick him in bed with a hot-water bottle. He could do with some relaxation after working late all last week.

I spread out on the sofa, plucking a piece of fluff from my leg. It feels so good to sit after being on my feet lecturing all afternoon, although I really do need to stir those onions before 'caramelised' becomes 'charred' . . .

'What's up?' I ask, flexing my toes to stretch my calf muscles. *Ah, that feels divine.*

Mark clears his throat and shifts on the armchair, his chest rising as he takes a deep breath. 'I need to leave, Anna.'

My head snaps up. 'Leave? What do you mean?' Mark doesn't go anywhere. Neither do I, for that matter. Our life is together, *here*, and that's all we need. I reach into the recesses of my mind, and a memory filters in of Mark saying something about a corporate away day for branch managers. That must be what he's talking about.

'Is it the away day?' An idea strikes me, and my mind starts whirling. 'You know, if it's in a nice hotel, maybe I can get tomorrow off work and come with you. We could spend the weekend there.' I've never taken so much as a sick day and I should spend more time reviewing my notes for the next week's lectures, but I don't teach on Fridays, and I'm sure I could manage to escape my research and marking for a day. A smile builds as I picture the two of us, hand in hand, strolling through a country garden.

And maybe . . . maybe we might get lucky there; maybe we might finally get pregnant. It will be the right time of the month for me, and the more we can try, the better. *More than 'better', actually,* I think as I picture me and Mark tangled up in perfectly crisp white linen, the windows wide open to the rolling green lawns . . .

My smile fades when I notice Mark's head shaking back and forth, back and forth, like he's trying to stop my waterfall of words from pouring over him. 'No, no. You don't understand. I'm leaving *you*, Anna.' He goes still, and his eyes lock on to mine.

'What?' My jaw slackens, my breath coming quickly as his words try their best to burrow into me, pushing and prickling at my skin. I want to move away from them, but I'm frozen in place.

Mark gets to his feet, pacing back and forth across our creaky floorboards. Every step is punctuated by a sharp squeak, and I wince. I keep meaning to get those fixed, maybe I'll look into it tomorrow – I jerk my head. What the hell am I doing? My husband's just told me he's leaving, and I'm worrying about the floorboards. But I still can't believe it's true. It's like he's speaking another language that I'll never understand.

Finally, Mark stops and sits on the armchair again. His cheeks are flushed now, two circles of red standing out against his chalky complexion, like a toddler who's got into his mum's blusher. Before I know what I'm doing, I squeeze into the chair with him until my body aches – that's how close I am to him. I need to touch him, to feel that he's solid and real. That *we're* solid and real, despite the words he's just uttered.

I reach out to take his hand. His palm is sweaty, but his fingers are cold, and I rub them between mine like I have countless times in our life together. But instead of drawing me close and burying his head in my neck, breathing me in as if I'm a power source for his draining battery, he jemmies himself out of the chair and crosses the room to the sofa, away from me.

I watch mutely as Mark runs a hand through his salt-and-pepper hair – the hair that's morphed from a sandy brown into this sexy version – and swallows. His Adam's apple bobs up and down, and I think how I know every inch of him so well, both inside and out. That's how I'm sure that whatever he's saying right now, it can't be how he really feels. How could it? We've done practically everything together these past ten years, from morning to night – building a life. Our world is each other. I meant it when I pledged my heart and soul, and I know he did, too: he's proved it in every single one of his actions, from the moment we met. I didn't wait years for someone like him to come along in vain.

I get to my feet, my legs trembling beneath me. 'Mark, you're being silly!' My laugh is less of a warble and more a distress cry. 'Right, I'd better go stir those onions before they stick to the pan.' I take a step towards the kitchen, but before I can escape, Mark grasps my shoulders.

'Anna, stop.' He looks me straight in the eyes. My gaze is glued to his, as if we're engaged in a staring contest and whoever blinks first loses.

I try to slip from his grip, but he won't let me. 'I can't . . . I can't be here any more,' he says finally. He glances around the room, at the cocoon we've spun together, and my heart starts beating fast as fear courses through me.

'What do you mean?' I can barely get my tongue to form the words. My mouth feels like the Sahara. 'But . . . *why*?'

Suddenly Mark is the one twisting away from me. 'Please.' His voice is like a plea, and it goes straight through my heart. 'Let me go. I have to go.' The words drift over the top of him, hanging in the air like a poisonous cloud. I try not to breathe them in, but they settle, cold and clammy, tainting every surface they touch. I step towards him, knowing there's no way – not in a million years – I'll let him go. We're too together, too *happy*, to fall apart.

'No.' I take his shoulders now, trying to make him face me. His muscles are like cement beneath my fingers, refusing to yield. 'I won't. I won't let you go.' I shake my head so hard that pain shoots through my neck. 'Sit down, okay? Just . . . sit, and we can talk.' If I can get him to tell me what's wrong, I'm sure we can fix it. Together, like we always have. I try to tug Mark on to the sofa. For a second he tilts towards me, like he's going to give in. And then he pulls away and ducks his head, his chest heaving like he's fighting with something inside of him.

'I need to go now,' he says. He turns towards me again, and I draw in a breath at his expression. It's something I've never seen before: a kind of defeat, maybe, mixed with pain and longing. 'Please don't try to contact me. It'll be easier if you don't. I've transferred some money into your personal account. There's plenty of money in our joint account for bills, and—'

'Mark, stop!' I put up a hand. 'I don't care about any of that. I don't need to know any of that. Come on, just sit down for a second.'

But he continues as if he hasn't even heard me. 'If there are any problems with the boiler, Asher can sort it out. He knows where the manual is. Anything else, look in the drawer by the kitchen sink. All the numbers you'll need are there.'

I shake my head, his words flying around me. *Boiler? Kitchen sink?* I can barely decipher what he's saying.

And then, because I don't know what else to do – I can't do anything else right now, anyway; it's all I can do to keep breathing – I watch as Mark puts on his coat – the coat he took off just minutes past, though that already feels like a lifetime ago – picks up his keys, yanks open the door, then closes it behind him.

Just like that, my husband is gone.

CHAPTER TWO

Anna

I don't know how long I sit on the sofa after Mark leaves. I barely move, waiting for the creak of the door as it opens again. Waiting for my husband to come home, to throw his arms around me and to say he didn't know what he was thinking – that of course he's not leaving. How could he?

The acrid odour of burnt onions taints the air, and I shuffle to the kitchen to remove them from the hob. The late-October sky is pitch black now, the streetlights bathing our lounge in an orange glow I used to think was so romantic. Now it seems alien, like something that's invaded my space and changed the world around me.

Just like Mark's words.

Let me go. I have to go. Let me go. I have to go. The horrific phrases bounce through my head like a twisted nursery rhyme whose upbeat tune belies its sinister meaning. I can't believe Mark has left me, I really can't. For goodness' sake, we've been trying like crazy to make a family, something I know he's keen on. *Very* keen, if the last few months are anything to go by. You can't morph from ardent family man to deserter in a matter of seconds, and the thought of Mark skipping out on me is laughable, anyway.

Whatever's happened, whatever the reason he *thinks* he wants to leave me, we can get through it. Everyone always says they've never seen two people so into each other (Sophie accompanies this with a roll of her eyes), and although that sounds a little cringeworthy, it's true. Being married – and staying married – has always been our top priority. Thanks to our parents, we've both seen first-hand how relationships can collapse. We've always been careful to ensure our marriage is first on the list of everything we do, from dinner together each night to chatting for hours about everything under the sun.

I catch my breath as I realise Mark hasn't taken anything – no suitcase, just the clothes he was wearing and his keys. My legs unfurl as if they have a mind of their own and move me to the bedroom, where I pull out drawer after drawer, each still filled with Mark's neatly folded clothes. His coats are hanging on the back of the door, his umbrella and his backup one on the hook beside them. This means he's coming back – of course it does. My husband won't even walk the short distance to his car without carrying an umbrella . . . Wait, *is* his car here? He rarely uses it, but he refuses to sell it in case we need it in an emergency.

I race to the window and look down at the street, my heart rate slowing when I see its metallic hulk gleaming under the street lamp. I head back to the lounge and sink on to the sofa, relieved my certainty has been vindicated. Whatever happened obviously shook him, but he'll be home soon and we can talk then. I look at my watch: he'll be back in an hour if he wants to catch that movie on Film4 we've been looking forward to. I can't wait to curl up with him, to rest my head on his chest like I always do and hear his heart beating beneath me as everything else fades away . . . the same as we have done practically every night of the year.

As we've got older, we've been happy to stay in rather than face the battle of the Tube after work, fighting the city to meet people we haven't seen for months. It might have been fun to hit the cinema or head to the theatre, but as Mark always says, why go out when we have everything we need right here? When he first said that, the sentiment made me smile, and I couldn't help thinking how lucky I was with him: I never had to compete for his affections with loads of mates and boys' nights out, which I'd heard other women complain about.

Right from the moment we first met, he's been there for me whenever I needed him. In all the years we've been together, he's never given me any reason to doubt his love. And I'm not going to start now.

My mobile buzzes in my hand, and I catch my breath again. Any small hope it might be Mark fades when Sophie's name pops up, and before I can send her call to voicemail, my fingers have already swiped 'Answer'. My muscles tighten and I take a breath, telling myself to keep it together. There's no reason to make a fuss when Mark will be back soon. But Sophie can read me like an open book; she was the first to witness my excitement when I met Mark after all those duds.

I was worried at the time she might scare him off – she may be only eighteen months older than me, but she acts like a mother hen, clucking around me and making sure I'm okay. She's always been that way, at least since that terrible time when our father left us for almost a year. Mum went to pieces, retreating into herself and blocking off the world – blocking off *us*. Sophie was the one who made sure I was ready for school on time, that I had a packed lunch (I'll never forget her version: a piece of stale bread and a broken biscuit) and that I did my homework. Even though Dad came back – and Mum did, too – the role was ingrained in her, and she carried on.

I didn't mind, really. Having her watch over me was comforting, and her stamp of approval really meant something. She'd never sanction anyone who might hurt me; we both knew the pain that came alongside that. Thank God she and Mark clicked straight away. I'll never forget how she leaned over and whispered in my ear, 'He's a keeper,' within minutes of meeting him.

And she was right: he *is* a keeper. I know that with every fibre of my being. I won't let him go, he must realise that, the same way I know he wouldn't let me go, either.

'Hiya!' Sophie's boisterous voice bursts across the line. 'Just wanted to tell you don't worry about babysitting. Asher's actually going to be home tomorrow night, for once, so he can keep an eye on Flora.'

For a second, I've absolutely no idea what she's talking about. Then I remember that tomorrow's Friday and that Mark and I had promised to take care of my niece in the evening so my sister could go to a friend's baby shower. With a husband who works every God-given hour in a City law firm, I know how much Sophie looks forward to any child-free excursion. And Mark always jumps at the chance to babysit Flora, which has lodged him even more firmly into Sophie's good books.

Eight-year-old Flora absolutely dotes on Mark and always has done . . . and Mark dotes on her just as much. Mark can spend hours playing with her menagerie of toys, watching endless YouTube videos and even singing karaoke to One Direction (shudder). It's surprising, given that Mark isn't exactly a paragon of pop knowledge, but it's so endearing. Watching Mark with my niece always makes me excited for the day when we might have kids – the day we *will* have kids.

'Oh, okay,' I say, happy that she's cancelled before I had to. I can't imagine Mark spending the whole night away from me, but even if he does come home in the next hour, there's no way I'd have the mental or physical stamina now to make it through the evening with Flora. Mark and I will both be exhausted after tonight, and we'll need to regroup – to pull ourselves in tightly again and remember what it is that makes us so good: our connectedness, how we're so in sync with the other's wants and desires and how we hold our marriage sacred.

'Mark will be disappointed,' I say to keep up the ruse. It's not a lie. He *would* be disappointed. Just yesterday he was saying that he hadn't seen Flora for ages and he couldn't wait to hear her news. I shake my head so hard my neck throbs with pain. What could have changed since then? What happened?

Maybe an argument with someone at the bank? Or . . . I shake my head again, wincing at the pain. Mark would never let anything from work spill over into our relationship; he's not the type to release his stress at home. If he does say anything about work, it's funny stories about customers or colleagues. I tried a few times, back when we first got together, to get his advice on department politics, or even just vent when one class gave me a particularly low score on my teaching evaluation, but Mark got so incredibly upset – almost more than I did – that I took a page from his book, keeping any work worries away from us. I like how our place is untainted, how our relationship is a refuge. And anyway, I can talk to Sophie about work if I need to.

He'll be back any minute, I tell myself for the millionth time, staring at the door handle as if it might turn this instant.

'Everything all right?' Sophie's voice interrupts my thoughts and I jerk upright, like she has a direct line into my mind.

'Oh, fine. All good here.' My voice trembles a bit, and I cross my fingers, hoping she hasn't picked up on it. 'Just busy . . . You know.'

'Do I ever. Work has been crazy.' Sophie runs her own online children's clothing shop since being made redundant from a marketing job a few years ago. 'And Asher hasn't been much help lately, either. I don't even know where he is half the time. Sometimes I'd give my right arm for a job like yours, to escape to a proper office every day.'

I stay silent, because even though a university setting is far from a 'proper office', it *is* an escape. I can't think of a better job than one where you get to read, research and discuss books all day. And actually, the university brought Mark and me together. I was giving a public lecture at the department one evening on Thomas Hardy and Mark approached me afterwards to say how much he'd enjoyed it. He'd never had the chance to go to university, he'd said, and he wanted to start reading the classics to make up for lost time.

We talked for a few minutes before he asked me out for coffee, and despite hearing Sophie in my mind (he's a stranger! You've only just met him!), I couldn't help saying yes. His soft brown eyes seemed kind, and I could tell by his questions that he was definitely intelligent.

The night was wet and windy and, as usual, I'd forgotten my umbrella. As we stepped outside to make our way home, Mark sheltered me under his. A sudden gust flipped it inside out, leaving us exposed to the elements, and he quickly ushered me out of the storm and into the glowing lights of a nearby cafe. Dripping wet and cold, we sipped our steaming hot chocolates, hunkering down on a sofa as rain lashed the windowpanes. The chocolate warmed our insides, the mugs our fingers, and it seemed so natural when Mark reached out to take my hand. The staff started stacking chairs and sweeping the floor, but we didn't budge. Somehow, we knew we'd found what we'd been looking for.

About time, I'd thought.

There's a shriek in the background at Sophie's end followed by a loud bang.

'Oh God, what's she broken now? Right, I need to go. Have a good weekend. Talk soon.' And with that, Sophie clicks off.

'Bye,' I say, staring at the phone as silence throbs in my ears. We used to love the quiet of our place, lying on the sofa with our bodies intertwined . . . no need for words to cloud the air. But now the silence presses down on me, a void that needs to be filled. I get up slowly and cross to the window. I stare hard at the street, *willing* my husband to appear from around the corner, but the pavement below stays empty.

I sit down. I stretch out on the sofa, I curl up, then I gaze down at the mobile again, my fingers itching to touch the screen. I won't call him – I don't need to. He'll be home soon – back here. Back with me, in our world, where he belongs.

CHAPTER THREE

Anna

Time ticks by, but the door doesn't open. I switch on the TV to view the film we'd planned to watch, an innocuous romantic comedy with a guaranteed happy ending, forcing myself to pay attention since I'll need to give Mark a summary when he returns. But all too soon the credits scroll up the screen, and I'm still alone.

Panic and fear swell inside of me when I realise it's almost midnight and Mark is still out there in the dark. Where on earth could he be? It's impossible to imagine him sleeping anywhere other than here. Since we married, I can count the nights we have each spent away from home on two hands . . . all for work-related events. I would have loved to travel and see the world together – I'd have done a gap year in a heartbeat if I'd had the nerve (and the money) – but Mark wanted to use any extra income to pay down the mortgage on our flat and save for a house. I had to agree it was the most mature, if not *adventurous*, option.

'This is ridiculous,' I mumble, grabbing my mobile that's resting on a cushion by my head. Whatever the reason he left – whatever the reason he asked me not to contact him – this is still the same man who is building a future with me. I hold my breath as I bring up his contact details and hit 'Call', my heart beating so loudly I can feel it pounding in my ears. As I listen to the phone ring, an odd buzzing sound comes from beside the door. I follow the noise to the side table, my mouth falling open when I open a drawer to see . . . Mark's mobile.

His voicemail clicks in and I end the call, reaching down slowly to draw out his phone. *That settles it, then – he's definitely coming home,* I think with a smile, remembering how he's forever telling me to make sure I have my phone with me in case I need to call. Any minute now he'll burst back inside, shaking his head with that warm smile of his and telling me he must have lost his mind. Not only did he leave me, but he left his phone, too! I'll roll my eyes – Mark has a way of making even the worst situations into fodder for cheesy sayings – and throw my arms around him, banishing the past few hours from my mind.

I sink down on to the sofa, my phone on one side of me and Mark's on the other, and stare at the door. Another film ends, and then another, and as the morning breakfast shows cheerily chirp their way into the new day, my certainty is punctured by little darts of doubt . . . and fear. It's almost eight o'clock now and Mark is still gone. My husband left suddenly, taking nothing with him – not even his mobile, his connection to the outside world. Leaving everything I know he holds dear. Leaving *me*.

I stand up and stare out the window, trying not to panic. Mark has never been one to share his feelings. He's generally always in a good mood, but there are times when he sinks into himself, turning quiet and sombre. His silences make me nervous and jittery, and I used to try to talk to him, to coax him to open up. Gradually, though, I learned to trust him . . . trust that he'd return to himself – return to me – and he always did. But now . . . could this be the one time he's shut himself off for good?

No, I can't think that. I won't.

I drop back on to the sofa and take a deep breath. I know my husband. I know he loves me and loves our life. Whatever has happened – whatever he believes has happened – I have absolute certainty that we can fix it, that we'll want to fix it . . . together. Nothing is as important as *us*.

My mind flips back to our second date. Mark had asked me out for dinner just two days after we'd first met, saying he couldn't wait to see me again. Sophie had smirked when I'd told her that, telling me to make sure I'd actually shaved my legs for once (it'd been a while, I'd had to admit) because I was finally going to get some action. I'd rolled my eyes, because even if it had been ages, I hadn't been ready to jump into bed with a man I'd only had coffee with – unlike Sophie, who'd shagged her way through half of Reading Uni, if her stories were anything to go by. I'd never been into one-night stands. I found it hard to let myself go and just have fun.

But Mark, well . . . Mark had been different from all those other guys who'd filled our dates with talking about themselves, as if I were simply an add-on to their world. Mark had looked at me (not my cleavage). He'd asked questions and actually listened to my answers. My job, my life: he'd wanted to know it all. And after we'd polished off our delicious chocolate bombes, he'd taken my hand and told me he wasn't interested in mucking around. He wanted to find a person who was real, a person to spend his future with.

I'd nodded, relief flooding through me that I'd finally found someone on the same page – someone I could really see myself with twenty years from now. Someone I could trust.

I still trust him. I still trust us. And even if I've no idea where he spent the night (God, that sounds strange), when nine o'clock strikes, I know where to find him. Come hell or high water – which did happen once when the bank flooded – he's always made it to work well before the opening time. He has the keys and he hates to keep people waiting outside. Whatever's happening in his personal life, he'll be there in about an hour.

And so will I.

I grab my mobile and leave a quick message that I won't be coming in to work today – thankfully, I don't have lectures – then pad into the bedroom, relief making my muscles less rigid. Soon all this will be over. Soon my husband will put his arms around me, will tell me whatever's plaguing him, will let me in. And then, together, we'll go home again.

I run a hand through my hair, grimacing as it meets with tangles and knots. Mark's never particularly cared about what I wear, saying I look gorgeous whatever state I'm in. But I can hardly show up at his work looking like I've been dragged through a hedge backwards, although after my restless night and in the aftermath of the adrenaline that had been coursing through me, that's exactly how I feel. I wrinkle my nose as I examine my sweat-stained T-shirt: I don't smell so great, either. I need a quick shower, something to wash away the horror of last night and start afresh.

I peel off my clothes, my skin looking even paler than usual in the grey morning light filtering into the bedroom. A memory bubbles up of how Mark would often stand behind me here as I undressed, wrapping his arms around my stomach and pulling me up against him, whispering into my ear that he liked me best with nothing on. And then . . . then he'd lower me on to the bed and we'd make love, the soft, dove-grey duvet cushioning our bodies.

Sophie was right – I *did* get lucky that night with Mark, and the sex ten years later is every bit as wonderful as it was that first time. He has a way of making me feel so cherished, like I'm the most important and valuable thing in the world to him, and even though I was beyond nervous all that time ago, I couldn't help opening up and abandoning my fears and worries under his thorough ministrations. The bond between us felt so real – so solid – that I gave myself to him completely.

I throw open the wardrobe now, averting my eyes from the row upon row of Mark's shirts – shirts he hasn't taken with him. For a second I wonder what he's wearing to work today, then I push the thought from my mind. I can't linger on any doubts or uncertainties; I need to keep moving. I dress quickly in jeans and a jumper, then run a brush through my hair, grab my keys and close the door behind me.

Outside, the air is heavy and still, smelling of damp, diesel and the pungent odour of rotting leaves. I hurry down the quiet, tree-lined roads towards the high street, past huge houses hiding behind high iron gates. Even though we've lived here for almost all of our ten years together, I still can't believe how lucky we were to nab a spacious two-bedroom flat in this area.

'It really is an ideal place to raise a family,' the estate agent had said, and Mark had squeezed my hand as we'd smiled at each other like one of those happy couples straight from a TV property show. With good schools, proximity to one of the biggest open spaces in London and a villagey feel about it, it was everything the estate agent had promised. Highgate *is* the perfect place to start a family – fingers crossed it happens soon. Mark tries to hide it, but I can tell he's getting a little anxious that nothing's happened yet. Sophie doesn't help – she's always regaling us with stories of how she got pregnant on the first try. It's normal for it to take a while, though, as I keep telling Mark.

Sweat drips down my brow and I wipe it away as I climb the steep incline towards the row of shops. Rooftops rear up in front of me and I hurry over the crest of the hill, eager to glimpse the lights of the bank on this dark autumn morning – a beacon guiding me to my husband. But the closer I get, the more that panic scrabbles at my gut. There's no welcoming brightness; no lit-up adverts on the bank's windows featuring smiling faces of happy customers. The building is dark and sullen, like it's crossing its arms and frowning at me.

'Where is he?' I ask one of Mark's colleagues hovering outside the locked door. The smoke from her cigarette clogs the air and the smell turns my stomach. 'Where's Mark?' I crane my neck to look inside the building, hoping to catch sight of something, but the foyer is shadowy and still.

The woman stubs out her cigarette and shakes her head. 'You tell me. Wherever he is, he's not here.'

I lean back against the door, my heart sinking so fast it feels like I'm going to pass out. I was so sure he'd be here, so certain this would be the end of that terrible night – a night in which we were cut off from each other. If he's not at work, then where the hell *is* he? *Maybe he's just taking the day off,* I tell myself, despite the fact that, like me, Mark hasn't had a sick day in forever.

The rattle of keys makes me straighten up, and for a second, hope leaps inside me. 'Mark?'

'Just me.'

I turn my head and see that it's the assistant manager (Ahmed, I think it is).

'Sorry I'm late,' he says to his colleague, who just nods and pops some chewing gum in her mouth. 'I only got the call to come and open up this morning.' He turns towards me. 'I just heard that Mark resigned. Head office called me about eight. Bit sudden – I hope everything's all right. Are you here to pick up his things?'

Resigned? I stare at Ahmed and gulp in air, but my breath still comes shallow and fast. Mark has quit? My husband doesn't love this job, that much is true, but he *does* love what it provides: a pay cheque, security and savings for the future. The Mark I know wouldn't trade those in for anything. I gulp as my heart starts beating fast, and the fear I've tried to keep at bay balloons inside me.

'Anna?' Ahmed unlocks the door and motions me forwards, then flicks on the lights. 'Come in. Do you remember where Mark's office is? This way.'

I blink against the harsh fluorescent lighting, numbly following Ahmed past the tellers' counter and through a glass door, where Mark's metallic desk gleams. The empty walls and barren desktop are in sharp contrast to the comfortably cluttered environs of our flat. Just our engagement photo perched by the computer monitor graces the room's clean confines. I catch my breath as I look down at it, trying not to read too much into the fact that he has left this behind, too.

We both prefer this photo to our official wedding picture, which looks tense and staged – in fact, I don't even know where it is right now. I squint down at our two glowing faces. God, we look young. My cheeks are flushed with happiness and cheap cava, and Mark's eyes stare steadily at the camera as if he's trying to telegraph that this, right here, is exactly what he wants.

I close my eyes, and I can almost feel the soft air of that summer evening – hear the *swoosh* of traffic on the road outside my tiny studio flat. We were drinking kir and stretched out on the sofa after stuffing ourselves with the gnocchi I'd managed not to burn in my minuscule kitchen. Something about the tropical temperatures – and, okay, maybe the bottle of cava we'd shared earlier – had cast a spell on us, making the night seem almost otherworldly. Out of nowhere, Mark pulled me on to his lap and whispered into my ear that he wanted to make me his wife.

We'd only been dating for a few months and we'd never even talked about marriage, but I didn't pause before saying yes. I loved him, I loved what we had together and I wanted it to stay that way . . . forever. And when he slid the ring on to my finger, something clicked into place within me: a sense of security, of safety. Finally, my life felt anchored.

The rest of the night was a blur. We finished our kir, then Mark offered to pop down to the off-licence for some celebratory bubbles. I went with him, not wanting to let him out of my sight for an instant. I just wanted to clutch him close, to feel the bond between us – the bond that would always be there.

It was at the off-licence that the photo was taken. Unable to stop my happiness from spilling over, I blurted out our news to the man behind the counter, who offered to snap the picture. We posed against the streetlight outside, on the corner of a busy road – not exactly the most romantic location, but it didn't matter. The glow of our faces bathed in the soft light from the lamp above us made the photo seem like pure magic. And that's what I want to hang on to: that bubble of happiness, unsullied by anything. That's what I need to protect.

'Not much to take with you, I guess,' Ahmed says, cutting into my thoughts. 'Mark was never one to linger here. He'd just finish the work and go home. He always said he had something better to get back to.' He grins at me, and despite everything, I can't help smiling back. I can picture Mark saying just that – Sophie would always tell me he'd win the award when it came to cheesy sayings. I have to admit, I quite like it.

'He was a great boss,' Ahmed says. 'Although I did notice he was a bit off his game these past couple of weeks. I'd never seen him take so much time off in all the years I've known him. Sneaking away to interviews, I guess?' He winks. 'Anyway, we'll miss him around here. Please give him our best, and tell him to pop by and visit.'

Mark took time off? I nod at Ahmed in a daze as his words float over me, then I scoop up the photo. I say goodbye and stumble out to the street. My legs weaken and I slump down on to a grimy bench, struggling to absorb the fact that my husband has left his job. What the hell happened? Because it has to be something, right? People don't make such radical moves without a reason, especially not someone as steady as Mark. He's been at the bank for years; he's been with me for years. What on earth would compel him to throw that away?

Throw *me* away?

I try to breathe through the confusion and worry crashing through me. However much I don't want to believe it, this *isn't* like those other times when Mark simply went quiet, then came back, and our wonderful world remained intact. Now it seems my husband is trying to dismantle the life we carefully built, the life we cherish. I can't believe it's true, but it is. And I won't stay quiet. I won't let him do this to us. Whatever he's going through, he needs me to be strong for him . . . for us. I glance down at the photo and our two smiling faces.

'Till death do us part,' I say, shivering in the cool autumn air. I meant the pledge then, and no matter what my husband is going through, I mean it even more now.

CHAPTER FOUR

Anna

I hurry back to our flat, as if the space we inhabit might tell me something about where Mark's gone – as if being surrounded by our treasured items will impart clarity. I set down our engagement photo in pride of place on the oak coffee table and gaze around our lounge. The corners are crammed with bookcases stuffed full of novels we've devoured and discussed, and the walls are covered in paintings we've carefully selected. We even hemmed the stupidly long curtains together, swearing as we pricked our fingers with needles (it's safe to say neither of us is a skilled sewer).

I've never lived somewhere I've loved so much, and even though I know Mark longs for a proper house when we have kids, this flat will always be the first place I finally felt . . . safe, I guess. Even after my father came back, it seemed like we were living on the edge, as if one wrong move might send him off again.

I close my eyes as memories swarm my brain, memories of the day my father left. It was summer, and Sophie and I shared a room back then. We woke up early, like we always did in the school holidays, full of excitement at the day ahead. Mum always had something wonderful planned; she had a way of making even a walk in the woods feel magical.

But that day we didn't spring from our beds. That day we stayed inside our room with the door closed, the duvet up to our ears as we tried to block out the sound of our mother sobbing. We didn't know why she was crying, of course – not until we finally crawled from our safe haven and padded down the stairs, still in our pyjamas. Not until our mother faced us, eyes red and swollen, and said our father had gone.

We stared at her, not sure what she meant, until she gathered us in her arms and started crying again. Then we knew. He had left her . . . left us. She said he'd be in touch with us, and he was – every few weeks or so, by phone. But of course it wasn't the same. He really had gone.

I shake my head now, thinking that, all these years later, I still don't understand why my father left so suddenly. We asked, of course, but Mum would only say they needed a break from each other. *A break?* I thought. How do you take a break from marriage? Sophie just scoffed, saying Dad wanted to 'dick around' – that of course there was another woman. Wasn't there always? The words sounded funny coming from a twelve-year-old's mouth.

I wrap my arms around myself, as if I can shield my heart from the questions battering my brain. Has Mark taken off like my father? Does he want a break . . . a break from me, from our marriage? And try as I might, I can't stop Sophie's words from ringing in my head, her words about another woman. She's wrong, I know she is. There *isn't* always another woman, but . . .

A memory from a few days ago niggles at my brain. Mark's mobile rang, and I went to answer it like I usually do if it's closest to me. But this time he lunged at it before I could get there, then took the phone into the bedroom. I couldn't hear much through the door – the high buzz of a woman's voice, and then his own lower tone – and when I asked casually who it was, he just shrugged and told me it was one of those annoying telemarketers. He looked so tense that I hadn't wanted to force the issue, so I let it go, even though I knew he was hiding something.

I grab Mark's phone and enter the password, my cheeks burning. I'd never felt the urge to snoop on his mobile, not even last night when I first found his phone. But back then I'd believed he'd be home again in a matter of hours. Now, after discovering he's quit his job, I realise it may not be that simple.

I can't believe I'm doing this, I think, holding my breath as I scan his texts and phone calls. There's not much there, just a few messages and missed calls from me in the past couple of days, and then nothing before that. That's not uncommon: Mark always kept his mobile 'neat and tidy', unlike my phone, which is crammed with texts from years ago.

I look though his recent numbers, but once again there's nothing . . . everything has been deleted, as per usual. I bite my lip as Ahmed's voice runs through my mind, saying how Mark has had a lot of time off lately – time off I knew nothing about. There *have* been a few days when Mark had said he needed to work late, which is odd since he rarely works past six. And he did beg off making love a couple of times recently, which is also completely unlike him, especially when we've been trying so hard to have a baby.

My head pounds and nausea churns my stomach. I put my hands to my temples and focus on breathing in and out, in and out. I can't actually suspect Mark of cheating on me, can I? Mark, my husband, who has spent the past ten years making me – making us – his number one priority?

I jump up and grab our laptop, the computer we share at home. I don't know what I'm looking for and I still can't believe I'm doing this, but I just need to . . . check. Sophie always says it's strange that we share a computer, but I don't think so. We even have the same password: our anniversary, of course. Like Mark's phone, though, I've never delved into his email. I've never needed to.

I type in Mark's username and password, my face hot – not with the shame of snooping this time, but with a mix of fear and panic. As I click through his messages, I don't know whether to cover my eyes or strain even harder to see, but there's nothing there, anyway . . . even his junk mail has been emptied. If he *was* up to something, though, it wouldn't be the brightest idea to leave evidence lying around on a shared computer. I log in to our joint bank account on the off-chance he's withdrawn money – a long shot since we never touch it for anything other than household expenses, using our personal accounts for everything else. The usual mortgage, bills and grocery debits fill the screen, and I slam the laptop lid closed.

A mad kind of desperation sweeps through me and I jump to my feet. I start upending the sofa cushions, rummaging through the cupboards, flipping through books . . . looking for something, anything, to sweep away my fears – something that will give me a clue to my husband's whereabouts. Inside the bedroom, I shake out socks and pants, unfold trousers and T-shirts and rifle through shirts. But all I uncover is a forest of folded receipts: this one from the Chinese takeaway around the corner that gave us both stomach pains for the rest of the weekend; this one for the extra bookcase from IKEA we had to order for our overflow of novels. Snippets of an ordinary, wonderful life that are now tainted with uncertainty.

I slump to the floor, staring at the mess around me as despair and frustration filter in. I've torn the place to bits and I've found nothing either to fuel or allay my doubts; nothing to bring me closer to finding or understanding my husband. I'm surrounded by the unremarkable minutiae of our usual life, but everything has changed.

CHAPTER FIVE

Anna

Somehow, I make it through the weekend. I hole up inside the flat, not even leaving when I run out of milk, just on the off-chance Mark might return. Thoughts spin through my head and I clutch at each one, trying desperately to make sense of my husband's disappearance – without thinking it might be another woman, that is.

Has he had some kind of nervous breakdown? Is he one of those people you sometimes hear about . . . someone who seems perfectly normal, but then suddenly cracks? I shake my head, struggling to apply that theory to my calm, steady husband. But then, it couldn't have been my calm, steady husband who jacked in his life, could it? Fear shoots into me as I wonder if he *has* cracked – and if maybe he's done something to hurt himself.

Mark wouldn't do that, I tell myself as my heart beats fast. He can't bear to hurt a fly, let alone inflict pain on himself. Even so, I reach for my mobile and google the numbers of the local hospitals, foot tapping as I call and wait for them to tell me if he's there or not. I'm not quite sure which answer to hope for: I want to find him and hold him close, but I can't bear the thought of him injuring himself, for whatever reason.

I let out a breath when I put down the phone twenty minutes later. Wherever Mark is, he's not lying alone in a hospital bed. Maybe . . . maybe I should try the police? But say what? *My husband told me he was leaving me, and – surprise! – he left!* It's not like he's vanished unexpectedly.

Try as I might to keep my doubts from growing, I can't stop thinking of that phone call I overheard, of Mark's time off work, of the nights Mark didn't want to have sex. It's impossible to picture my loyal husband cheating on me, but . . . I could never have pictured him leaving our life, either. I barely sleep, unable to get comfortable in the huge, empty expanse of our bed, and after calling in sick again on Monday morning, I decide I finally need to talk to Sophie.

It's been strange keeping all this to myself for so long – Sophie's the one I always chat to when I'm upset or need help. I've never talked to her about Mark, though . . . I've never needed to, and somehow it would've felt like breaching the boundaries of my marriage. But I know she loves him, and she loves us together. And right now, I'm in desperate need of reassurance, not to mention direction.

I throw on an old jumper and a pair of jeans, then grab my jacket and head for the door. Sunlight streams through the trees and the air is so fresh it hurts my lungs. It's a gorgeous day, but I'm too tired to contemplate walking the short distance to my sister's, so instead I head to the car. I fit the key into the lock and swing open the door, sliding into the driver's seat. I'm miles from the wheel and I ratchet the seat forward, thinking it's been ages since I've driven. There's no need to in London – it'd take about twice as long for me to get to work, anyway – and Mark's always driven us on the odd times we have taken the car anywhere. This is fine by me, since the only time we came close to arguing was when Mark taught me to drive.

I was happy to take public transport, but Mark insisted I learn to drive, just in case I was ever caught in a situation where I might need to. I was surprised by just how much I enjoyed it: the wheel in my hand, the rumble of the engine in front of me, the way the tyres hugged the road as it curved. I loved to accelerate, watching the trees and houses blur as the car gained speed.

But Mark had other ideas, urging me to slow down if the speedometer crept anywhere near the speed limit. I longed to sit back and enjoy the drive, but he peppered me with constant reminders to pay better attention, turn the indicator on earlier, watch for the upcoming zebra crossing . . . I had to clamp my lips closed to stop my growing impatience spilling out. I had never been more relieved than when I finally got my licence and the lessons came to an end.

I'm about to put the key in the ignition when I catch sight of the satnav. Mark usually keeps it tucked away in the glove compartment, but for some reason it's still stuck to the dash. I bite my lip, wondering if it might give me some clue as to Mark's whereabouts. Mark has driven this car somewhere recently; the satnav wouldn't still be out if he hadn't. I flick it on, mentally crossing my fingers. The screen comes to life and I touch 'Recent Trips', my legs jiggling as I wait for the information to appear. Finally, one name comes up: 'Margo'. I blink at the letters, trying to breathe through the nausea swirling inside of me – through the questions and dread now hammering at my skull. *Margo?* Who the hell is that?

My hand shakes as I reach out to touch the screen, and an address in East Finchley – just minutes from here – pops up. I sink back into the seat, my mouth suddenly dry, my stomach churning. I've never heard Mark mention the name Margo – I would have remembered, because he rarely talks about other people, not even his mum and dad. And to the best of my knowledge, he doesn't know anyone in East Finchley. I didn't think he'd ever been there . . . although this satnav clearly proves me wrong.

So who is she? Is he there with her now? Was my sister right and there *is* always another woman?

Before I can even think about it, I pull away from the kerb and into the street, following the satnav's calm directions towards East Finchley. Rush-hour traffic clogs the streets, and I go as fast as I can, lurching around cars and running through amber lights. Mark's voice rings in my mind, admonishing me, telling me to slow down, but I can't. I need to get there, to prove that whoever Margo is, my husband wouldn't betray me – wouldn't betray us and the life we are building together.

The closer I get to Margo's, the harder it is to breathe. I want to find my husband; I need to make sure he's okay. But what if . . . ? I swallow as I turn the car down a quiet street, the satnav showing I'm only a minute away. I slow as the screen indicates another turn, then spin the wheel and stop.

I must have gone the wrong way because I'm faced with a sign saying 'East Finchley Cemetery'. I stare at the satnav, then back at the sign, and then at the screen again. No, the arrow is showing that I've reached my destination, the very point that Mark has called 'Margo'.

I start up the engine and drive slowly down the path, pulling up in front of a stone chapel. Even though it's warm inside the car, I shiver. Today is a journey into the unknown – into a place I never even knew existed . . . a place Mark hid from me. And I'm not sure I'm ready for what I'll find.

CHAPTER SIX

Anna

I turn off the engine and yank on the handbrake – Mark constantly reminded me of its crucial importance – then open the car door. Cold air swirls around me and I pull my jacket closer, as if to protect myself from what is ahead. I don't know what I'll uncover here, but I do know one thing: my husband has been places and seen people that I never knew about. He's kept things from me, and the relationship I was so sure of, so *proud* of being one hundred per cent honest and open . . . wasn't.

Part of me wants to get in the car again and drive home, but I know that even if I do that, I can't go back. Whether there's someone else in his life or not, things are different now. Our world *has* changed. I take a deep breath, trying to stay steady despite feeling like the ground is shaking beneath my feet.

I head towards the chapel and push open the heavy wooden door, praying there's someone inside. Thankfully, I'm in luck: a bespectacled man is sweeping the floor in front of the altar. His lifts his head as I approach.

'Can I help you?'

'I hope so.' I swallow. 'I'm looking for someone called Margo?' It's an idiotic question, I know, but I've no idea if she's an employee, if this is where Mark meets her . . . or if she's even alive, given the location.

'Well, I'm the only person here . . . still breathing, that is.' He smiles and the corners of his eyes crinkle.

'Okay, well, could you help me find a gravestone?' I might as well start there.

'Surname?' The man shoves his specs further up the bridge of his nose.

Shit. 'Um, I don't know.'

'Come this way.' He beckons me up the aisle and into a small office that's crammed with yellowing books. The air is heavy with the smell of old paper and must. 'Any idea when she might have passed?' he asks.

I shake my head. 'No, sorry. I guess any time in the past sixty years or so?' I'm not sure if this Margo is related to Mark, if she's someone he knew, if . . . God, this is so surreal. I feel like I'm groping in the dark, unsure which way to turn.

'Well, this may take a while,' the man says, 'but I like a challenge. At least it's not a very common name, so we might be able to find the person you're looking for.'

'I'll wait. As long as it takes.' I sink on to a hard pew outside the office, every part of me humming with exhaustion. After what feels like forever but is probably only an hour or so, the man pokes his head out of the little room.

'I've found a Margo.'

I jerk to my feet and let out my breath as relief sweeps through me. If it's the right Margo, then at least she's no longer living – at least she's not someone Mark's with right now. But . . . who is she?

'What's her surname?' I ask.

'Margo Lewis,' the man says. 'Born 1981, died 2003.'

'Margo *Lewis*?' The same surname and just a couple of years younger than Mark? This is definitely the right person, but who is she?

Mark rarely talks about his family, but I know he's an only child, so was Margo a cousin? Or maybe . . . I swallow hard as a thought bubbles up inside me. Could she have been his *wife*? They would have been very young when they married, but I guess it's possible. Why on earth wouldn't Mark tell me, though? I comb through my memories, trying to remember if he'd given any *hint* of another marriage, but there's nothing. Mark's never even mentioned ex-girlfriends . . . It's just not something we ever needed to talk about. Now, I wish we had.

'Come on.' The man is shrugging on his jacket. 'I'm not busy today. I'll show you where the grave is.'

I nod mutely and follow him out of the church. Wind whips through the trees, leaves falling around us like crispy confetti. I shudder as I walk between the graves, picturing Mark coming here on his own . . . coming to mourn someone close to him, someone he never told me about. *Why?* The word seems to echo with every footstep as we crunch down gravelled pathways.

'Here it is.' The man stops after a few minutes, pointing to a plot. 'I'll leave you on your own now.'

'Thank you,' I whisper, barely able to speak as I stare at the gravestone in front of me. There's nothing remarkable about it: Margo's name carved in stone, along with the dates of her birth and death. A simple posy of marigolds graces the base, their vibrant blossoms a splotch of colour against the white granite.

My eyes trace the engraved letters like I can burn them into my soul, pleading with them to tell me something. *Who are you?* I scream inside my head.

I lean even closer, as if the stone might respond. Whoever she is – because it does feel like she's still here, a third person who's been present in our relationship – she must have been someone very special, very dear to Mark, to exercise such a pull on him all these years later. Someone he loved . . . someone with the same surname who was just a couple of years younger . . .

I catch my breath, pain slicing through me as the unavoidable knowledge sinks in: Margo must have been his wife – no other answer makes sense. I collapse on to the cold ground, images tearing at my brain, each picture carving itself into the sacred place we'd created.

Mark, smiling at her in that tender way I thought was reserved only for me.

The two of them exchanging a kiss as the registrar pronounces them husband and wife.

Them both cosying up in a flat just like ours, dreaming of their future.

Margo dying, leaving Mark all alone . . .

Did he find it too painful to even begin to tell me – me, the person closest to him? I shake my head, wondering if I'm as close to him as Margo was . . . wondering if *our* marriage is as good. I let out a puff of air, thinking that of course it's not. If it was, Mark wouldn't have left. After all, he wouldn't even be with me if Margo was still living.

I get to my feet and stare at Margo's grave, feeling for the first time that perhaps Mark and I are on different pages when it comes to our partnership. I'd always held our marriage in such high esteem, but maybe for my husband it was a kind of consolation prize. Anger flares inside me, and I stride away from the grave. Mark didn't cheat, but it still feels like he betrayed me – betrayed us – by keeping things hidden.

I climb into the car, feeling disorientated and lost . . . as if I'm gazing at my life through a different lens and can't make sense of anything. I'm no closer to finding my husband. If anything, he feels even further away.

CHAPTER SEVEN

Anna

I battle the traffic on the road, my mind spinning. I'm too full of emotion and questions to even speak, so instead of heading to Sophie's, I drive straight home. I need to get a grip on what I'm feeling – need to sit down and find my way in this strange, shaky world.

Mark was married. Mark had a wife before me. Mark is a widower. It all sounds so surreal that I can barely grasp it, let alone begin to understand why he didn't tell me. There *must* be an explanation for why he held back. Anger hits me and I pound the steering wheel with my hands. God, I'm tired of trying to read my husband's mind! I thought I knew him, but right now I don't have a clue what he might be thinking.

I drag myself up the stairs to our flat and flop on to the sofa, staring around at our home. Did Mark read lots of books with Margo, too? Did he choose the same colour scheme – sleep on the same firm mattress? Did she take the right-hand side of the bed as well – drink her coffee with the extra amount of milk he sometimes slops into mine? Did he kiss her neck in that perfect spot, too? Anger and something like jealousy burst inside me once again, and I roll my neck to ease the tension. I hate that I'm second guessing our whole life together now.

I lower my head on to a cushion, staring up at the ceiling. Could Margo have anything to do with Mark's disappearance or is it just a coincidence that he left me after visiting her grave? Did she know his family in a way I never did? Did she even meet his parents, to whom I've never been introduced? I never gave much thought to the fact that he kept me at arm's length from his family. His parents divorced when Mark was in his late teens, and Mark explained that he hasn't been close to his mother or father ever since – a situation I could completely relate to, since I'm not close to mine, either. The trauma of my dad leaving cast a shadow over our family, and none of us wants to unearth those feelings – and if I'm being honest, I'm not sure I can understand or forgive my mother for failing Sophie and me when my father disappeared. She came back to life once he returned, but it was too late – we'd already learned to cope without her.

The fact that we both lacked the steady presence of our parents in our lives drew me and Mark even closer together – made us even more dear to each other. We've always joked that at least we'll never have problems with the in-laws. But now . . . Now I wonder if he kept me from his parents because he didn't want me to know about Margo.

I drum my fingers on my chest, running through what I *do* know about his family. His mother went off to Australia after the divorce and his father remarried, making a new life in the commuter belt. The divorce blew the family apart . . . an outcome I can fully understand, even if my own parents are still together.

It's unlikely he's reached out to them, but they are a link to Mark's past. And right now, I can't help feeling that Mark's past has something to do with his present.

I grab the laptop and crack it open to see if I can find his mum and dad's contact information, email or otherwise. I click on 'Contacts' and scroll down the list of email addresses, thinking it's rather . . . short. A few people from the bank, identifiable only by the domain name; Sophie and Asher; Flora – I smile, remembering how she begged to have an email account so she and Mark could write back and forth to each other. Warmth rushes through me as I recall the two of them sitting here a couple of months ago, with Mark on this very laptop and Flora on her tablet, typing little messages, bursts of laughter coming from them.

'Like peas in a pod, those two,' Sophie'd said, shaking her head as she'd watched them. 'He's going to be great with kids, lucky thing. Asher didn't have a clue. Still doesn't, most of the time.'

I'd nodded, my hand sliding down to my belly, and I remember thinking that my period was due that day and it still hadn't come. Could this be it? I'd gazed over at my husband, his face creased with happiness, and pictured our child in this place, bringing even more light and joy to our lives. Like Mark, I couldn't wait to have a baby and give it the perfect childhood I'd never had.

But I wasn't pregnant. My period came that night, just as I was about to duck into the loo and take a test. I wonder . . . I wonder if Mark would have left me if I was having a baby. I shake my head as the answer resounds in my mind: no. I may not know everything about him like I thought, but I'm certain he wouldn't have walked away from his unborn child.

Right, here's his father: Richard Lewis. I jot down the email then scroll through the short list of contacts to find his mother, Helen. I stare at the names and tap my fingers on the table, the sound loud in the empty space. What on earth should I say? *Hi, I know we've never met, but have you talked to your son lately?* I shake my head and let out a breath. It feels so strange to finally be making contact with his parents all on my own – without Mark by my side.

I quickly type out a generic message to each of them from my own email account, asking how they're doing and if they've heard from Mark. I know it sounds strange and will likely open up a whole can of worms, but I don't have time to faff around. If only I had their phone numbers! I cross my fingers, hoping that I won't have to wait long for a response. As much as I'm dying to ask about Margo, I don't want to toss out that question in an email. I don't know exactly what happened, and I don't want to give them a reason not to respond.

I sink down on to the sofa and pick up our engagement photo, waiting for love and certainty to filter through me – feelings that this photo usually inspires. But as I stare down at our glowing faces, the swirling questions and doubts block out everything else, like fog shrouding the sun. My image in the photo morphs into the face I've been constructing of Margo, and I screw my eyes shut and turn away.

I just need to find Mark, I tell myself. I need to find my husband, and then everything will be okay. Right now, though, I'm not even sure I believe that myself.

CHAPTER EIGHT

Mark

The noise of buses and cars whooshing past the grimy window assaults my ears, and I roll over in bed without opening my eyes. I don't need to; I know exactly where I am. This dingy guest house in the bowels of Euston couldn't be further from our lovely flat in a quiet, leafy road. Images fill my head of Anna and me curled up on the brand-new sofa, indulging in our favourite weekend pastime. Not sex (although we loved that, too): online shopping, in the comfort of our own home.

After we first bought the flat, we'd open the laptop and cuddle for hours as the wonderful world of domesticity unfurled on the screen in front of us. No need to push through crowds at IKEA or dodge pushy furniture salesmen on Tottenham Court Road – we could make our home our own without having to leave it. Men aren't supposed to love shopping, I know, but this wasn't just browsing objects. This was choosing a life, a way to live.

A way to live that's behind me now.

I let out a puff of air, thinking how ironic it is that the dismantling of our world began with a desire to expand it: we wanted a child. It took a few years – almost ten, to be exact – until I was ready to contemplate having a baby. After Anna and I married, I was still too fearful, too worried that, despite my efforts, something would happen to burst the bubble we'd created. I was always watching, always waiting . . . for what, exactly, I didn't know. I just needed to be on guard – to protect what we had. I knew how it could be yanked away all too quickly.

But finally, with our life unfurling day after day – each new morning repeating the same comfortable patterns – I began to relax. The tension inside me – the tension that had been there for so long that it felt like an extra limb – started to shrivel, loosening its grip. It would never disappear, I knew that for sure, but perhaps I could risk stretching the barriers of our world even more. The walls were thick enough now to protect a baby. A baby I'd never, ever let down . . . not this time.

And then, despite our numerous efforts, nothing happened. Perhaps I was too eager – too impatient. The bottle of elderflower pressé was already chilling in the fridge, awaiting the big announcement of a positive test (if Anna couldn't drink, I wouldn't, either). We'd begun researching the best car seats, prams and Moses baskets, diving headlong into our dreams for our baby. Sure, we'd just started trying, but it's never too early to start planning, right?

Anna didn't seem worried. *It will happen,* she told me. *We're still relatively young, we're healthy* – although I'd been feeling so incredibly tired, with weight dropping off me despite forcing myself to eat. But I, well . . . somewhere deep inside of me, I couldn't help wondering if this was repayment for the past; if this inability to conceive was my punishment for letting go of that child all those years ago, despite the circumstances. That niggling fear drove me to the GP, who half-listened to my concerns while tapping on her keyboard, then she told me she'd do a physical and go from there.

'Go from there' didn't exactly lead in the direction I'd expected. 'Go from there' destroyed everything I'd built in one fell swoop, the pieces of my life that I'd thought were solid disintegrating into dust.

I won't have the child I so desperately wanted. I won't have my wife by my side. I won't have the world I carefully created.

I close my eyes, remembering the moment of diagnosis. I'd hoped – *prayed*, even, although to what I don't know – for my life to remain untouched by illness. Through the scans, the multiple tests and the agonising wait for results, I sent up plea after plea for everything to be fine. I should have known that you can't bargain with life, though. It'll give you up when it's ready.

Primary liver cancer . . . advanced, spread to the lymph nodes . . . four to eight months if I don't have treatment; six to eleven months with treatment that *might* slow the tumours' growth. The words washed over me, each one like a violent wave breaching the dam I'd constructed. I'd done everything I could to keep my life with Anna safe, but my body had betrayed me. The one thing I couldn't control was myself – and it's killing me.

A wave of pain sweeps over me, and automatically my hand reaches out for my phone as if I can connect to Anna right now, before I remember I left it behind. I didn't mean to – thank *God* I deleted all the text reminders of appointments and the histories of my phone calls and queries to try to understand my disease – but I was in such a rush to get away before my willpower faltered. I could hardly stand up that terrible night – hardly bear to carry on – but I had to. I had to remove myself from our world – to cut myself off with surgical precision, like a blackened limb to be amputated so the body survives.

Pain slices through me as Anna's image fills my head: the curve of her neck, soft and tender, those flyaway wisps waving from her ponytail like a halo. The swell of her arse, so sexy even in the hideous jogging bottoms she likes to wear. The feel of her in my arms, and the scent of fresh soap as I pull her close.

I couldn't be further away from Anna now, even though she works nearby. I didn't want to be this close to her university, but the doctor left little room to argue: this was one of the best centres for my disease, and if I wanted a shot at a few extra weeks (months, if I'm lucky), it was where I needed to be.

Apart from the many doctor's appointments, the only time I'd ventured out these past few days was to buy new clothes from the shop around the corner. Everything I'd worn on the night I left is bundled up in a carrier bag, shoved to the back of the cheap wardrobe . . . leftovers of another time – another me. I can't bear to even look at them now, let alone have the fabric touch my skin. I took nothing from home except my keys and wallet, and it comforts me to think of our flat stuffed with all those things we bought, my wardrobe still full . . . as if I could slip back there at any second. I won't, of course, but I like to picture our world intact, with Anna nestling inside that perfect place. It's part of the reason I didn't tell my wife I'm ill.

My wife.

Anguish grabs my gut, and I swing my legs over the side of the bed. I know she'll struggle; I know she'll hurt. If she's anything like me – and she is, I know she is – the searing pain will sting her soul, as if a limb *was* surgically removed. She'd struggle even more with me around, though. I have to keep reminding myself of that. I know first-hand the suffering that comes from watching someone you love die; the horror of knowing that whatever you do – whatever you say – nothing will change.

I get to my feet, shivering at the cold in the room, and pick up the pen and paper resting on the tiny table that's shoved under the window. Ever since I left, I've been trying to write my wife a letter – a letter to be opened once I'm gone; a letter explaining why I had to leave the way I did . . . that I did it for her. But every time I sit down, the words flee my mind. It's as if the connection between my brain and my fingers has broken down, the words lodged in my faulty, cancerous cells.

Cancer. I shiver again, not sure if it's from the chill in the air or the word itself. It hasn't quite sunk in, despite the battery of tests and grim conversations. It hasn't hit me that my life is over, despite leaving Anna and my job. There *is* something I have to do, though. It's the very reason I'm even bothering with chemo, in the hope that it gives me some longevity. I'll never have a child of my own, but there's a baby

I'm desperate to find; a baby Anna knows nothing about – a baby from another life I've tried to shut out.

Not a baby any longer, I think, shaking my head and trying my best to visualise that squalling, warm bundle as a teenager. Now that my carefully built barrier has tumbled down, the past feels so much closer than all those years would suggest, as if I could reach through time and gather that child in my arms.

Pain slices into me again. If only. If *only* I had done that – helped when I could have, instead of turning a deaf ear. Maybe then things would have turned out differently. Maybe . . . I don't know. All I know is that I need to take that child in my guilty embrace and say I'm sorry. Sorry for failing her and sorry for failing her mother. It will never be enough; it will never change what happened. But if I can find that baby, then maybe I can find a way to take hold of the past, one final time.

CHAPTER NINE

Anna

I twist and turn in bed, trying to sleep as images assault me. Margo and Mark hugging and laughing, then Mark grieving at her grave. Mark running away from me and tumbling into the yawning hole that swallowed Margo . . . then me yanking him out, pulling him back into the light and anchoring him in our world.

As the days pass with no word from Mark's parents, I'm struggling to take steps in any direction, rotating between worry, fear and anger . . . then love, and finally a trust that somehow, despite what Mark didn't tell me, everything will be okay. And then I'm straight back to worry and fear when I realise it's almost a week since my husband left and I've no idea where he is. I'm trapped in a no-man's land: the past has cracked, I can't recognise the present and I don't know the future, either.

I'm jolted awake one morning by a ringing mobile. It takes a few seconds before I realise the noise is coming from Mark's phone. I grab the handset, brow furrowing as I stare at the unknown number on the screen. Could it be Mark's mother or father, calling him to get in touch? Have they seen my email?

'Hello?'

'Can I speak with Mark Lewis, please?' A man's voice comes through the phone and my heart crashes – it's not Mark's father.

'I'm sorry, he's not here right now. Can I ask who's calling? Or take a message?'

'Just the nurse returning his call. I'll ring again. Goodbye.' The line goes dead.

I stare at the phone for a second. The *nurse*? From where? I hit the number to call it back, the mobile sweaty in my grasp. The phone rings once, then clicks as someone picks up.

'Hello, Macmillan Cancer Support. Can I help?'

Macmillan Cancer Support?

'Hello? Can I help?'

'Yes.' I push out the word. 'One of your nurses just called my husband, Mark Lewis?' Silence falls on the line as I realise I don't know who or what to ask for.

'I'm sorry.' The woman's voice is low and sympathetic. 'I can only speak to Mark Lewis.'

'Is there a reason you're calling him?' My pulse is racing now and my mouth is dry.

'I'm very sorry,' the woman says again. 'Goodbye.'

The phone clicks off. I sit there staring down at the screen as my mind whirls, trying to compute what's happened. A nurse from Macmillan Cancer Support called my husband . . . but why? Maybe for a donation? But then I'm sure they would have tried their spiel on me – or at least have told me why they were calling. And I don't think they use nurses to canvass for money, either.

My heart beats fast as I snatch the laptop and google the charity. A colourful website fills the screen containing lots of tabs and links for people who have been diagnosed with cancer. My eyes pop at one line offering anyone with questions the chance to call an information line.

But why would Mark be in touch with Macmillan Cancer Support?

I swallow hard against the fear rising up inside me. Mark can't be ill, can he? He's never even had a cold, for God's sake. He's the healthiest person I know, always eating his greens, taking vitamins and making sure I do the same.

Maybe it's not for him, I tell myself. Maybe it's . . . My thought trails off as I blink slowly. Pieces fall into place, slotting neatly into a jigsaw of horror. Those secretive phone calls and the time off work. The nights he didn't want to make love . . . the weight I wasn't sure he'd lost.

Mark leaving his job – leaving me.

My husband has cancer.

Every part of me starts vibrating with terror, with panic, with a love so strong – so visceral – that I feel like I could conjure Mark up right here. Whatever doubts and fears the past few days have thrown up about our marriage – whatever secrets Mark has kept – none of it matters now. There may have been a few cracks in our perfect world, but this news has blown it apart.

Our protected safe space is forever behind us, but it doesn't matter. All I care about now is Mark. I don't know why he hid things from me and I don't know why he left. But I do know one thing: I want to find him and be there with him – through this, and whatever else may come.

CHAPTER TEN

Anna

A restless energy flows through me, sweeping away any hint of fatigue. I can't stay in the flat. I need to move – need to do something. I need to find my husband and gather him close to me, but I don't know where to look. I throw on my coat and grab my keys, not even sure where I'm going. My feet move forward, one and then the other, faster and faster, until I'm almost jogging.

Mark has cancer. Mark has cancer. I breathe in and out, the cold air searing my lungs as questions tear at my brain. Is it serious? Is he in hospital right now? Is it something minor – easily treatable – and he's just panicked? Maybe he was planning to come back to me once the cancer is gone.

But then . . . why would he quit his job, just like that? And why did he need to leave me?

I swivel in the direction of Hampstead Heath, the scent of wet leaves and damp earth filling my nose as I enter the park. The sky looms large above me and long grass tangles around my feet, making it even more difficult to push ahead. But I'm desperate to keep going, as if stopping will let everything catch up with me and pile on top of me, forcing me down.

The horns and screeching brakes of buses fade as I make my way across the broad expanse. There's something so different about this park from any other: it's untidy – untamed – and you could wander for hours, pretending you're not in London but some ancient, otherworldly forest. Mark and I are lucky to have it practically in our back garden.

Every Saturday and Sunday morning, we'd head here when the streets were still quiet, before the Heath filled with families and tourists. We'd run through the underbrush, taking the back route into the park. I'm nowhere near as athletic as Mark, but I loved moving beside him through the empty fields as if we were alone in the world. He could have surged ahead, but he matched me step for step as we huffed up the steep incline of the park. London would spread out beneath us, and it felt like we'd conquered the city.

I stop for a second, thinking back to a few weekends ago. We'd had our usual run and Mark didn't seem any weaker, any more tired than usual. I wonder if he knew about his diagnosis then. I wonder if he was hurting inside, full of questions and fear. No, surely not. I would have noticed something was wrong; I would have seen he wasn't himself. Maybe you can hide your past, but you can't hide an illness from the person who knows you best . . . can you? And why on earth would you want to? God, if I was sick, I'd take all the help I could get, particularly from those closest to me.

Before I know it I'm across the park and just steps from Sophie's. Her house isn't exactly what you'd call big, but it's worth an insane amount of money. Glossy blue shutters stand out against a white stucco front, ivy crawls up a trellis on one side and, even in autumn, the front garden is filled with green. Set back from the hustle and bustle of the high street, you almost feel like you've stepped into another world. Sophie's constantly complaining about all its quirks and foibles – the doors that don't shut properly, the mismatched floorboards – but I love it. It's exactly the kind of place I can picture Mark and myself living, even if it's well beyond our price range.

I stare up at her house and a desperate urge to fall into her arms sweeps over me, as if she can make everything better. I rush up the little path to her door and bang the knocker on the bright blue wood, praying she's home. Never have I wanted to see my big sister more, not even during those dark days after our father left.

'Anna?' Sophie swings open the door and I practically fall into her. She sways under the force of my embrace, but manages to stay upright and wrap her arms around me. I let my head drop on to her shoulder, breathing in the familiar scent of vanilla musk that she's worn since she was a teen.

Finally, I lift my head, then wipe away the tears I didn't even know I'd cried. She gazes at me, waiting for me to speak – waiting until I'm ready, even though I don't think I'll ever be ready to say the words. But I need to. I need her strength, even if just for a minute.

'It's Mark,' I say, my voice raspy. 'He's left.'

'*What?*' Her eyebrows fly up, and she takes my arm. 'Come on, sit down. Tell me what's going on.'

I let her guide me into a chair at the kitchen table, suddenly feeling so, so tired. All I want is to put my head down on the solid wood and let myself drift off – drift away, even if just for five minutes – to a place where this nightmare doesn't exist. But I can't, because somewhere out there, Mark needs me – more than he ever has before.

'Mark has cancer,' I say quickly, afraid I'll halt halfway through the sentence if I don't get it out fast. 'At least I think he does. He didn't tell me. He just left . . . almost a week ago now.'

'A *week*?' Sophie's voice rises, but I can't stop.

'I only found out when I called a number on his phone,' I continue, 'and it turned out to be Macmillan Cancer Support.'

'Okay,' Sophie says slowly, processing the information. 'Okay. But that doesn't necessarily mean he has cancer. Right?'

'No, but a nurse from there said they were returning his call. I tried to find out more, but they wouldn't tell me anything. Mark has lost weight, and . . .' I close my eyes, as if I can block all this out, then force them open. 'I went to his work, but he's resigned.' Sophie's eyebrows shoot up again, and I look away. I can't bear it. 'His colleague said he'd been taking a lot of time off.'

'Oh my God,' she says, reaching across the table and grasping my hand. 'Poor Mark. Poor *you*.' She falls silent, and all I can hear is the ticking clock on the wall. 'Do you know where he is?'

'No. No idea.' I shake my head, staring down at the table as confusion rushes into me. 'I can't believe he left. He knows I'd do anything for him. I mean, he's my husband, after all. I love him.'

'I know you do,' Sophie says softly. 'And I'm sure he knows that, too.' She's quiet again for a minute. 'But people don't always think sensibly after being diagnosed with a serious illness. It's such a huge thing, isn't it? The first reaction is probably to run away. Especially for men.' She rolls her eyes, and the corners of my mouth lift, despite everything. That's exactly what I'm hoping: that he's just panicked and he'll come back soon. 'But if I know one thing it's that Mark loves you. The man practically worships you, Anna. I wouldn't have let him marry you if he didn't.'

She squeezes my hand, and I think for a minute about telling her about Margo. But I can't bear to have her pick over Mark's past – I can't stand any more speculation about why my husband would hide Margo from me. I don't want to focus on uncertainty and doubt, and whatever happened with him and Margo isn't important now. I shove her name from my brain, focusing back on Mark.

'Do you think the cancer must be serious, though?' I ask, barely able to get the question out for the fear clutching my throat. 'I mean, if he's left me, left his job . . .'

'Look, let's not get ahead of ourselves,' Sophie says in a practical tone. 'There are so many different kinds of cancer, and many of them are treatable. Let's just focus on finding him.'

Several hours later, though, finding my husband doesn't seem like an easy task. My ever-efficient sister has sat us down at the table, opening her trusty laptop and making a list of all the places we should ring. B & Bs, hotels, our doctor's surgery, hospitals with cancer centres, Harley Street clinics . . . the list is endless, and I'd be lying if I said it wasn't daunting. London is a city of over eight million people, and there are plenty of places to hide if you don't want to be found.

Don't want to be found. I wrap my arms around myself, barely able to believe that phrase applies to my husband. I always thought we were each other's ultimate security blanket – at least, I felt that way about Mark. An image of Mark kneeling at Margo's grave fills my head again, and I try once more to push it away. It's wispy and ethereal, though, and I can't get hold of it. Confusion and panic wash over me and my gut twists. Mark didn't let me into his past and he hasn't let me be here for him now, either. But *why*?

My stomach lurches with panic and I rush up the stairs to the toilet, dry-heaving into the sparkling toilet bowl. I've barely eaten these past few days – I couldn't face making a meal for one in the kitchen. I wipe my mouth and shakily make my way back downstairs.

The front door bangs closed, and Flora rushes into the kitchen.

'Hi, Mum.' She spots me, then streaks into my arms. 'Auntie Anna! Is Uncle Mark here, too?' Her ponytail bobs as her head swings back and forth in a bid to find him. If only it were that easy.

I tighten my arms around her soft body, loving that she's still so squeezable. Sophie told me that lately the girls at her school have started playing 'dieting', where they 'cut out carbs'. Goodness knows where they got this from – at Flora's age, I was more worried about where to *get* sweets than cutting them from my diet. I relayed this to Mark one day over dinner and was surprised and touched at the vehemence of his reaction.

'That's crazy,' he'd said, anger twisting his face. 'The teachers need to put a stop to that before it gets out of hand.'

'Mark's . . .' I falter, unable to even complete the sentence. I don't even know a plausible place that he might be. The thought makes my gut twist again.

'Mark's busy just now,' Sophie says firmly. 'Now, how was your day?'

Sophie sits Flora at the table with a plate of toast and I close my eyes as Flora's stream of consciousness washes over me. The cosy domestic scene makes my heart ache. I'd give anything to have this right now – to be sitting with Mark in our flat, looking forward to our future with absolute certainty and trust.

Flora runs upstairs to start on her homework and Sophie plonks down beside me with the laptop again.

'Right,' she says, swivelling it round so I can see it. 'We've got lots of numbers to call, but . . . it is something of a long shot. We don't know if he's checked in under his own name, and it's unlikely the cancer centres will tell us if he's their patient. We can try the GP, but they probably won't tell us anything, either. And you've already contacted his parents . . . is there anyone else you can think of getting in touch with?'

I shake my head. 'No, not really.' For some reason I don't want to tell Sophie I've already checked his phone and laptop.

The door bangs again and Sophie's head snaps up. Asher sweeps through the kitchen, briefcase in one hand and suit jacket in the other. His eyebrows rise when he spots me.

'Oh, hi, Anna,' he says, leaning down to give me a quick kiss. 'Everything all right?'

I open my mouth to answer, but he's already halfway up the stairs.

'Flora home?' he calls over his shoulder, his footsteps thumping on the stairs.

'In her room,' Sophie answers, then shakes her head. 'Hello to you, too,' she says in a low voice. She busies herself with typing out more numbers, but I can see from the set of her shoulders and the way her mouth has tightened that she's anything but happy. I certainly wouldn't be if Mark came back after a long day at work and didn't even say hello or kiss me. But maybe it's just been a stressful day for Asher. Sophie's always saying how hard he works.

Footsteps thud on the stairs again, then Asher reappears in a cloud of cologne. 'Right, I'm off,' he says. 'Sorry I can't stay and catch up, Anna.' He flashes me a smile.

'Wait!' Sophie says before he can dash out the door. 'Where are you going? You said you'd be home tonight, remember? Flora really wanted to play that game on her tablet with you.'

Irritation streaks across his face. 'Oh, sorry, I must have got mixed up. I am busy tonight, after all. I just talked to Flora, don't worry.' And the door bangs behind him before Sophie can say anything else.

Silence falls in the small kitchen and, for the first time, I don't really know what to say to my sister. She complains about Asher a lot, but I never suspected such . . . *coldness*.

'Well, that's him gone, then.' Her tone is breezy, but I can see the hurt in her eyes. 'Do you want to crash here tonight? God knows what time he'll be back, and it would be nice to have some company – for once.'

'Actually . . . yes, thanks. I'd love to.' I don't fancy crossing the Heath in the dark – Mark's admonitions ring in my mind – and I don't want to spend another night alone at the flat with my torturous thoughts. I want to be here at the epicentre of our search.

'Great.' Sophie gets up and stretches. 'I'll make another cup of tea, and then we can add some more numbers to our list so we're ready to start in the morning.' She puts her arms around me and, for a second, it feels like we're kids again, just the two of us against the world. 'Don't worry,' she says into my ear. 'We'll find him. Everything will be all right.'

Tears blur my vision and I nod my head against her shoulder, hoping – praying – she's right.

CHAPTER ELEVEN

Anna

I'm tucked up in Sophie's spare bedroom later that night, every muscle throbbing with fatigue. My head is buzzing and I know I should sleep, but each time I close my eyes, all I can see is Mark's face on the day he left, so pale and tense. I wish I had held on to him now – I wish I had somehow stopped him going. But how could I have known he was leaving because he was ill? If only he'd told me . . .

My mobile jangles, and I grab at it so fast it skitters off the bed and bounces across the floor. Cursing, I lunge for it and say hello into the receiver breathlessly.

'Anna, it's Margaret.'

Oh. My heart sinks as I recognise the voice of our university department head. I'd hoped it was someone returning an earlier call, or something to do with Mark. 'Hi, Margaret.'

'Just wanted to ring and make sure everything is all right. I can't remember the last time you were off sick.' Her tone is warm and concerned, like the mother you always wanted to have. In a way, she *is* like a mother . . . at work, anyway. A staunch feminist, she's determined to help other women succeed in the male-dominated world of the university. When I was an undergraduate, she took me and several other women on the course under her wing, doing everything she could to propel us forward. It's thanks to her support that I made it to where I am now. Without her encouragement, I might have opted out of the academic life after my undergraduate degree – to do what, exactly, I didn't know. I just knew I wanted to do *something* – to live.

Back in my early twenties, I'd felt so alone. My parents had set up camp on an island off the Scottish coast – they didn't have a phone signal half the time, and I wouldn't have known what to say to them anyway. Our relationship had been reduced to birthday cards and a phone call at Christmas . . . if I could reach them. Sophie was busy enjoying the hectic life of an intern in a Soho ad agency, and although I still saw her regularly and I knew she'd be there in the blink of an eye if I needed her, she had a whole new world that was separate from me. Meanwhile, I was in my last year of an undergraduate degree, living in a tiny, cramped flat with three other girls after answering an advert for a 'quiet person – no party animals allowed'.

The three were in medical school and if they weren't in hospitals or labs they were furiously studying. While I didn't aspire to be a party animal – not by a long shot – it would have been nice to hang out in the kitchen with a mug of tea at night, or even have a few drinks together. Instead, I felt even more alone. Hadn't Sophie promised uni would be the best years of my life? Where were the pub crawls, the boozy student union nights, the *men*? I didn't envy Sophie's hit-and-run relationships, but having someone to lean on would have been lovely . . . someone to trust.

The ratio of women to men in my English classes was pathetic; the lone male was sure to be paired up within days of the academic year starting, if he wasn't already taken. I did register with a few dating websites under Sophie's duress, just to give them a try and to get out every once in a while. But the men I met seemed unsure of what to say and how to behave – from the one-kiss/two-kiss dance at the beginning of the date to the 'Can I see you again?' at the end. I wasn't going to entrust my heart to someone who dithered over whether or not to split the bill.

Life rolled on and, thanks to Margaret's encouragement, a few years later I'd almost finished my doctorate. I had a studio flat of my own, a few articles published in reputable journals and a roster of students who seemed to enjoy my first attempts at lecturing. After a long and intensive campaign Asher finally convinced Sophie to marry him, and despite her attempts to pair me up with his best man, I remained single. I got a post-doc position and loved my job, I was happy enough and, although I was starting to give up hope on finding someone, I wasn't about to compromise. Better to be alone than with a man who'd hurt me.

Then I met Mark.

It sounds so clichéd, but Mark was such a bright light in my life he put everything else in shadow. I still enjoyed work, of course, but the intensity I'd put into it – the hours in the office, the seminars I'd attended – diminished. I caught up with Margaret less and less, until our relationship became mainly a passing-in-the-hallway affair, unless she wanted to speak with me specifically. London's attractions receded into the background, since we stayed in most of the time . . . usually snuggling up in the cosy confines of my tiny place because I had to be at work much earlier than Mark. Nothing else mattered, nothing but us and this wonderful connection we'd somehow managed to find. Nothing would change that.

And until Mark left, nothing did.

Margo's gravestone floats into my head, accompanied by the endless list of questions about Mark's past. I shove the thoughts away, reminding myself that I need to focus on finding my husband because whatever is in his past, he is just that – my husband. He is still the man I married, the man I pledged heart and soul to . . . until death do us part. My mouth goes dry as I realise I don't know how much time he – we – have left.

'I need to take a leave of absence,' I say to Margaret.

The words leave my mouth in a rush and silence falls on the line. I cross my fingers, hoping that Margaret will be all right with me taking time off. Despite her motherly persona, she rules our department with an iron fist. She'll defend you to the end if you're in her good books – which, thankfully, I've managed to be – but if you're not . . .

'I know it's sudden,' I continue. 'But Mark, well . . .' I take a deep breath, knowing I'll never – not in a million years – be able to get these words out easily. 'Mark has cancer, and he needs me.' Whatever he thinks – whatever he's doing – I know that much is true.

'Oh, Anna.' Margaret's voice is so laden with sympathy that my eyes tear up. 'I'm sorry. Please take the time that you need. I'll get in touch with the HR department and let them know. Just keep me updated on everything, all right? Is there anything I can do to help?'

I wish, I think, but I shake my head. 'No, thanks.' I squint and try to think about my work, which seems so far away from me now. I should care; I've worked so hard to get to where I am. But right now, it's faded into total insignificance. 'My lecture notes are all on the desktop, organised by date, and—'

'Don't worry.' Margaret's voice cuts me off. 'I'll do the lectures myself if I need to. You just focus on what you need to do, all right? And take good care of yourself,' she adds. 'Cancer can be a tough road . . . for the family, too.'

'Okay,' I say, although I couldn't care less about my well-being. What's good for me is what's good for Mark: being together.

'Give my best to Mark,' Margaret says warmly, and I remember just how much the two of them liked each other when they first met. Margaret's been trying to convince Mark to do a degree at uni ever since that day, saying his mind is wasted at the bank.

'I will.' I say goodbye and hang up, then I huddle under the duvet and close my eyes, desperately wishing that, when I open them, Mark will be by my side again.

CHAPTER TWELVE

Mark

A few days have passed since I was last out of bed . . . apart from crawling to the toilet to throw up, that is. The doctors didn't know how I'd react to the chemo. 'Let's just see,' they said, as if I was an exotic slab of meat that might emerge golden brown or black and crispy. I feel more soggy than crispy, I have to say. Every muscle is heavy, as if my body has been welded to the sweaty bedsheets. And despite the anti-nausea drugs they gave me, my stomach has been emptied so many times it's actually concave.

This is the first of three chemo cycles I'll endure over the next ten weeks and – I wince as the incision for the catheter throbs – I pray that it works, that it gives me the extra months I may need to find this child. I won't even know if it *is* working until they scan me when all these cycles are done, but I'll take my chances. I'll do whatever is needed to track down the baby.

The room swings around me as I sit up, but I force myself to stand and teeter to the bathroom. I've wasted enough time now, and I need to get moving, to do something to continue my search – not that I've had much success. So far, I've spent hours on the Internet and phone, trying to figure out where to start, which direction to turn in to find this child. I've tried the Adoption Contact Register, but you have to be eighteen to register, and the child I'm looking for would only be thirteen. I've called councils and social workers, left endless messages on robotic answering machines . . . nothing.

For the first time in my life I wish I watched more reality TV. You know those shows where people track down long-lost family members so quickly and easily? How the *hell* do they do it? Maybe if I'd tuned in for some mind-numbing telly instead of chatting with my wife – bodies entwined on the velour sofa that felt like we were lying on clouds – I'd know where to go from here. I'd make a great show, actually: dying man seeking long-lost baby, a final punt at life. Even I'd watch that.

Gazing into the mirror, I *do* look like a dying man, although my ghostly pallor could be due to the terrible fluorescent light above me. Grey stubble covers my cheeks – I haven't had the energy to shave. My face is pale and sweat beads on my brow. My T-shirt is wrinkled and stained and I'm not even wearing pyjama bottoms.

But none of that is what makes me look different – or at least *feel* like I look different. It's my eyes: they're dull and flat, as if the sheen has already gone out of them . . . as if I'm already dead.

I step into the shower for the first time in days and make the water as hot as it can go, hoping the warmth can reach right into the very heart of me where it feels so, so cold. I clumsily remove the soap from its soggy paper wrapper, cursing when it slips from my grasp. I lean down to grab it, dizziness swamping me again, and I fall to my knees. Water beats on to my back, and anger kicks in my gut, too. I can't even have a bloody shower now without falling over? *Shit.*

And this is nothing, I remind myself. This is one cycle of chemo, which the doctors don't even know will work. This isn't the litany of horrors that dying from this disease will entail . . . the pain, the swelling, the wasting away.

This isn't death. Not yet.

I close my eyes and a yearning for my wife's cool hands on my clammy head – for her tender voice as she guides my shaking limbs back to bed – grips me with such force that a cry escapes from me. I miss our creature comforts, yes – the wonderfully firm bed, the thick carpet underfoot, the pillows that wrap themselves around me – but it's *her* I miss a trillion times more. I miss her so much that my heart feels like it's on fire, consumed with longing and love.

The claustrophobic confines of this room remind me of Anna's studio flat, the place where we first made love. I had an actual bedroom that wasn't bordered by a hotplate on one side and a minuscule loo on the other, but my place in Finsbury Park was too full of memories . . . and none of them were good. I was still sleeping on my sofa at that stage, unable to even touch the bed, and I didn't want to take Anna there. I couldn't bear to have our two worlds mix: the fresh and hopeful colliding with the dark, draining remnants of the old.

Anna felt like a gift to me, a chance to begin again. I grabbed on to that with all my might, blotting out everything that came before her. And luckily, she didn't mind my hazy past, seeming to be just as keen to build a life together. We fitted perfectly – we didn't have many extraneous bits that would clash, anyway.

That first night we made love, I unwrapped her slowly. We were both nervous – a little reticent, I guess, to be so exposed, so vulnerable. I took deep breaths as I peeled off her layers, trying to calm myself down. It'd been ages since I'd had sex . . . ages since I'd dated. My life outside that flat barely existed.

This was my chance to live, finally, and I sensed that Anna felt the same. When we were both naked, I let my eyes slide over her body. Slender but curvy, she was almost luminescent in the glow of the street-lights outside. I couldn't wait to bury myself in her, to become one.

And now . . . now, we've been ripped apart.

The empty pages lie by my bed and every day I turn towards them, composing lines in my head, trying to explain to Anna why I left. This letter is my one remaining connection to my wife, even if she won't read it until after I'm gone. I've yet to write a word, though. I can't bring myself to. It's as if penning the letter will seal my fate – seal the fact that I won't see her again – and I'm still desperately struggling to accept that. I love her so much that the thought of not touching her – of not kissing her neck or seeing her smile – is like another death in itself, and every bit of me strains to rush back to her.

But then . . . but then I remember. I remember how disease sucks light from everything, even memories. When I'm forced to think of that terrible time – when the images crowd in and the only thing I can do is retreat into myself and try to bear it – all I can see is hollow eyes and freckles so dark they look like splotches of black paint against pale skin. Hair dropping out on the pillow, the dull rust colour a sharp contrast to its former vivid red. Wasted arms and legs, so different from the strong limbs that pumped beside me on our runs, matching my pace and even forcing me forwards. The voice that had chattered and laughed now barely a croak, the smile looking more skeletal than happy.

And finally . . . I screw my eyes shut, even though I know it won't help, because the longer I'm away from my life, the more memories tumble out, playing in awful Technicolor instead of a muted black-and-white.

I don't want Anna to be haunted like this. I don't want her to play the role of the carer, her world shrinking down to nothing but the person dying and the disease that will claim them. I've lived the half-life of waking in the morning and wondering if the person you love is still alive – checking their chest for the slightest hint of movement. It's a slow death for both of you, the carer and the patient, and I can't – I *won't* – expose my wife to that.

I love her too much to damage her that way . . . the way I've been damaged.

CHAPTER THIRTEEN

Anna

A couple of days later, I'm still caught in this terrible place: a place without my husband – a place where my husband is ill and I can't help him. No one ever thinks their loved one will get cancer, of course, and I'm still not sure I've fully absorbed it. I know Sophie's right and that many people survive . . . but I can't quite wrap my head around the idea that Mark would pack in his life if he knew he'd be okay. I hope with every fibre of my being that he *will* be fine, though, and our life together will continue.

And even though I tell myself it's not important now, Margo's face continues to invade my dreams . . . the one place I can't control my thoughts. She marches through my subconscious, taunting me with a grin and holding up Mark's hand from within her grave, as if she's claimed a trophy. I jerk awake each night drenched in sweat, mouth dry and heart pounding. I know Margo is dead, but somehow her presence in our present feels very real.

Thank God for Sophie's constant reassurance and her unwavering faith that Mark and I will get through this – that we'll find him. Because despite all our efforts, we aren't any closer. A curt response came in from Mark's mother saying she hasn't heard from her son in years, but there's still no answer from his father. Sophie and I spend hours together at her kitchen table, our voices intermingling in the silence as we make our way through hundreds of telephone numbers, dialling hospitals, cancer centres, private clinics on Harley Street and every hotel and B & B within a three-mile radius (and you won't believe how many of those there are!). But we find . . . nothing. Nothing except receptionists who could really use some training in customer service.

I've left my name and number with countless people across the city, just in case, but no one has called and no one has heard of my husband. And while part of me knows this is an exercise in futility, I can't help the jet of hope that spurts up at every 'Hello?' on the other end of the line, thinking that this could be the one – this could be the call that uncovers my husband, that puts an end to this nightmare, or at least brings us together. But it never is.

My mouth stretches into a giant yawn and I throw off the duvet, pulling on the jeans and jumper Sophie lent me. I haven't been back to our flat since the day I found out Mark has cancer. I can't bear to be there alone, without him – to wrap myself in the sheets that once held us, knowing he's sleeping somewhere else, ill and alone.

I roll my neck and open the laptop to check my email, the first thing I do each morning. I log in and click on to my inbox, a process I can almost perform with my eyes closed. I brace myself for nothing but junk mail, but this time it's different: Richard Lewis's name shows up on the screen in black, bold letters.

Mark's father has responded.

My heart starts pounding and, with shaking fingers, I click to open the message.

Dear Anna,
No, I haven't heard from Mark. Should I have? If something is wrong, I'd like to know. I might be able to help. Please call or, even better, come and see me.

I blink at the phone number and the address below this message, taking deep breaths as disappointment crashes through me. I knew it was unlikely that Mark would reach out to his parents, given how little they know of his life now. But with no other direction to search in . . . I run my eyes over the words, wondering if Richard *could* help somehow. Margo's name pops into my head yet again, as if she's just loitering there, waiting for a chink in my mental armour. I let her linger for once, tilting my head as I stare at the screen. I know Mark left because he has cancer, but could there be something in his past with Margo to explain why he kept his illness to himself – a past that his father may know better than me? I don't know if it will help me find Mark, but right now, I have nothing to lose.

I run down the stairs to the kitchen, where Sophie is plaiting Flora's hair. As usual, Asher is nowhere to be found. I'm beginning to think Sophie's litany of complaints about his lack of parental participation really does have some merit.

'Mark's father responded!' I say, my voice hoarse with sleep.

'Brilliant!' Sophie responds through a mouthful of grips. 'So does he know where Mark is?'

I shake my head. 'No, but he wants to help. He lives in Berkhamsted, and I'm going to go and see him.' This is way too important for a simple phone call. I need to connect with Richard face to face.

Sophie sets down the brush. 'Do you want me to come with you? I'll drop this one off at school and then we can go together.'

I ponder the idea for a second, but this journey, and whatever I might uncover, feels like something I need to do on my own. Besides, Sophie still doesn't know about Margo and I can't take the time to explain now. 'No, that's all right. Thanks, though.' I take the cup of coffee she offers, then sit at the table and draw her laptop close to me. I pull up the train journey planner website, hoping the trip won't take too long. Thankfully, there are plenty of direct trains to Berkhamsted, and it looks like it'll only take about an hour to get there from here, if I'm lucky.

A few minutes later I head out into the drizzly, grey morning. Mist swirls around the chimney tops and the whole world feels dark and foreign. As I walk down the deserted path to the Tube station, I realise I am heading to a foreign place . . . somewhere I had never even thought about until a few days ago – somewhere I had never suspected played a part in our present.

My husband's past.

CHAPTER FOURTEEN

Anna

I sit numbly on the train as the landscape flashes by, unable to read or even gaze out the window. I stare at the seat in front of me, eyes gritty and head humming. For the first time I'm going to meet someone who knew my husband before me – someone who raised him and made him into the man he is today . . . and someone who knows his past. I was so eager to see Richard, but the closer that I get, the more uncertain I become. What if he tells me things I don't want to hear? What if . . . I shake my head. I need to do this. I need to *know*, to break down the barriers between Mark and me and build us up even stronger – strong enough to face illness and get through it together.

Finally, the tannoy announces the train is approaching Berkhamsted. I haul myself to my feet and push through the throng towards the door. As I step from the train and on to the platform, the skies open up. Rain sluices through the air and wind slices into me, plastering my jacket to me like a second skin. In a way, it feels like the town is protesting my arrival, and I shudder – from the cold or the thought, I'm not sure.

According to the map on my phone, Mark's father lives close to the station, so I hurry in what I hope is the right direction. A few minutes later, I'm standing on a quiet street with sprawling brick houses on either side. For a second, it almost feels like I'm back in the neighbourhood where I grew up. The same sensations are in the air: the distant buzz of a lawnmower, the smell of damp earth and flowers. The whole place feels *safe*, tucked away from the crime and noise of central London.

I spot the right house number and hurry down the path, then bang the heavy brass knocker against the door. My heart beats fast as I wait for it to open, and I smooth back my damp hair. *Maybe I should have called first,* I think, biting my lip. It is the middle of the day, after all, and I've no idea what Mark's father does for a living, or if he even still works.

The door swings open and I'm faced with a frazzled-looking woman. Inside the house, children's laughter mixes with shrieking and the sound of something crashing on to the floor.

'Yes?' She cranes her neck to look past me. 'Where's the van? The natives want their lunch, and these groceries were supposed to be here hours ago.'

Groceries? I shake my head. 'I'm sorry, but I'm not here to deliver groceries. I'm Anna. I'm here to see Richard?' Instinctively I draw back, wondering if I have the wrong house. No, it's number 42, the same as Richard wrote in the email. Can this woman be his new wife? She looks like she's only a few years older than me.

'Oh.' The woman lets out an embarrassed laugh. 'I'm so sorry, of course you're not. The doorbell rang, and I just assumed without even looking . . .' She shakes her head, hair flying out at all angles. 'Come in, come in. Too late to escape the madhouse here. It's not usually this wild, but the kids have an inset day and the nanny's stuck in traffic. I'll tell Richard that you're here.' And with that she disappears up the stairs, looking all too eager for a second of peace and quiet.

I stay in the hall, not wanting to encounter the pack of wild hyenas that now sound like they're attacking a piano keyboard in the room next door. I wince at the clashing chords that crash through the air, then peer down a narrow hallway where several photos of seemingly angelic children smile out at me: a girl hovering on the cusp of adolescence, two young boys who look a few years apart and then a toddler girl.

I shake my head, wondering who these children are. I knew Mark's father remarried, but this young brood can't be his, can it? If so, he and his wife have certainly been busy. I catch my breath as sadness sinks into me – sadness that Mark and I don't have a family. Will we ever? Can we ever, given his illness?

A thought flies into my head, and I pause: is that why he left – because he won't be able to have kids? I don't know much about chemotherapy, but I remember hearing it could make men infertile. Whatever the consequence of his treatment, we can face all that once he's well again. I want a child, yes, but I want my husband more: healthy and happy. And I'll tell him that as soon as I find him.

'Come on up, Anna.' The woman's voice interrupts my thoughts. She beckons me up the stairs with a warm smile. 'I'm so sorry. I'd no idea you were Mark's wife – Richard just filled me in. I'm Jude, Richard's wife. It's so nice to finally meet you! We would love to see Mark, too – the kids would be beyond excited if he came by. Anyway, follow me.'

I pad up the stairs, trying to absorb the fact that Mark has a whole bevvy of step-sisters and step-brothers I never knew about. I wonder if he did. It's hard to imagine my husband, who loves children so much, turning his back on this family if he *was* aware they existed. But then . . . Jude must be about thirty years younger than his father! Is that why Mark doesn't talk to him?

It's quieter upstairs, and Jude shows me into the study. A thickset man with a bushy white beard and eyes exactly the same shade as Mark's is sitting at a heavy oak desk behind his laptop. He gets to his feet and extends a hand and, for a second, I almost feel like my husband is here. Mark has the exact same way of standing, slightly bent at the shoulders, and his brow furrows like his father's, too. A longing to find my husband – to straighten out those little wrinkles in his forehead one more time – sweeps over me, and I pray that Richard can help.

'Anna. I'm Richard,' he says, his grip strong. 'So nice to finally meet you.'

'You, too.' No matter the reason that they don't talk now – and no matter what Richard might tell me – it *is* nice to meet someone connected to my husband. I meet Richard's eyes, wondering what it's like to be so cut off from your son's life. Did he try to reach out? Does he care? My own father doesn't seem bothered, but then our distance was more of a mutual decision. I'd always assumed Mark's situation was much like mine.

'Have a seat.' Richard points to a chair on the other side of his desk. 'I'd suggest moving to the lounge, but we probably wouldn't get two words in without my kids jumping all over us. Can I get you a drink? Water?'

I nod. It's the last thing I want, but I need time to absorb this whole family scenario. He returns with some chilled water for us both and I grasp the clammy glass and gulp it down, wondering where to start. Mark hasn't talked to Richard for years, and I can hardly open by informing him that his son has cancer. Besides, I'm not sure how much Mark would want me to tell him.

'So is everything all right?' Richard asks, cutting through the silence that's descended. 'I'm guessing not, since you wouldn't be here if it was.' He shakes his head. 'I can't even remember the last time I saw my son. I only found out he got married because one of our old neighbours ran into him at the bank where he works.'

I stare down at my hands, uncertain what to say.

'I did try, you know.' Richard leans back, as if he's heard my unasked questions. 'I tried to contact Mark many times, but he never responded.'

I shift in my chair, wondering yet again what drove them apart. 'You said you might be able to help.' I swallow, praying he can tell me something, although the possibility is looking very slim. 'Mark is missing. Well, he left,' I add hastily. I don't want Richard to think Mark might have had an accident or something. 'That was over a week ago now, and I haven't been able to find him. Do you have any idea where he might have gone? Friends, other relatives . . . ?'

He shakes his head, and even though I knew it was a long shot, disappointment crashes through me. 'I'm sorry. I wish I could tell you something. Like I said, I'm not in touch with his life. I've no idea who his friends are now or where he might go.'

I hold Richard's gaze, my heart pounding. Maybe he can't tell me much about Mark's present, but . . .

'Did you . . . ?' I draw in a breath, my pulse whooshing in my ears. 'Did you ever meet Margo?'

'Margo?' Richard's face twists and his voice emerges in a rasp, as if he hasn't said her name in years. My chest squeezes as I watch the colour drain from his face. However she died, it must have been something terrible.

'Did Mark mention her?' he asks finally, taking a sip of water.

'He visited her grave,' I say, avoiding the question. I don't want to lie, but now that I'm in front of Richard, I'm desperate to know what happened . . . to see if there's something that will help find Mark, yes, but also to help understand why Mark hid her from me – why our perfect marriage wasn't what I thought it was.

Richard's shoulders lift in a sigh. 'Well, I'm glad. He's never talked about her death, and I'd always hoped that maybe, with time, he could accept it.'

'What happened?' I ask, biting my lip as Richard's face tightens. I don't want to make him delve into painful memories, but . . .

'He never said?' Richard sips his water again. 'I'm not surprised, I guess. It was a lot for a young man to handle.' He pauses and meets my eyes, as if weighing up how much he should tell me. I sit still, willing him to talk . . . to fill in the missing pieces of my husband's past, the pieces I didn't even know *were* missing until a few days ago.

'Margo was very ill,' Richard says. 'And Mark, well . . . he tried everything to help, but he couldn't. She passed away after a long struggle.' He swallows hard. 'It was a terrible time for us. The family had pretty much fallen apart already, but losing a daughter . . .' He turns his head to look out the window, his eyes glazed with tears.

A daughter? Margo was Richard's *daughter*? I jerk as I realise my mistake. Margo wasn't Mark's wife; she was his sister. Relief shoots through me, so intensely that I nearly slump over. Mark wasn't married before – I wasn't his consolation prize after his true love died. Instantly, the images that have been parading through my brain these past few days disappear, as if I've flicked off a switch. Yes, my husband still hid things from me, but it's not even close to what I thought was going on. I feel almost light-headed as I process this information, my relief giving way to grief that my husband lost his sister.

'I'm so sorry.' My words are beyond inadequate, but I can't think of anything else to say.

'It was thirteen years ago now,' Richard says, still gazing out the window. 'And although life goes on – life *has* to go on – sometimes I still can't believe she's not here any more. If it hadn't been for Jude, I'd probably be downing half a bottle of whisky every night. Thank God for her . . . and the kids. I really wish Mark could meet them, but I understand. It's part of the reason why I've let him be. He needs to have his own life away from what happened.' He tilts his head like he wants to say more, but shifts in his chair and stays quiet.

God, poor Mark, I think, watching through the window as clouds scud across the sky. No wonder he didn't want to talk about his past. The impact of his sister's illness on the family must have been truly horrific for him to shut out his parents like that. Imagine watching a sibling waste away. I wince, unable to even picture going through that with Sophie. Is it any surprise he went quiet from time to time? If it had been me, I'd have fallen to pieces. Tenderness swells inside me, along with admiration for his strength and an urgent desire to reach out and hug him close – to heal whatever wounds are inside him . . . emotionally and physically.

I take a deep breath, deciding that Richard should know about Mark's condition. He's already lost one child, and he deserves the chance to find his son.

I pause for a second, conjuring up the terrible words. 'Richard . . . Mark has cancer. And he's missing. I don't know why he left, but I need to find him – I need to be with him to help him through this. I can't let him go through it on his own.'

Richard stares at me, then shakes his head back and forth, running a hand along the smooth surface of his desk. His eyes narrow and he sucks in air, as if someone has dealt him a silent but deadly punch to the stomach.

'What kind of cancer?' he asks. His eyes bore through mine, as if I might have the answers. I wish I did.

'I don't know,' I respond. 'Mark didn't even tell me he was ill – he just said he was leaving. I only found out when someone from Macmillan Cancer Support rang him . . . it was a nurse, returning his call. I begged them to tell me something, but they wouldn't.' I pause, hoping Richard might give me another reason for why Mark received that phone call, but he stays silent. 'And everything started to make sense. Mark leaving me, him quitting his job . . . he'd had a lot of time off, apparently. And he'd lost some weight.' I try to keep my voice level through the fear kicking at my insides. I can't lose him. I won't.

'*Cancer*,' Richard says, swiping a hand over his face. 'Christ.' He reaches across the desk towards me, narrowing the gap between his world and mine. 'But look, there are many kinds of cancer, and there have been many advances in treatment. Whatever Mark has, he may not have left because of its severity.'

'So why would he leave, then?' I ask, desperate to believe that Richard's right. Is it what Sophie has said about some people being thrown off course by their diagnosis and just running away?

Richard sits back and lets out a heavy sigh. 'Mark, well . . . he knows how difficult it is to care for someone with an illness.' He grimaces, as if the memories are clawing at his insides. 'I can't claim to know my son after all these years, but he's always been very protective of the ones he loves – at least, he was with his sister. So if I had to guess, I'd say he left to keep you away from all of this – away from his disease and all the worry that comes with it.'

I hold Richard's gaze, my mind whirring. Is he right? Mark *has* always erred on the side of caution when it comes to both me and our relationship. Even Sophie – my uber-protective older sister – jokes that he'd wrap me in cotton wool if he could. He always checks that I have my pepper spray on the rare occasions when I go out on my own, and that I'm eating enough veggies and getting enough sleep. It can be a little irritating, I have to admit. But it's always signalled his depth of care and attention to our world . . . to me.

Mark has always pledged to go to the ends of the earth to keep me safe, and I guess – in light of what's happened with his sister – it makes sense that he'd hide away from me now. Margo *does* have something to do with him leaving, and I wish he'd told me about her. But now that I know who she is – now that everything is out in the open – we can face any obstacle that lies in front us and build an even stronger marriage. It won't be easy, I know, but I'm certain we can do it.

'I've let my son live his life for the past thirteen years,' Richard says, cutting into my thoughts. 'I've let him make his own way, left him alone. But I can't stand back now and watch him go through this by himself.' He leans forward. 'We need to find him. We need to make sure he's getting the help he needs from the very best doctors.'

He falls silent for a minute and I can almost see the wheels turning in his head. 'I know some doctors who specialise in cancer – there's a network of doctors who all went to medical school with me years ago. We *might* be able to find out where Mark's getting treatment, although it's a very slim possibility.'

'I've rung up most of the centres around London,' I say, and Richard shakes his head.

'They'll tell you nothing,' he responds. 'Legally, they wouldn't be able to. I'm not even sure what my colleagues can do. No one wants to risk being struck off. But having an in like I do always helps.'

'Sweetie?' Jude pokes her head around the side of the door. 'We're about to have lunch. The children are asking for you.'

Richard's heavy face lifts into a smile, one that's so full of warmth and love I have to look away. 'Thanks, honey. I'll be right down.'

'Anna, would you like to stay?' Jude asks.

The tantalising, homely scent of chicken soup and toast drifts towards me and, despite my whirling emotions, my tummy grumbles. But as much as I'd like to fill my stomach and my heart with this world, I need to get back to finding my husband.

'No, thanks. I'd better go.' I stand, and Richard gets to his feet, too.

'I'll call as soon as I hear anything. Don't worry, Anna. We'll find him,' he says. 'We're both on the case now.'

I nod, then say goodbye. The air is crisp and leaves glide from the trees as I walk to the railway station, feeling almost dizzy with hope and relief. Now that I understand why my husband left, the distance between us has narrowed. The endless questions have stopped, too, replaced once again by determination . . . and certainty. I quicken my pace, eager to get back to London now and resume the search – to find Mark and bring him home.

Home to me, and to the new world we will create together.

CHAPTER FIFTEEN

Mark

I move like a robot in the cold, dim light while pulling on my clothes. I'm desperate now for my energy to return – to sink into the past and find my sister's child, the tiny girl that was taken away when Margo slipped back into the clutches of anorexia . . . the baby only I and her father know about, and the baby I could have – should have – tried harder to keep in our family, although I was consumed with the daily struggle of helping my sister recover.

The baby that might have saved her life, if only I'd helped her get her back.

I know it's too late to change things. My sister is dead and the child is gone. But if I can somehow know that she is all right – that she went on to have the life her mother would have wanted for her and that she's loved and cared for – then maybe, just maybe, this hole that's burned into the fabric of me might finally fill in.

I lower myself on to the bed again, my eyes sinking closed as I try to picture that squalling, bald bundle as a proper person. Would she be like her mother at thirteen, filled with boundless energy and surrounded by a gaggle of giggling girls? My chest squeezes as I remember Margo throwing her arms around me, introducing me to all her friends as 'the best brother ever'. I'd roll my eyes and feign embarrassment, but secretly

I loved it – loved having a little sister look up to me, loved playing the role of the older, protective brother . . . even if she was barely two years younger than me.

So much for that, I think, pain slicing through me, because it was me who set her off on the path to her destruction, right from the start. I introduced her to running when she was barely a teen, laughingly urging her to go faster and faster, to do everything she could to beat me. I encouraged her obsession, timing our runs and planning our training sessions. I thought I was helping – I was so proud when she made the cross-country team at school – but I hadn't realised it had gone so far. Not until it was too late. Not until Margo had collapsed one day while out on yet another run. Our neighbour brought her home, and I'll never forget seeing my sister's pale face as she hobbled in, her legs moving so slowly . . . She sank on to the sofa, her chest heaving, her voice shaking as she reassured me – over and over – that she was fine. Just a touch of the flu, that was all. She begged me not to tell Mum and Dad, since they'd keep her home from school and she needed to go to one of the endless activities she was involved in.

I believed her. Why wouldn't I? Sure, she'd lost some weight, but anyone would with the same amount of training. With all that exercise, she was in great shape. Give her a few days and she'd be back to normal.

But she wasn't – she never was again. And I'll always remember that as the day anorexia entered our house, even though I didn't know it then.

I shake my head, wishing for the millionth time that I *had* told Mum and Dad. They picked up on it as time wore on, of course . . . as my sister got thinner and thinner, as their pleas to eat grew louder and louder until they finally dragged her off to a specialist. But if Margo had started treatment sooner, maybe it would have stuck. Maybe it would have stopped the disease from taking over her life, blotting out everything except her obsession with calories – even the art she loved. Despite being so social, she used to spend hours in her room, sketching everything from the obligatory ponies and rainbows to fantastical, otherworldly scenes. I shudder to remember the last drawing I saw in her sketchbook right before she went into treatment for the first time: the page was slathered in charcoal with a skeletal face leering out from the black.

She never sketched again, although she was always drawn to artistic people . . . like the father of her child, the man who abandoned both her and his baby when the anorexia returned.

My eyelids fly open as a thought enters my mind. Would he know anything about where the child might be? Surely the father would need to sign something to allow the adoption to take place. Ben – I can barely even bring myself to think of his name, that's how much I've tried to block him from my thoughts. I vowed never to speak to him again, but it's not like I have many other options to investigate or much time to do it in.

I grab my new cheap mobile and connect to the hotel's painfully slow wireless Internet. Then I google his name, as snippets of memories ping into my head. Ben was an 'artist', or so he said . . . if you can call scavenging skips and fashioning strange objects from rubbish 'art'. He spent half his time combing building sites and the other half crashing trendy east London art shows, getting drunk on warm white wine. I remember this because the first time I met him he told me he'd done just that.

My eyes widen as I see that now he's considered one of London's most respected artists specialising in 'found objects', at least according to his website (which he appears to have written himself). I click on the 'Contact' tab, noting that his art studio is at the same address where he used to live with my sister.

I can still picture so clearly the one-bedroom place above the chicken shop that Margo moved in to, full of hope and optimism as her belly swelled. It was strange to see her frame take on added weight as the baby grew – strange to see her *happy*. She'd been doing so well and her weight had been steadily creeping upwards. After years of recovery centres, counselling and relapses, I was finally feeling hopeful. Maybe now – maybe after all this time – I could start to worry less and relax a bit. Maybe now the lingering guilt that I'd started this whole thing by encouraging her to run would fade. Maybe I could start to form a life, too.

And then she told me she was pregnant.

'Are you sure you're ready for a baby?' I asked her, feeling terrible as the smile faded from her face, but knowing that no one else would ask the question. Mum and Dad had stepped back from managing her illness years ago after endless conflicts over sticking to treatment plans. Margo was over eighteen by then, and our parents had become increasingly frustrated by her lackadaisical attitude towards recovery. They'd had a huge bust-up one night after she'd skipped yet another counselling session – they told her to commit to a programme or to move out. She'd chosen to leave, turning up at my door with a rucksack slung over one shoulder.

My heart had sunk as I'd beckoned her in. I'd never seen her look so frail, shoulders hunched as if she was staggering under the weight of her bag. Her hair was limp and lifeless – her eyes sunken into her head. In an instant, every tiny joy I'd managed to accumulate in the past couple of years since leaving home vanished, like they'd never existed in the first place. Illness had found me – had invaded my home yet again.

But that hadn't mattered, because this was my sister standing in front of me and needing my help. I was her big brother, the one who should have been able to make everything okay.

'What happened?' I'd asked, sliding the rucksack from her shoulder and guiding her into a chair. Her shoulder blade was sharp beneath my hand, like a rudder for a captain to steer.

She sank down, pulling her cardigan even closer around her. 'Mum and Dad have had enough, I guess,' she'd said, her face contorting with anger. 'Can you believe they told me to get out?'

I'd raised my eyebrows. *Could* they have asked her to leave? I hadn't talked to my parents about Margo's treatment since moving out – not the all-consuming, hours-long discussions we used to have, anyway. I'd heard a few things from Margo here and there and I was always keen to help if I could, but Dad assured me he had things perfectly under control. It was his default position, although almost every visit home proved the opposite: my parents constantly arguing over the best way to get Margo to eat; my sister locked away in her room; the house falling down around us as repairs were neglected to pay for any and every possible solution to my sister's illness. I'd told myself things would get better when I left – that Mum and Dad could then focus solely on Margo – but if anything, matters seemed to get worse.

I'd wanted to believe my father, though. I'd wanted to believe he could help her, that Margo would be well again. And – I swallow, guilt sweeping through me – I'd wanted to live a life with illness no longer dragging me down.

But now . . .

'I'm better off without them, anyway,' Margo had said, her face tightening. I winced as the skin stretched across her bones. 'They don't know the first thing about helping me. Not like you.'

I'd nodded, thinking that maybe she was right. Maybe I *could* help her in a way my parents couldn't. After all, when I'd lived at home, I'd usually been the one to convince her to eat in the end. Maybe she'd be better off with me.

'Can I stay here?' she'd asked. 'Just for a bit?'

'Of course.' The answer had been automatic. *Just a few months,* I'd thought, and then she'd be well again. I focused all my energy on her, rushing home from work to make sure she'd eaten something during the day and spending hours each night coaxing her to eat another bite. I knew every website on her illness inside out – visited every counsellor within a mile radius of our flat, only for Margo to proclaim them 'useless'. She'd have a good couple of months and I'd be elated, certain that this was the moment she'd conquer anorexia, but then she'd stop eating again. Frustration and despair latched on to me wherever I went, constant reminders that I was useless.

Months turned into years, and Margo and her illness became my world. Sometimes, when the weeks spun by on a carousel of worry and fear, I'd encourage my sister to reach out to our parents once again . . . hoping – *praying* – that they'd agree to step in. My sister would have none of it, though, bitterly saying that they only wanted her if she was well. And my father held firm against my pleas for help, too, telling me in our final conversation that nothing else had worked and that by giving her a safe place to crash, I was only preventing her recovery.

'What am I supposed to do?' I'd asked, shaking with rage. 'Kick her out on the street?' I'd always got on with my father – always admired his confident authority, how people would naturally follow his instructions. Everyone but Margo, that is. But at that moment, I couldn't have hated him more. He must have known Margo would go to me – that she'd seek my support. He must have realised I'd take her in. Is that how he could chuck her out so easily, because he knew I was there to shoulder the burden? He understood how difficult things were with Margo. How could he just leave us alone like that?

Time ticked on. My parents got divorced – I'm surprised my mother even had the strength, since Margo's illness had shrunk her, too. My father remarried, and neither Margo nor I went to the wedding, both too angry and bitter to wish him well. Margo was my family now – anorexia the place we lived in.

Until she met Ben and started building her own life.

'I'm lucky I was even able to get pregnant, given how I've treated my body,' Margo responded, with the defiant look I knew so well. 'Okay, so I'm young and it wasn't planned, but what is in life? Look at the past few years.' She made a face. 'Ben's happy. I'm happy. And I'm feeling better than I have in ages.' She put an arm around me, drawing me close, and I had to admit she did feel much more solid – much more alive – than the bird-like woman I'd grown used to and was scared would snap in two. 'I'm ready for this – I really am. And God, you must be ready to get rid of me by now, too! When's the last time you had a shag?' She pulled away and smiled, almost glowing with joy. Despite my misgivings, I couldn't help smiling back. 'You're going to be an uncle! Uncle Mark. It has such a nice ring to it. And I know that you're going to be the best uncle ever, watching over this child and making sure nothing bad happens to them. Just like you have with me.'

Pain floods into me now and I press my hands against my eyes, desperately trying not to let it overwhelm me. Because I wasn't the best brother ever, and I wasn't the best uncle – not by far. I let down my sister. I let down my niece. I couldn't be a worse uncle if I tried.

Tomorrow, when I can walk further than the shower, I'll head to east London. I'll start my journey into the past, and I'll try to reclaim a bit of the faith my sister once had in me . . . the faith that she lost in the end.

CHAPTER SIXTEEN

Anna

I practically run from the Tube back to Sophie's flat after visiting Mark's father, itching to hit the spreadsheets and track down my husband. Energy and hope burst inside me as I recall Richard saying there's a very good chance Mark will be all right. And with Richard on the case, hopefully it won't be too long until we find him.

I fit the key in the lock and push my way inside, standing in the kitchen as voices drift from upstairs. Angry voices: my sister and Asher are arguing about something I can't make out. Whatever it is, it certainly sounds heated. Asher doesn't even see me as he rushes down the stairs, slamming the door behind him.

'Soph?' I call, wanting to let her know I'm here.

She comes downstairs a few seconds later, shaking her head. 'Did you hear that?'

'Well, I couldn't hear what you were saying, but . . . Is everything okay?' Sophie and Asher always argue – or 'discuss', as Asher puts it – but this seemed like more than that.

'It's fine. He'll be away on business for a few days, so at least we won't have to talk.' Sophie rolls her eyes and I bite my lip. He's going to be away for a few days and that's how he left? What on earth is going on with them? Sophie and Asher have never been the world's most together couple – they're two very different people – but I thought it worked for them. Sophie's practical and organised, running the family like a well-oiled machine. It's a good thing she does, because despite his success in the business world, Asher's a little scatty, as if his mind is moving a mile a minute.

They seem to function in two different spheres, and although I wouldn't want that kind of relationship, I always thought Sophie was at the very least content with her marriage. Now, though, I'm beginning to wonder.

'So how did today go? Was Mark's dad able to help?' She settles into a chair at the table.

'No. Well, a bit. He's a doctor, and he's going to try to use his contacts to find out if Mark's at a London cancer centre.' I pause, debating again whether I should tell Sophie about Mark's sister. There's no reason not to now – any doubt about why Mark left is behind me, and I don't want to hide things from her.

I take a deep breath and relay what Richard told me. Sophie's silent until I come to the end.

'Wow,' she says, sitting back and shaking her head. 'And Mark never told you any of this?'

'No. Nothing.' I sigh. 'There were times he went quiet, but I never thought . . .'

'Well, you wouldn't, would you?' She reaches out to touch my hand. '*God.* You know, I used to think our family was the only one with something horrible in our past . . . Dad leaving and all. But as I got older, I realised we're not. Everyone has something, I think. Something they can either put behind them or that affects how they are today.' She gets up to flick on the kettle, then settles back into her chair. 'It looks like Mark tried to put it behind him . . . until this cancer thing reminded him of all that. I guess it makes sense now why he left, although of course he should have talked to you.' She looks closely at me. 'How are you feeling about all of this?'

'I wish he'd told me about Margo and the cancer,' I say. 'But Soph, I love him. I love him, no matter what.' I meet her eyes, realising that despite all the uncertainty and fear of the last couple of weeks, that much is true. I might have been jealous and angry that Mark hid Margo from me, but I didn't love him any less. 'We need to find him.'

'We will,' she says, and her confidence buoys me up even more. 'Listen, I've almost finished all the numbers on our list—'

'But there were loads left to call!' I interrupt, my eyebrows rising. She must have spent hours on the phone.

'Yeah, but that's okay,' she says quickly. 'Work is a little slow and I've got time on my hands. I'm going to broaden our scope and add more hotels, looking beyond this area. Down into south London, maybe, and beyond.'

'That'd be fantastic,' I say, thanking my lucky stars that I have such a supportive sister. 'I'll just grab my laptop from my room and be right down to help.'

I head up the stairs, passing by Asher and Sophie's bedroom. Their heated words echo in my ears, and Sophie's pinched expression floats into my mind. Every marriage has its fault lines – I'm learning that much. But Mark and me . . . well, this is our chance to start over. And I'm not going to give up on that, no matter what lies ahead.

CHAPTER SEVENTEEN

Mark

When I open my eyes the next morning I actually feel okay – I can move without feeling like the floor is a rolling ocean keen to knock me off my feet. I take a quick shower, get dressed, then pull on my trainers, a stark contrast to the shiny black shoes I wore to the bank each morning.

I head down the creaky stairs, a cloud of dust rising from the carpet with every step. The scent of instant coffee from the dingy breakfast room turns my stomach and I hurry away from it. I need to eat, but the thought of rubbery over-boiled eggs and limp toast sends a wave of nausea through me. I should be staying in – giving my body a chance to recover from the blast of drugs – but I can't, of course. I don't know how much time I have, and I need to find out what I can about my niece while I'm still able to move.

Out on the street I pause, unsure which way to turn for the nearest Tube. Anna's worked in this part of London for ages, but apart from a few faculty parties and the lecture where we first met, I haven't been here much. The streets are dirty and people rush by, heads down and chins tucked in against the cold, and I struggle to place my warm, friendly wife amidst this cityscape. Her sphere is the university, where she can sink comfortably into the world of books and the ever-present stack of papers to be marked.

I picture her there now, head bent over her work with that cute little furrow in her brow as she puzzles over what on earth a student is trying to say . . . life proceeding as usual. My gut twists, but I know I've done the right thing by leaving. She loves her job, and I couldn't bear it if my illness took her away from that.

Wind whips down the street and I yank up the hood of my thick padded parka. I force my legs through the damp, chilly air and then down the Tube stairs for the journey east to Whitechapel. The Underground is clammy and warm, filled with the breath of a thousand commuters and the smell of wet wool. I board a train and, as it rattles through the dark tunnels, I try to breathe through my mouth and will myself not to be sick.

The train pulls into Whitechapel several minutes later and I stand up gingerly from my seat. Without any food in my gut, I feel so insubstantial, like I'm floating through the air – like I might drift off and stick to the grimy station ceiling above me. Did Margo feel this way most days, I wonder? Like she was struggling to keep her feet on the ground – struggling to focus?

I go through the turnstile and stand still for a second. I haven't been here for years, not since that terrible day when Ben called me. I was kicking back, watching a terrible action film Margo always made fun of, relishing having the flat to myself after years of sharing it with my sister. I loved her, but keeping track of her food intake, making sure she was taking care of herself and that she didn't relapse, well . . . I felt like a weight had been lifted off my shoulders. I'd been worried about the pregnancy and how she'd adjust to the pressures of motherhood, but so far everything seemed fine.

Her baby girl, Grace, arrived safe and sound in the middle of one of the hottest days of the year and Margo and Ben were both smitten. Ben was transformed, even staying in and changing nappies. I was thrilled for them, relief filtering through me that finally I could relinquish my role as protector. I'd always be Margo's big brother, but she had her own little family now – a family that would hold on to her tightly if anorexia came calling.

I'd been by several times to visit, bringing gifts and laying my claim as the world's greatest uncle. Margo was tired, naturally, and the baby liked to scream, but apart from that they resembled any other couple with a newborn: happy and in love with their child, but exhausted. Margo was even thinking of getting back in touch with our parents and telling them the news, that's how proud she was of Grace and how far she'd come.

So when my mobile rang that night I ignored it, shoving it away from me and hunkering down in front of the screen, luxuriating in the feeling of being able to shut off the outside world. I let the on-screen action play out, switched off the lights then staggered practically comatose into my bed . . . the bed Margo had given up only months before.

I remembered the phone call when I awoke the next morning. I grabbed my mobile, brow wrinkling as Ben's recorded voice came down the line.

'It's me, mate. You need to get over here and sort out your sister, all right? I can't do any more. I'm done.'

The message ended abruptly and I stared at the phone, instantly alert. What the hell? I pulled on my clothes, called in sick to the bank and jumped on the Tube to Whitechapel.

I rushed up the escalator and down the street into the early autumn sunshine, the golden rays illuminating empty crisp packets on the street like jewels. Chicken bones crunched under my feet as I lurched past the window of the chicken shop. I pressed the buzzer to Ben's flat. Finally, after I'd leaned on the buzzer for what felt like hours, the door unlocked. I opened the door and rushed in, stumbling forwards, the sharp edge of the grimy stairs cutting into my shins, then took the steps two at a time. My heart beat fast and I wondered what I might find, the old worry settling like a shroud around my stiff shoulders.

'Margo? Margo!' The door was half open and I pushed inside. The small room was rammed with baby gear: a bouncer, a swing, a mat. Bottles and other baby paraphernalia clogged each surface, and bibs and tiny Babygros were draped over the ancient iron radiators, but the place was silent and still, with no sign of the family who lived there.

'In here.' Margo's faint voice came from the bedroom and I raced towards it. My sister was an unmoving lump on the bed, her body pressed up against the wall. Despite the heat of the day, she was swaddled in blankets.

'Margo? You okay?' I put a hand on her shoulder and turned her towards me, my heart sinking when I saw her face: eyes glazed over, cheeks pale. Had she relapsed again? *Shit.*

'Where's Grace? Where's the baby?' I asked, my eyes furiously scanning the silent room.

'Gone,' Margo said, her voice emerging creaky and low, as if speaking from beyond the grave. 'Just like Ben. They've all gone away.'

'What do you mean?' I shook my head, struggling to make sense of her words. 'Margo? What do you mean?'

But Margo just stared through me, refusing to even answer.

I dashed back out to the lounge. *The baby must be here somewhere,* I'd thought, furiously pushing aside clothes, nappies and blankets . . . although I'd never known an infant to be so quiet. Fear coursed through me as it fleetingly crossed my mind that the baby might not be breathing any more – you always hear such horrible things about cot death.

But finally, after searching practically every corner of the flat, I had to concede defeat. Margo was right: Grace was gone.

CHAPTER EIGHTEEN

Anna

I swing my legs off the side of the bed, my mouth stretching in a yawn. It's still dark outside, but downstairs I can hear Sophie's voice on the phone as she continues our hunt to find my husband. We start every morning with a vengeance, fuelled by countless cups of tea and multiple slices of sugar-laden carrot cake from the bakery around the corner. Oddly, it's the only thing I can manage to choke down these days, which is good because I need the energy to match Sophie call for call. Her relentless drive to find Mark pushes me forwards, too . . . partially blocking out the voice that's taken up residence in the very back of my brain, bleating like a distressed lamb whose volume increases every time I close my eyes. I may know who Margo is now – I may understand why Mark left – but that doesn't change the fact that my husband has cancer.

And he's going through it alone.

The only thing that will silence that voice is finding him, and every day I cross my fingers that this will be it – that this will be the day that the voice finally stops. I stand now and head to the bathroom, splashing cold water on my face. In the mirror, my reflection looks more zombie than human: dark circles ring my eyes, my hair is limp and my face is pale. I stare at the woman in front of me, wondering what Mark looks like now. Will the disease have changed him or will he be unmarked? Is it too soon for any effects to show? I *hate* knowing nothing.

I open the cupboard below the washbasin to take out a fresh bar of soap, catching sight of a box of tampons. I pause, realising that I haven't bought any in a while. When was my period due? My foot taps as my brain works furiously, trying to remember. With everything that's happened, it's been the last thing on my mind, but I think it should have been a few days ago. Mark had my cycle mapped out on his phone . . .

I rush to the bedroom and grab his mobile from my bag, flipping through the mostly empty calendars until I see 'Anna due' . . . yes, a few days back. I stare at the screen, my heart pounding. *Could* I be pregnant? I've been late a few times, but I'm usually pretty regular. Nothing can throw off your body like your husband's abrupt departure, though, and things haven't exactly been normal around here.

I throw on my jacket and rush down the stairs, then jam my feet into my shoes. If I was at home, I'd have ten different pregnancy tests to choose from. Mark was always keen to have plenty on hand so I could check at any hour. But I'm not at home, my husband's not at hand and thankfully there's a twenty-four-hour chemist just down the street.

'Back in a sec!' I call, then close the door before Sophie even has a chance to answer.

Outside, a cold November wind whips down the street, biting the tip of my nose and cutting through my thin coat. I shiver and walk faster, bile rising inside me. This is not how I want to find out I'm pregnant; alone, with my husband missing – missing and with cancer. I want to be back in our flat, warm and cosy . . . back in my husband's arms. I gulp in air and shove away the anger, telling myself that everything will be all right. God, I'm getting tired of that phrase.

My breath comes fast and my pulse is racing, but I'm not sure if that's from the exertion or the thought that, finally, I could be pregnant. I *have* been tired, but mostly because I hardly sleep. And while my stomach's been off, that could be because of stress and my carrot-cake-only diet. My last period was over a month ago, so that would make me barely one month pregnant . . . if the test is positive, that is.

The chemist is just down the street, but by the time I get there, my insides are frozen. *I* barely feel alive, let alone able to sustain another life. In a daze, I pluck a test from the shelf and pay, then shove it into my coat and rush to Sophie's.

'Anna?' Sophie's voice follows me as I head up the stairs. 'Everything okay?'

'Fine!' My voice sounds strangled and, despite the cold, I'm sweating now.

I close the bathroom door behind me and peel off my jacket. My fingers shake as I unwrap the foil from the test, but I don't know whether it's from hope or fear. I want to have a baby. I want to have *Mark's* baby, and I know he was just as desperate for a child as me. But would he still feel the same now, facing what could be the biggest challenge of his life? A child is a huge commitment, and when I find him, we're going to need every bit of energy to fight his cancer . . . even if it isn't serious. Can we cope with cancer *and* a child?

And – I swallow as the thought wraps itself around me like a coil – what if we *can't* find Mark? Will I raise this baby on my own?

We will find Mark, I remind myself. And as for the baby, well . . . there's no need to worry until I find out if I *am* pregnant or not.

I lower myself on to the loo and aim for the stick, holding my breath. I feel light-headed, as if I'm watching all this happen to someone else – as if this isn't my reality. I pop the cap on the top of the stick and set it down on the sink, forcing air in and out of my lungs as I watch the liquid creep up inside the observation window. The control line appears, and my legs start to shake. I get to my feet, unable to stay sitting, then sink back down again as the room swings in front of me. God, I can't bear this.

And then . . . and then another line appears, and I close my eyes.

I'm pregnant.

I keep my eyelids closed – that line imprinted on my vision – as emotions tumble through me, each hitting with the strength of a freight train until I feel almost flattened from their force. Surprise that I really am pregnant after all this time. Sadness laced with anger that this Hallmark moment I've dreamed of so many times – bursting into the lounge holding a positive test and being swept up into my loving husband's arms – has been taken away from me so very brutally, in such an unimaginable way . . . taken away by life, yes, but by my husband's actions, too. And finally, layered on top of everything else, is *hope*. I breathe in, letting it fill my every pore – letting it push back all the fear and doubt. In the midst of this nightmare, there is light. There's a baby, a perfect mix of me and Mark. A baby that will remind us both in such tough times that life can be joyous – that it's not just illness and pain. Mark is sick, yes, but he may not have fled because the cancer is so serious. He may have fled because of what happened with Margo and his urge to protect me. He will recover, and we'll have a child.

Maybe the timing *is* perfect after all.

I open my eyes as a slow smile lifts my lips. I picture the three of us back in our flat, a Moses basket in the corner and a play mat on the floor. Baby giggles burst like bubbles in the air, showering the place in happiness and joy.

This is the new life we will build: a world of *family*. A perfect little trio, and we'll be even stronger as a unit. We will face the world together.

CHAPTER NINETEEN

Mark

Ben's flat is only a short walk from the Tube station, but every step feels like death is at my heels, just waiting to pull me under. I could have waited another day, I suppose, until I felt stronger. But right now, a day means everything. Funny how, until just recently, I used to long for the days to pass . . . for the month to pass, so that Anna could take that test and tell me there's life inside her.

I pause for a second, wondering what I would have done if she *was* pregnant. Could I have torn myself away, leaving her and my unborn baby behind? Pictures rush through my mind of Anna sponging my brow, bringing me a sick bucket then dashing over to feed our child, moving from one helpless being to the next – if I even managed to live long enough to see the baby. I shake my head, shrugging off the images. There's no point even wasting time thinking about it.

I'm sweating despite the cool temperature and I unzip my jacket, staring up at Ben's flat. The chicken place has morphed into a smart coffee shop. Even Whitechapel can't escape the effects of gentrification, I guess. The buzzer to the flats above is broken and the door hangs open, so I poke inside and struggle up the stairs. The air still reeks with the scent of frying chicken despite the shop's departure, and I try not to breathe in too deeply. I stop at the top of the stairs, listening to a bass drum thump from the flat. At least my journey here hasn't been in vain – Ben is home.

I knock on the door, then bang harder when I realise he probably can't hear me over the music. I guess the *artiste* doesn't need silence to work.

The door opens, and Ben's eyes widen in shock. 'What are you doing here?'

Not exactly a warm welcome, but then I didn't expect one. Ben and I were never the best of friends, not even from the start. I remember the day Margo brought him to my place in Finsbury Park, a few weeks after they first started dating. She was so excited for me to meet him, and I wanted to like him, I really did.

At that time, she was doing fine. She was working in one of those army surplus shops down in Camden Market, and he'd come into her shop looking for some combat boots. Alarm bells started ringing as soon as she told me this story – I mean, the kind of man who wears combat boots in their day-to-day life probably isn't someone you want dating your sister, especially when they're as fragile as Margo. Funnily enough, Margo seemed to attract the kind of man who *would* wear combat boots . . . I guess they were eager to scoop her up and fulfil their Prince Charming fantasies or something.

Anyway, she brought him round for drinks one night. I'd bought a nice bottle of red and he turned up with a bottle of foul white wine he'd 'pinched last night from the gallery down the street'. Ben's large frame and scraggy, dark curly hair made him look almost ogre-like next to Margo's small-boned figure, but it *was* good to watch her laugh and joke with him as they devoured the white wine while I sipped from my red. She'd always hidden away from men, being too ill to even focus on a world outside of her own internal battle and too insecure about her body and the ravages of her disease. But something about Ben brought her out of herself in a way she hadn't been even with me.

Still, I had my doubts. I fully admit I was a little snobby, but she was my sister after all. Ben didn't have a steady job – I'd no clue how he even made a living with his 'work'. But Margo didn't mind. She'd always loved art and painting herself, and Ben's artistic nature appealed to her. She liked his easy come, easy go lifestyle, too. The worry-free way he floated through life was completely different from how she'd struggled until meeting him. Within months she'd moved in with him, and then a few months later she was pregnant.

And then . . .

I blink to reconcile the image of Ben in my mind's eye with the man facing me now. His curls are grey and the once-youthful face – with almost-chubby cheeks that Margo had loved to pinch – has sagged. He's still dressing the same, though: black T-shirt, combat boots and army fatigue trousers. Some things never change, I guess.

I hold up my hands to show I come in peace. 'I just want to ask you something, and then I'll go.'

He raises an eyebrow, and for a second I wonder if he'll even let me in. Then he shakes his head and motions me inside. 'Come on, then.'

I enter the flat, surprised at its tidiness – in complete contrast to the last time I saw it. A leather sofa graces one wall and an armchair rests in the corner. Fresh flowers brighten the top of the dining table, and there's even *wallpaper* on one of the walls. Ben makes a face as he clocks my expression.

'I know,' he says. 'It's not exactly my taste, but . . .' He shrugs. 'Sometimes it's easier to just go with it than argue, you know? Anyway, I moved into my own art studio last week, just down the street. Finally.' He smiles, and I notice a photo perched on a side table of him with a dark-haired woman. 'So why are you here? After what happened at the funeral, I never thought I'd see you again.'

I bow my head as memories wash over me. *The funeral.* Oh, God. I've tried so hard to blank out that day. But suddenly it's clear, as if film has been peeled off a window, letting light – or darkness – stream through.

My father looking small and deflated, crouched in the corner of a pew beside his new wife, as if the further away from Margo's body he is, the further removed he could be from this reality.

My mother on the opposite side of the church from my father, holding herself so stiffly, like she might crack with just one movement.

And Margo's coffin in the middle, at the front of the church. The focus of our vison now, just as she'd been the focus of all our lives for . . . well, for what felt like forever.

But no more.

I was climbing the steps to give the eulogy when I spotted him: Ben, at the back of the church, dressed in his usual uniform of combat fatigues. I can't even identify what happened to me at that moment. All I know is that my vision blurred and rage scalded my insides. Words spewed out of me, mangled and contorted, darkened by anger and grief.

'Get out,' I said, my voice echoing around the sanctuary. 'Get out of here. You left Margo. You're the reason she's dead. *Go.*'

And without a word – without a sound, almost – Ben did leave. I never saw him again – never wanted to think of him again.

Until now.

'You know, you were right.' Ben meets my gaze, then shakes his head. 'I shouldn't have been there. I shouldn't have gone that day. I *was* the reason she died.'

I jerk in surprise, stunned both at his words and at the pain now pulling at his face. Has he lived with guilt all these years, too? Despite what I said at the time, I never really thought anyone else was to blame . . . anyone but me. Ben may have played a small part in what drove Margo to her death, but ultimately the failure to protect her lay with me.

Ben motions me on to a sofa, then sinks into an armchair. 'I tried, mate. I really did try.' He falls silent, and the only sound in the flat is the ticking of the radiator. It's so warm I peel off my coat, and I can't help remembering how stifling it was that day, too, so long ago, when I came here to find my sister.

'I didn't even know Margo had an eating problem until after she got pregnant,' Ben says. 'I'm not sure she would have told me if it wasn't for that – she'd read somewhere that a history of anorexia could affect the baby's development, and she wanted to make sure everything would be okay. And for a while it was.' He sighs. 'I'm not going to lie – I was a little unsure about wanting a baby. But seeing her so excited, hearing her talk about how wonderful it would be, well . . . it made me excited, too, even though I don't think I'd ever even *held* a baby before.'

I nod – that makes two of us. Grace was the first baby that I'd held, too.

'Watching the birth, that blew my mind. I had no clue what to do after that – Margo neither, but we muddled through. It was all going fine for the first few weeks.' He drops his head. 'And then she started going on about losing her baby weight. I might have made a few comments about laying off the cake.' He winces. 'I had no idea how that would affect her, you know? I just thought she would get back in shape . . . a bit faster. You always see those birds in the paper and on TV just weeks after having their baby and they look exactly the same.'

I can't help sucking in my breath. I can only imagine how Margo took that.

'I know, mate. *Christ*, I know.' Ben runs a hand over his face. 'But shit, I was only young. I didn't realise – didn't understand what could happen. Didn't know she would just stop eating, that her milk would dry up, that she wouldn't be able to feed the baby and it would just *scream* for hours on end . . . I tried to help her, I really did. But I couldn't take any more. Before I left, she promised to call you, to get you to come and take care of her and the baby.' He shakes his head. 'She wouldn't even move from the bed at that point. I don't know if she was too weak or depressed or what, but I knew I couldn't stay there, couldn't try any more. I just . . . I had to get out. So I called that health visitor who'd been keeping tabs on us – because she knew about Margo's history and all that – and I left.'

He takes a deep breath, his huge chest heaving under the T-shirt. As strong as he looks right now, he seems weighed down, almost *crushed* by all that's happened. A flash of sympathy goes through me, and I blink in surprise.

'It's a tough disease for anyone to handle,' I say, thinking how bizarre it is that I'm trying to comfort this man – this man I drove from my sister's funeral, who hurt her so deeply. 'She needed more than what you could give her.' She needed *me*, and I let her down.

'I had no idea the health visitor would call social services,' he continues, as if he hasn't heard me. 'No clue the baby had been taken away. I only found that out when I dropped by a couple of weeks later to collect some of my things . . . and to talk about what to do with the flat. That's when I called you.'

'Do you have any idea what happened to the baby? To Grace?' I ask, holding my breath.

He shakes his head and my heart crashes. 'No. All I know is that she was adopted. A few months after Margo died, I think it was. I had to sign something giving up my parental rights. I did think about keeping her, just for a second. But I couldn't give her a good life, not the kind of life two parents who really wanted her could. I could barely take care of myself back then, let alone a baby. It was Margo who did everything, until—'

The door opens and a woman with long dark hair comes in. She bustles into the room without turning to face us, plopping her bags on the table. 'God, that took ages. The queue was massive, some idiot wanted a refund, which dragged on forever, and . . . Oh, hi.' She smiles as she spots me on the sofa. 'Sorry, I didn't see you there.' She throws off her coat and I try to keep my expression neutral as I notice a tiny bump underneath her clothes.

She's pregnant.

I can feel Ben's gaze on me now, and I wonder how much he's told this woman. Has he told her he has another child out there somewhere . . . a child he abandoned, signed away to someone else? Has he told her the story of Margo and how he left after setting her off on a path to despair? Or has he kept all that locked inside, like me?

My lips lift automatically to return the woman's smile, and I can't help thinking that however Ben has chosen to handle the past, his life has moved on. This flat is almost unrecognisable, and he's with a new woman now . . . and with a baby on the way. A wave of jealousy and anger sweeps over me – it's so strong I have to lean back and breathe deeply, waiting for it to pass. Ben has the life I wanted to have – the life I tried to live. The life I *should* have, for all my sacrifices. Because I didn't run. I'm the one who stayed and nurtured my sister all those years. I'm the one who cajoled her to eat, who carried her to the loo when she was too weak to go on her own, fragile and weightless in my arms.

But I'm also the one who didn't save her child – who didn't even *try* to find the baby, despite Margo's desperate pleas. I'm the one who brought about her death. How could I even think of happiness after that? I don't deserve it. I don't even know why I tried.

'I'd better go,' I say, shuffling to my feet, my muscles crying out in pain.

Ben gets up, too. 'Will you . . . will you let me know if you find anything?' he asks, his face still tight and his shoulders hunched up around his neck. None of us has escaped the past unscathed, it seems.

I nod. 'I will.' I lift a hand to say goodbye, then plod down the stairs and back on to the street. It feels even colder after the closeness of the flat, and tiny shards of ice fly through the air, needling my skin. I duck my head, burrowing my chin into the softness of my jacket. Cars and buses lurch by me, but I barely hear them. I've opened the door to the past with this visit, willingly stepping inside this place of pain and grief that I have barred myself from for so long. But the one thing I long to find – the one piece of the puzzle I need to slot into position – seems determined to elude my efforts.

But it won't stay hidden for long. It can't. No matter how much you may try to run, the past is always there, waiting.

Just like, I hope, Margo's baby is waiting somewhere for me.

CHAPTER TWENTY

Anna

I'm bursting to tell Mark that we're having a child – bursting to lift him up from the dark place he must be in, to bring us even closer together – but we still haven't found him. It's been over two weeks now since he left, and with every passing day my desire grows and grows until I can barely stand it. I need to make this real, as if the baby growing inside me won't exist until its father is aware of its presence.

I'm desperate to tell anyone, actually, but I can't – not even Sophie. I won't . . . not until I tell my husband first. This child is our wonderful secret, our token of hope for the future, and I can't break that hope by sharing the news with anyone other than Mark. Even though we still have no idea where he is, he feels closer to me now than ever before. Part of him is inside me, and despite my initial fears about this pregnancy, I've never been more thankful. This baby will bring such joy to our lives, no matter what the challenges ahead.

I smile, thinking of the cute T-shirt I bought as a way of breaking the news to Mark. I tore myself away one afternoon from manning the phones and headed up to the high street and into one of those exclusive baby shops where one scrap of cotton costs about as much as a jumper from Boden. I'd only ever been in here to buy things for Flora, and it was so surreal picking out something for my own child . . . *our* own child.

As soon as I saw the T-shirt hanging at the back of the shop, I knew it was perfect. So tiny it was hard to imagine a baby fitting inside, it was such a soft blue I wanted to wrap the fabric around me. But it wasn't the colour that drew me in – it was the slogan 'Mummy + Daddy = Me' emblazoned in bright letters across the front. As I held it in my hands, happiness washed over me and a smile lifted my lips. Everything *will* be all right. This baby is the perfect combination of me and Mark, and he or she will keep us strong – will *make* us strong, together.

I carried the T-shirt home inside my coat, right next to my heart – right next to our baby – just in case my sister decided to pop out of the house and spotted me. Back at Sophie's, I folded the T-shirt into a slim box, then wrapped it in blue and pink tissue. I wrote a little card saying that Mark will be the greatest father ever, then stuck the box in my bag, longing for the day I could give it to him. We will find him, because it's not just for me now. It's for this child, too.

Mark's father has rung every morning this week to give me an update and to see if I've made any progress. So far, Richard has called the west London hospital he used to work at on the off-chance his oncologist contact there might tell him something. He's reached out to hospital admins he knows and to specialists he's met at conferences. But he's made the same amount of progress as me and Sophie: none.

I emerge from the bathroom then pad down the hallway and into the chill of the bedroom to shrug on another jumper. Sophie keeps the house nearly frigid, and no matter how many clothes I put on I'm always cold. I remember Sophie saying she was always hot when she was pregnant, but I guess it's too early for that to happen yet. I'm about to head down the stairs when my phone rings.

'Hello?'

'It's Richard.' The low, rich voice comes through the handset and for a second I think how much it sounds like Mark.

'Oh, hi.' I pause, wondering what to say today. It's becoming harder and harder to maintain an upbeat front. 'Still nothing I'm afraid. But my sister has put together a whole new list of B & Bs and hotels to try, so we're going to dive into that.'

'I need to meet this sister of yours,' Richard says. 'She sounds like she might even be able to organise my office. Jude's long since given up, but she's not exactly the most organised person herself.'

'Sophie probably could,' I say, thinking that she's certainly organised her house to within an inch of its life. No speck of dust would even think of settling on a surface here – it would be whisked away before making contact.

'Anyway, look. I'll keep ringing hospitals, but I've pretty much exhausted my contacts. It was worth a try, though.'

I nod and stay silent, something like despair pressing down on me.

'I've been thinking that perhaps we should try to talk to Mark's primary-care physician,' Richard says.

'Primary-care physician?' I ask, wondering who on earth that is.

'The GP,' Richard responds.

'Oh.' My heart sinks – I'd thought it was someone new who might have answers. 'I did try them, right after we first found out Mark was ill. They wouldn't tell me anything . . . confidentiality and all that, just like you said.'

'I know,' Richard responds. 'But if I see them, as Mark's father and a fellow colleague, they might extend me the professional courtesy of at least telling me what centre they've referred my son to.' He sighs. 'It's something I can try, anyway.' I hear a thump on the table. 'I can't stand sitting here, doing nothing.'

I nod silently, wondering how a parent gets through the death of one child . . . only to be hit by the serious illness of another. And I can certainly understand Richard's desire for action – staying still feels like giving up. That's part of the reason why I keep dialling number after number.

I quickly tell him the name and address of our GP. 'Can you let me know how it goes, even if you don't find out anything?' I ask, praying he has more success than I did. *Anything* would help at this stage.

Richard says yes, then we hang up. I bang down the stairs, sniffing the air in anticipation of coffee. The kitchen is deserted – odd, since Sophie's usually back from the school run by now, beavering away on the phone even before I arrive.

'Soph?' I call.

I hear a noise, then Sophie emerges from the downstairs loo.

'Okay, let's get started,' she says. Her tone is brisk and efficient, but her cheeks are red and her eyes are wet. She sits down at the table and picks up the phone, then clicks on the computer to bring up the screen.

'Wait.' I put a hand on hers. 'Is everything okay?' I wait for her usual torrent of complaints about Asher and his job, but she just nods. 'Oh yes, everything's fine. Just these bloody allergies.'

I know for a fact that Sophie's hay fever only acts up in June. 'Really?' I ask, eyeing her carefully. I'm sure she won't say anything – she's never been the emotional type, preferring to crack sarcastic jokes instead of wading into sentiment. I wait for her brusque response, so I'm stunned when tears start seeping from her eyes and she gets up and spins away.

'Sophie? Soph!' I touch her shoulder, trying to turn her towards me. I don't think I've ever seen her cry, not even when Dad left. She's always been the practical older sister I could lean on.

'I'm sorry. God, I'm sorry.' She pulls away and wipes her eyes, then blows her nose loudly. 'I told myself I wasn't going to do this. God knows you have bigger issues than what's going on with me right now.'

'What *is* going on with you?' I ask, biting my lip. Does this have something to do with Asher? My mind flashes back to her comment on how he's always away, the coldness between them and the argument I overheard.

'Asher and I are separating,' she says, and my heart sinks. I knew something was wrong – I've been around here so much lately and, despite my own problems, I'd have to be blind not to see it – but I never imagined it could be so serious.

'Oh, Soph.' She lets me pull her in for a hug, then moves away. 'Why?' I ask.

Sophie sighs. 'It's nothing . . . and it's everything,' she says. 'We just don't connect the way we used to, you know? I used to love being with him, and I knew beyond a shadow of a doubt that he loved me. He certainly tried hard enough to convince me of that in the beginning.' She smiles sadly. 'And I believed him. But lately . . . well, lately it feels like he couldn't care less – about me, anyway. He always asks about Flora. I'm just a cog in the machine that keeps things ticking over.'

'I'm sure he doesn't feel that way,' I say. I'm *not* sure, actually, but I need to say something.

Sophie shakes her head. 'Sometimes I feel like I could disappear and the only thing he'd notice was the lack of clean pants in the drawer. I mean, seriously! And when he is around, all we do is fight. We can't even discuss what to have for dinner without arguing. Not that he's ever home for dinner now, anyway.'

'But can't you just talk to him about all of this?' I ask. It doesn't sound like a happy relationship, but it doesn't sound *terrible*, either. 'I mean, you have been married for so long. And you have Flora . . .'

'I know, I know. And I never wanted Flora to grow up in a divorced family – or to have to go through something like we did. That was brutal. God knows I've tried to give her a good home life. That was part of the reason I decided to start up my own business and work from home so I could be here for her. For Christ's sake, I even sew all her clothes! And you know I didn't exactly begin life as a domestic goddess.' She smiles, and I remember all those times she made 'soup' for me from a horrible concoction of ketchup and onion powder.

'Maybe if I'd stayed in an office job, maybe if I hadn't taken on all the house stuff . . . maybe things would have stayed more *equal*. But I feel like now I've become the bitter stay-at-home mum while he's out swanning around enjoying life.' She sighs. 'And I *did* try to talk to him. I told him how I felt, suggested we get you guys to babysit and go out more often – start to have a life together again.'

'And?' I ask.

'And that was two years ago now and nothing changed.' She rubs her eyes. 'He'd say sure, good idea, but whenever I tried to book something, he was always busy. As far as priorities go, I don't even think I'm on the list.'

'I can't believe he doesn't care, Soph.' Okay, so things might point to that now, but they have such history together. I remember when they first met: how Sophie's face had lit up, and how she couldn't stop talking about this guy who didn't let her get away with her usual trick of creeping off after a one-night stand, who asked her out again and again until she said yes. When they married in a huge ceremony with practically half of London in attendance, she screamed out 'yes' with such force and conviction that everyone burst out laughing.

And then when Flora was born, Asher had gazed at the two of them with such love and joy . . .

How can all that be gone?

Sophie shrugs. 'I didn't want to believe it either, trust me. But how many times can one person keep trying to keep a marriage alive if the other one just doesn't seem interested?' Tears come to her eyes again, and she wipes them away. 'I don't know what's worse: to stay and keep banging your head against a brick wall or just accept defeat and move on. No, wait, I do know what's worse: to keep banging. I can't do that any longer, Anna . . . I can't. I can't just hang around and wait for him to say he's leaving, like Dad did to Mum.'

I put an arm around her, searching for something to say. I don't even know where to begin.

'The worst bit is, when I told Asher I thought we should separate, all he said was fine, if that's what I wanted.' She lets out a bitter laugh. 'As if that's what I want! He couldn't even be bothered to ask me *why*.'

'I'm so sorry, Soph,' I say. Guilt washes over me as I realise I've been so busy, so driven to find my husband that I never even attempted to talk to Sophie about her marriage. But then I never – not in a million years – dreamed it would come to this. 'Listen, please don't worry about any of this.' I wave a hand at the computers and lists and mobiles littering the table.

'No, no.' She shakes her head. 'Focusing on finding Mark is giving me something to do. It's something to think about, other than what's happening with me and Asher. Besides' – she smiles up at me – 'I know your marriage will make it through this . . . unlike what's happened with mine. If I have faith in anything, it's you two.'

I nod, grateful for her faith that mirrors my own. Our little family *will* make it through this intact, I know that much for sure. It's one thing for Mark to have left in order to protect me from his illness, but there's a baby involved now, and my husband would never dream of cutting himself off from our child.

'Right.' Sophie clears her throat. 'Let's start making some calls.'

We spend the next few hours ringing hotel after hotel, breaking only for cups of tea. I jump when my phone rings later that afternoon, and I remember I've been waiting to hear from Richard. I grab the mobile and answer before I can see who's calling.

'Hello?'

'It's Richard,' he says, and my heart starts beating faster. Sophie raises her eyebrows at me and I nod. She looks as tense as I do, and just as desperate for some good news.

'And?' I realise how abrupt that sounds, but I don't care. I need to know if he's managed to get anything out of the GP. I hold my breath, bracing myself for his answer.

'We've found him, Anna,' Richard says, his voice ringing with triumph. 'We've found Mark.'

'You found him?' I nearly drop the phone, and Sophie punches the air in victory.

'Well, I've found out where he's receiving treatment,' Richard says. 'And since we know that, we know where to look.'

'That's fantastic!' I say, happiness filtering through me for the first time since Mark left. *We found him.* I can barely believe it's true. 'So where is he?'

'He's a patient at Euston Central Hospital, at the cancer centre there,' Richard says.

'Euston Central Hospital?' My voice rises and I swallow hard. That's just around the corner from my office – my everyday world. I pause, picturing Mark walking those familiar streets. Did he hope he'd see me? Did he walk past my building on the off-chance of running into me? Or did he keep his head low, scuttling around corners in fear? *How* could he be so close to me yet hold himself so separate?

He's trying to protect me, I remind myself. That's all. Once he realises I want to be there for him . . . I think of the tiny T-shirt wrapped up in my bag and I grin in excitement and anticipation. Finally, we will have our Hallmark moment. I can't wait to see Mark's face when he opens my gift. He *is* going to be the greatest father ever.

'Why Euston Central Hospital?' I ask Richard. 'Sophie and I figured Mark would most likely be in north London. Wouldn't the GP refer him to the nearest centre?' I make a note to redouble our efforts to focus on all the hotels and B & Bs around Euston. There are loads, and I'm not even sure we've made it that far on the list.

'There could be several reasons.' Richard clears his throat. 'He might have been referred there because of the type of cancer he has. Different centres often specialise in certain cancers.'

I nod, cursing the fact that I still don't know what cancer Mark has.

'But listen, Anna,' Richard continues. 'If anyone can help get him through whatever he's facing, it's them. I have every confidence in their medical ability.'

I take a breath, clutching his words close to me. Richard's right. He *has* to be, especially now that we're having a baby.

'So here's what I propose,' Richard says. 'Depending on Mark's treatment plan, he could be in the cancer centre anywhere from every week to every month. And he'll likely have tests and appointments in between, too.'

'Every week to every *month*?' My heart drops. Somehow, I thought we could just swan over and he'd be there.

'The body needs time to rest between the treatments,' Richard says. 'The side effects can be fairly brutal.'

I cringe, picturing the man I love lying prostrate on a bed, unable to move or take care of himself.

'Couldn't you just ring them up and ask when his next appointment is?' I ask. If the GP had told Richard which centre Mark's at, perhaps the doctors will give him more information, too.

'I wish it were that easy,' Richard says. 'But it's one thing for a professional colleague to tell me where a family member has been referred, and another to ask for specifics of their medical treatment. No receptionist or administrator would risk their job that way.' He's silent for a minute. 'Why don't we set up a rota and take turns to watch out for him? I know it sounds a little cloak-and-dagger, but if that's what it takes to find my son, that's what I'm willing to do.'

'Oh, me too,' I say without a second thought. Knowing that Mark could walk around the corner at any time would make me willing to watch for him every minute of every hour. 'But you don't need to do that, Richard. I'll stay there as long as it takes.'

'Well, the outpatient centre is only open during daytime hours,' Richard says. 'And hopefully we won't have to wait too long until we find him. But . . .' I hear him draw in a breath. 'I need to do this. I need to be there for Mark this time.'

'Okay. Well, I'm going to head to the outpatient centre right now,' I say. 'Can you come too?'

'Yes, I'll meet you there.'

'Great,' I say, relieved I wouldn't be alone in this. 'You've got my number – just ring and I'll let you know where I am. I'll be there before you.'

'All right. I'll see you soon.' And with that, he's gone.

I turn towards Sophie, who's watching me eagerly, and a huge smile crosses my face. 'We've found him,' I say, tears filling my eyes. This whole ordeal will be over soon. I know the road ahead won't be easy, but I don't care, because no matter what happens, Mark and I will make it . . . together. I take a deep breath and touch my tummy. *We'll make it together*, I think again. For this baby, and for the family we always dreamed of.

CHAPTER TWENTY-ONE

Mark

One day melds into the next in this timeless void I'm now inhabiting. Apart from the cleaner who ducks in and out of the room (likely to check if I'm still alive), I feel like I'm alone in this place. In a way, I guess I am. How many others are caught in the terrible twilight between life and death, knowing that even if treatment *does* work, this is their final autumn, final winter . . . ? Maybe I'll see spring, and possibly summer – if I'm lucky. How many others have shut down their lives before life shuts them down? I turn over on the bed, wondering how I'd have reacted to this illness if Margo had lived – if things had been different. Would I have bravely faced it head-on with a confident smile, fully embracing life for the time that remained? I'd like to think so. I'd like to think I could be that person.

But there's no point dwelling on that. I'm not that person and I never can be. Margo is gone and the only thing I can do – apart from protecting Anna from my illness – is find Grace and make sure she's all right, despite my failure to watch over her. I should give my body a chance to rest and to eat and drink. But even if I wanted to, nothing tastes good any more. It's as if I've lost my taste for life, like my senses have started to turn themselves off in preparation for the end.

I can't sleep either, even though I'm absolutely knackered. I lie on the bed, eyes wide open, my mind spinning as I try to come up with a way to track Grace down. If only . . . Christ, if *only* I'd tried to get Grace back when Margo came to live with me again in my flat after I'd taken her away from Ben's. She'd begged and pleaded for me to get in touch with social services, to back up her story that she was in a safe place now and with someone who could help – that she was getting the assistance she needed.

But I *couldn't*. I couldn't see how my sister could cope with a baby just then. She was so weak, so tired, hardly able to care for herself. I couldn't deal with caring for her and the baby. I had to focus on one of them, and I chose her. Besides, I figured it would just be a couple of months before she was back on her feet. The child wouldn't be adopted that quickly, and surely social services would have to ask for Margo's consent . . . something I knew she would never give.

And for a while I thought I'd made the right choice. Margo appeared to be getting better, stronger. She was on different medications that seemed to ease her anxiety about gaining weight and she was talking about the future and how she might support Grace. Regular life resumed, and I went back to work. And then . . .

I close my eyes as the memory jolts into my brain. I remember the early morning sunshine streaming through the large sash windows, chasing away the lingering darkness; the birdsong outside making you believe you lived in the country rather than a crowded north London neighbourhood; and the peace of the street before the city awakened and the rush towards work and money began. I sat at the small breakfast bar that morning, like I had done on so many others, breathing in the rich, heady scent of my coffee and savouring the silence before another busy day.

And like always, after finishing my brew, I padded quietly towards my old bedroom where my sister now slept, taking care not to step on the loose floorboard that always squeaked. I cracked open the door, waiting until my eyes adjusted to the darkness, then crept across the threadbare carpet towards the bed, eyes peeled for any hint of movement. I stood there that day, waiting, as the niggling worry grew into fear and then panic.

'Margo?' I whispered, because I didn't want to think . . . '*Margo.*' My voice was louder, but my sister didn't move.

'Margo!' The shout escaped from me before I even had a chance to consider stopping it. I reached out to shake her, to feel the warmth of her breath on my palm, to sense her body twitch beneath me. But she was stiff, her skin cold and unyielding. I told myself it was too dark to see properly – that I was overreacting – and I flew to the window and yanked open the heavy curtains.

And in the streaming sunshine that bathed the room in gold and yellow, my sister lay still in the bed now awash with light – light that couldn't drag her back from the darkness she'd chosen to embrace.

I don't recall much about the hours that followed. I never wanted to – never tried. I do remember doctors saying Margo had died of an overdose brought on by taking too much of her medication, so much it couldn't have been accidental . . . *suicide*. I remember my mother and father telling me I'd done everything and more, and me turning away in disgust. How could they know – they, who'd left my sister to fend for herself . . . or me to fend for her, moving on with their own lives, taking off in separate directions. For God's sake, they didn't even know she'd had a baby.

And anyway, they were wrong. There *was* something I could have done. I could have got Grace back, or at least tried. I could have given Margo an iota of hope that there was a reason to carry on.

I turned my back on everything after that. I got a new phone, changed my email address and threw away any post from my parents unopened. I had to or I wouldn't have been able to move, to even start to function and pick up the pieces of my life. And the baby . . . well, I don't know what happened. I didn't want to know.

Until now.

But how can I find a thirteen-year-old girl if no one can even give me a hint as to where she might be? *Anna would have some ideas,* I think, as a longing for my wife darts through me. We'd sit down together, brainstorm for ages and come up with different paths to follow. It feels so strange to be engaged in such a big thing without her by my side.

I let out a bitter laugh, shaking my head. If Anna was by my side, then I wouldn't be doing this . . . would I? Would I – could I – ever have told her about Margo, about the baby? I grimace just imagining her stricken expression if I'd told her that I'd let my own niece go. No, I could never tell her that. I couldn't bear to have her think of me any differently from the man she believes I am.

There *is* a final place I can search for clues – a place I've been dreading . . . avoiding it until every other avenue is exhausted. After Margo died, I packed away all her things – and Grace's, too – and shoved the boxes in a storage unit. I'd drained a bottle of vodka I found stagnating at the back of a cupboard before even attempting to enter my old bedroom (sleeping there was out of the question – I hadn't been inside since Margo had died a month earlier). My father had offered to come and clear it out, but hell would have frozen over before I'd let him anywhere near her possessions. If he couldn't help her in life, then he could forget about offering assistance after her death.

I'd thrown things in boxes as fast as I could, trying not to touch any object for too long, as if they would burn my fingers. Stacks of unopened post, crumpled letters, magazines, her favourite soft toy, Lopsy, that I'd bought for her when she turned ten . . . and then all the baby stuff she'd hung on to. My chest squeezes as I remember the tiny baby clothes she'd laid out neatly in a drawer, the unopened pack of nappies, the cartons of formula. She'd wanted her baby back. She'd prepared for it. So why . . . ? Had she thought she would never recover? Had she thought I'd never help? *Would* I have?

When everything was packed, I stood back and stared at the pile of boxes. This was the whole of my sister's life, contained in only five boxes . . . packed away in a matter of minutes. But I couldn't stop and think for too long. I loaded the boxes into the boot of my car, drove to a storage centre and rented a locker. I could have kept them in the crawl space above the flat, but I wanted them away from me. I couldn't bear to think of all her things resting just above my head – as if they were silently judging me.

And to this day, they're still at that storage centre. Unopened, unexamined, untouched. Protected from time.

I take a deep breath and sit up in bed. I need to go there, after all these years. I need to comb through those papers, those things I packed away. To unearth the memories I've worked so hard to forget and to see if there's something that might help me find my sister's child.

I throw on my coat and head out into the blinding sunshine. My breath makes clouds in the air as I walk down the street to hail a black cab. My head is pounding and I know I should stop and take something for it, but I can't bear to slow down now. I climb in the back seat of a taxi, and as the cab slowly wends its way from central London to the north of the city, I remove my keys from my pocket.

Nestled against the others is a tiny key, almost lost in the forest of glinting metal – the key to the locker holding all of Margo's things. My fingers trace its sharp ridges as I ponder why I left it on my key ring for all these years. I glance down at the other keys, each one signalling a step forward: new home with my wife; new responsibilities at the bank; new *life*. Yet through the past thirteen years – through the changes and the moves – that locker key has remained. I barely even gave it a second glance. I mostly forgot it was there. But still, the thought of removing it never even crossed my mind.

You really can't disconnect from the past, no matter how much you try to convince yourself otherwise.

After a long journey across London, the minicab pulls up to a brightly painted building on the outskirts of the city. I gaze up at the exterior, but nothing looks familiar . . . I really *was* in a haze the last time I was here. My legs shake as I hand the driver some notes and get out, but I know my queasiness has nothing to do with my illness.

My breath comes fast as I make my way into the building, then through the labyrinth of corridors until I reach the right locker. I fit the key into the lock and steel myself to face what's inside – to face my past. But as I swing open the door, I'm not met with the wall of grief and pain I've prepared for. I'm met with . . . *nothing*.

The locker is empty.

CHAPTER TWENTY-TWO

Mark

I stare at the yawning space, my mouth open. I draw back and check the number on the locker door: yes, I'm sure it's the right one – it's burned into my mind. And the key did fit the lock after all. So why is there nothing here? Where has everything gone?

I'm sure there's a logical explanation, I tell myself as I retrace my steps back to the reception desk. *There must be.*

'Excuse me?' I say to the bored-looking teenager sitting behind a battered metallic counter. A few plastic chairs are dotted around, a dusty fake fern sits in one corner and a radio blares out the latest football match scores. The whole place couldn't be less inviting if it tried.

He glances up from his phone. 'Yeah?'

'I'm looking for the contents of locker number 103.' I gesture down the corridor, as if he doesn't already know where that is. 'I have the key' – I dangle it in front of his nose – 'but there's nothing inside.'

He sighs and plonks down his mobile. 'Let me see.'

I drum my fingers on the counter, the metallic noise like rain beating on a tin roof as he clacks away on the computer.

'Ahhhhhh.' He shoves his glasses further up the bridge of his nose and meets my eyes. 'Did no one tell you?'

'No one tell me *what*?' I ask, impatience tinging my voice. Anna always said I was the most patient man in the world – Margo said that, too – but I haven't the time for patience now.

'About two years ago there was a flood. A pipe burst or something and most of the units on the ground floor experienced some water damage. We would have tried to email or call . . .' He peers at the screen. 'Yes, we did try to reach you.' He tilts the monitor towards me. 'Is that your email and number?'

I lean in to examine the tiny text. It's my old number – the number I had before changing all my contact details – and the email is one I only use when I have to enter an address online. I never check it.

'So where are all my things now?' I ask, my chest tight. Surely he can't be telling me they've been thrown away, disposed of? They couldn't do that, could they? And how damaged could they be? Suddenly, I'm beginning to feel like the universe really is conspiring against me – like it doesn't want me to find Grace after all.

'Let me see . . .' He taps a few more buttons, then scrabbles in a drawer and pulls out another key. 'After drying everything out, we moved your stuff to an upstairs unit with more ventilation. But it says here to tell you that some items may have been damaged irreparably' – he stumbles over the word – 'and to offer you some vouchers.' He pushes up his specs again, then rips off a few luridly coloured coupons and hands them over.

'Keep them,' I say.

'Can I have the old key back?' the teen asks, but oddly I don't want to part with it. I manage to jemmy it off the key ring and I take the new one, then I follow the directions on the wall towards locker 237. As I climb some stairs, dizziness swoops over me, forcing me to grab on to the handrail and wait for it to pass. The fluorescent lights burn my eyes and I almost feel like I'm going to be sick, but I gulp in air and take another step up.

The second floor is a carbon copy of the first. I lurch down the corridor and fit the key into the lock, panic prickling my gut. What if everything inside is damaged? I'm not sure what I'm looking for exactly, but I'd hoped for something . . . maybe a letter from the social worker containing some sort of useful information or . . . I don't know. But while I'm worried that the damage may have erased a vital clue, my fear is so much more than just that. I packed away these precious things for safety's sake – to keep *me* safe, yes, but also as an attempt to preserve Margo untainted by time. But now . . . My sister's life is all hidden in this locker, but it's not been protected – untouched – like I'd imagined it would be.

I open the door, bracing myself once again. The overpowering odour of damp and mildew hits me like a wall, and I force myself to reach for the small stack of boxes, heart sinking as I examine the water-stained sides and sagging cardboard. I grab a box and rip it open, my stomach twisting as I take out Lopsy, the soft toy I'd given Margo so long ago. That rabbit had lived by Margo's side through each and every one of her treatments, it had rested in a cot with Grace, it had come to live in my flat . . . and it had been nestled by Margo's side when she died, the one constant in her terrible journey.

That rabbit is now covered in black mould. A huge patch stretches across one side of its face, transforming its perky, cheery grin into a sinister leer. I stare at the toy in horror, feeling the same mould creep over those very few happy memories I've managed to hang on to, pushed down deep inside me where nothing would reach them.

I drop the rabbit like it's scalded my fingers and collapse on to the floor, the cold, hard concrete seeming to bite at my bottom. The boxes loom over me, sneering at my weakness, taunting me with their damaged contents. I want to keep going – keep searching – on the off-chance that there's a random paper, some important letter tucked away or document I've missed.

But I can't. I can't do this now. I'll find another way to track down Grace . . . a way that doesn't involve combing through the desolation of my sister's life. I drag myself to my feet, throw Lopsy back in the box, and lock the door. I trudge down the stairs to the reception, then I ask the boy to call me a cab. A car pulls up and I walk as fast as I can towards it, escaping into the warmth of the back seat. I close my eyes and will the taxi to move.

It's not the storage centre I want to leave behind, though – it's this place inside me, full of darkness and death.

CHAPTER TWENTY-THREE

Anna

If I was desperate to find Mark before, now I feel like every cell of my body is on fire. I long to throw my arms around him – to tell him I want to be there for him and to let him know about this child growing inside me. I choke down food when I remember to, telling myself the baby needs it. I swallow awful prenatal vitamins and try to rest, but I barely sleep. My brain won't let me, envisioning again and again the moment we track down my husband. Because just knowing where he is – or at least where he's receiving treatment – means that the moment is imminent. It has to be, because I'd rather pluck out my eyeballs with hot tongs than wait any longer.

Will Mark be surprised to see me, I wonder? He *must* have known I would try to find him. What will he say when he finds out I know about Margo? I bite my lip remembering the times he'd retreat into himself, and my insides go all shivery as fear plunges through me. *He'll be relieved, I know,* I reassure myself. He will let me in this time. He won't push me away.

Not with the baby, I think, hope lifting me up again. Not with our child. I smile, picturing his shock and surprise morphing into happiness and joy as he takes me in his arms and holds me tightly . . . but then I wonder if he *can* even take me in his arms. Will he be so weak with the illness beating him down? Not yet, surely. It's only been a matter of weeks, and Richard seemed to think he'd be all right.

But what if – I swallow hard as fear rises up again. What if Mark *is* very ill? What if he doesn't even live long enough to see the baby? Or what if he dies when our child is so young . . . too young to even remember their father?

No. I shake my head, as if I can dislodge the doubt and worry ricocheting inside me. Mark will recover. We'll have a wonderful baby. And together, we will be a family.

Around and around my thoughts spin, on a merry-go-round that morphs from darkness to light with the flick of a switch. The dark circles under my eyes deepen, spots take up residence on my chin and my hair is greasy and lank. But I don't care about how I look. All I care about is keeping this baby healthy and finding Mark.

Sophie and Richard are just as anxious to locate him, and although there's not much left to say, it's good to have their company as we take up residence in the cafe across from the cancer centre's entrance (thank God there's somewhere to sit and wait – I'd crouch in the cold if I had to, but having fresh coffee on hand is so much better).

In the week we've been watching for Mark, we've developed a daily routine. Sophie joins me here almost every morning after sending Flora off to school. She bursts into the warmth of the cafe with a smile and without even asking, she grabs two mugs from the man at the counter who has our regular order ready for us (espresso for Sophie, decaf latte for me). Then she sits down, gets out her mobile, opens her laptop and continues calling every hotel and B & B close to the centre. She's about halfway through the list now and we still haven't had any luck, but at least we know we're in the right area because, as Richard says, Mark might not be able to handle much travel after his treatments, so he'd have to be nearby. I shudder, picturing my husband shrunken and in pain, clutching at himself tightly as he makes his way down the pavement.

Or would he stride down the street with his usual grin, standing up to the cancer with courage and certainty?

Either way, I wish I knew.

I've told Sophie to stay home if she wants to, but she's adamant that she wants to help me. I can't say I blame her wanting to get away from her empty house. Without Mark, I'm not keen to hang around at home either – I've taken up residence at Sophie's. Asher's apparently checked in to a hotel close to his work, and Sophie says that even though she was the one who brought up separating, she's finding it harder to adjust to his absence than she thought she would. I think she sleeps even less than I do.

Richard turns up just before lunch after his kids have been sent off to school and his train gets into London. Despite Sophie making up a rota so that each of us can take shifts, we all seem to spend as much time as we can here . . . each trying to find Mark for our own reasons. Sophie takes off first, heading back to Hampstead to greet Flora home from school, then Richard and I wait until the lights flick off in the chemotherapy centre on the first floor before heading our separate ways into the dark November night. As I trudge back to Sophie's, it strikes me that after keeping our marriage to ourselves for so long, it's ironic that these other people in my life – in *our* life – are helping to bring Mark and me together again.

My time with Richard has helped me get to know him, too. He's quiet yet warm, coming to life when he talks of his family. I long to ask him more about Margo – what she had, how she died and everything in between – but every time I contemplate bringing it up, I remember his expression back at his house that day . . . like someone had torn open his chest and mangled his heart. No matter how much I want to know, I can't ask. Not now, anyway. Someday, when Mark and I are together again, I'll understand what happened and why it had such an impact on his family.

I shiver now, watching the wind whip down the street, rustling the rubbish and sending it flying into the air. I follow the progress of an empty plastic bag wheeling and spinning before turning to Richard. The sky is darkening, and I cannot ignore the call of nature any longer. If ever I doubted I was pregnant, my constant need for the loo is certainly affirming it. My bladder is definitely getting a good workout.

'I'll be right back,' I say. 'Just heading to the loo.'

Richard nods and sips his coffee, his eyes never leaving the cancer centre across the street. As I head down the narrow stairs to the toilet, I hope that when we do finally find Mark he will let his father be a part of his life . . . and Richard's children, too. We need to throw open the doors of our closed-off world and let his family in – let it join with *our* little family. For the first time I can see that the more people we have around us, the stronger we will be. And I have a feeling we'll need every little bit of that strength in the future.

CHAPTER TWENTY-FOUR

Mark

It's time to head to the doctor for a check-up to see how my body is coping with the first cycle of chemotherapy. Even though it was over two weeks ago I still feel incredibly weak, and I thank God that I booked this B & B so close to the cancer centre. It's only a few streets away, so I might just be able to drag my sorry body over there.

It's obvious why I'm feeling so wretched (apart from this disease, of course). Ever since I returned from the storage centre, I haven't been able to sleep for longer than an hour or two. And when I do, I'm plagued by horrific visions of Margo's face covered with mould, filling her open mouth and forming lacy patterns on her distant eyes. Visions of the black earth heaving up to swallow her coffin . . . and of my final visit to her grave after learning I'd soon be joining her. It was there that I pledged to find Grace, my whisper torn away as the wind whipped past. But I know she heard me, and I won't fail her this time. I *won't*.

I haven't eaten nearly as much as I should, either. The cleaner, whose cheery face is the one thing I look forward to each day, is kind enough to bring me some fruit and yoghurt from the breakfast buffet downstairs. And sometimes I manage to make it to the off-licence next door to buy stale bread, sweaty cheese and ham made from God knows what. But everything tastes like sawdust, sticking in my throat with each attempt to swallow. I'm not sure whether that's down to the quality of the food or my changing taste buds.

In an odd twist of fate, this is the very same off-licence where I bought Anna and me a bottle of champagne just after we got engaged. She lived in a shabby studio a few streets away . . . I'll never forget that place. It was where we first made love, and where I realised that she was the one I'd been looking for – the one I'd make a fresh start with. I wasn't nervous and I wasn't scared. I was sure of the path forward, and certain Anna was it. And when I asked her to marry me and she said yes, I wasn't surprised. Together, we were secure and happy. I knew she felt that, too.

I glance down at the empty pages of my letter to Anna still awaiting my words, then shake my head: maybe later. I creep into the shower, standing under the tepid spray and trying not to look down at my body, at how the weight is dropping off me, how my skin is starting to pull across my bones in a way I know all too well from Margo. I picture my wife leaning her head on my chest and pulling me close, and I shudder. What would she make of my ribs beginning to poke out under my skin? How would she feel when I cringe and move away, the pain of her embrace outweighing the pleasure?

Thank God I left when I did. I couldn't bear her witnessing my transformation from man to cancer victim – from her husband to a weight around her neck, dragging her towards my death. Thank God she can't see me now . . . that she won't ever see me again.

I shake off the grief that grips me and run a hand over my chin. Bristles scrape against my palm in a comforting way, reassuring me that at least something is still growing. Something besides my tumours, that is . . . although I pray that the chemo has had some effect besides obliterating my appetite. I won't know if I'm closer to death or further away from it until all three rounds are over, and it's driving me crazy. Do I have weeks left, or months? I've always got through life by knowing my end goal: making Margo better, marrying Anna, having a family. Now

I'm operating blindly, a silent passenger inside my body. One thing's for sure, though: I don't have time to waste.

I step out from the shower and pull on my clothes, thinking for the millionth time of those boxes back at the storage locker. Despite lying on the bed for hours with my mind working like crazy, I still haven't hit on an idea to help me track down my niece. I should go back to that locker. I *need* to go back to that locker – to muster up the strength to open those boxes – but every bit of me baulks at the thought.

I close the door behind me and head out into the frigid afternoon, gathering my padded parka around me. Its warmth and comfort have been my saviours these past couple of weeks; the jacket is worlds away from the thin, formal overcoats of my old life that looked so professional, but offered no protection from damp, chilly winds.

My appointment's not until 5 p.m., but the sky is already darkening. Suddenly I long for a steaming cup of coffee, to duck into the warmth of a cafe and tuck myself up against the cold afternoon. There's a small coffee shop just across from the cancer centre – I saw it last time . . . I quicken my pace, hurrying as much as my shaky legs will allow towards the golden light streaming from its interior. I can almost taste the rich scent of coffee beans, almost feel the goodness of the hot liquid on my tongue. For the first time in what feels like forever, I don't feel like vomiting.

Ah, here it is. And good, it doesn't look very busy. I'm not sure I could take standing in a queue for very long. I lean closer to peer through the window – and I freeze.

Staring back at me is a face I haven't seen for a very long time – for thirteen years, to be exact, ever since Margo's funeral.

It's my father.

CHAPTER TWENTY-FIVE

Mark

At first I'm not sure if he recognises me. It has been a while after all, and I don't exactly look the same. My hair is greying for a start, and that's without the beard I've been growing for the past few weeks – not to mention this thick coat that looks more rapper than banker. But then his eyes widen. Shock and surprise sweep over his features, and I spin away, heart pounding.

What the hell is he doing here? I wonder, trying to force my legs to move faster. My muscles don't seem to be getting the message, though – it's like a bad dream in which you feel like you're moving through sludge. The bright lights of the cancer centre across the street beckon, looking for the first time more like a sanctuary than a death sentence. If I can just get in there – get beyond reception and up to the chemo floor – I'll be safe.

Safe from what, exactly, I don't know, but I need to get inside.

I slow at the pedestrian crossing, willing the light to turn green. I swivel this way and that, trying to find a safe route through the traffic clogging the road, but the cars keep coming. I pull up the hood of my coat and huddle inside it, hoping to shrink into myself, to hide away.

'Mark?'

My heart sinks when I hear my father's voice, feel his hand on my arm. *Shit.* Sighing, I pull down the hood and turn to face him, struggling to keep the surprise from my face. Close up and without the window to blur his features he looks like he's aged not thirteen years, but thirty. His hair is cropped short, tiny strands valiantly clinging on to the sides of his head, and his thick beard is now completely white. His face has changed, too, beyond just physical looks. He always seemed so sure of himself – so confident he was making the right choices. But now . . . there's something less solid about him – less certain.

'What are you doing here?' My voice emerges as a rasp and is swallowed up by the buses revving past us.

My father takes my arm and tries to pull me over to the side of the pavement where we won't be blocking the way and might actually have a hope in hell of hearing each other. But I won't let him. I stand still, rooted to the spot.

'I'm so glad we found you,' he says, gripping my arm despite my attempts to escape his grasp.

'We?' Oh, God. My pulse is racing so fast now that I feel even more light-headed. Who is *we*? Does he mean Anna?

He seems to read my mind and gestures towards the cafe. 'Anna's inside.'

My heart plummets. *Shit.* Do they both know about my cancer? They must do if they're waiting here just across from the centre.

'She's done everything possible to find you – to tell you that she wants to be with you.' My father draws in a breath. 'And so do I. Whatever cancer you have – whatever the prognosis – I want to be there for you and help support you through this. I need to be.'

Anger swirls through me like a tornado, almost lifting me off the ground with its intensity. '*You* need to be?' My voice cuts through the noise of the traffic whooshing past. 'I don't give a fuck about what you need, Dad.' I try to breathe, to steady myself. 'Where were you when Margo needed you all those years ago? Where were you when *I* needed you to help me with her?' Fury makes my legs shake as I picture all the days – the endless days – pleading with my sister to eat, to just get well again, to do whatever she could to beat the disease back into submission. Her fevered cries that I had to get her baby back – that she needed the child to be with her . . . a child my father still knows nothing about. I was alone; I'd felt all alone. And so had Margo, I'm sure, despite my useless attempts to help her.

My father recoils as if I've struck him, but he still doesn't let go of my arm. 'I made a mistake,' he says. 'Your mother and I . . . we made a mistake letting you deal with it by yourself. We know that now. But we thought she was doing all right, getting on with her life . . . finally recovered. We'd no idea how far things had gone. Until it was too late.'

'You're right, Dad,' I say, barely able to get out the words. 'You did make a mistake and it is too late. Too late for Margo, too late for me.' I finally manage to wrench myself from his grasp and step backwards. 'I don't want your help, not now. Go back to your life. Enjoy living – the same way you have for the past thirteen years.'

My father's face crumples like I've punched him, but I don't care. All my rage, all my fury and grief and pain is focused on him as if he's the cause of everything that's happened: Margo's disease, her death, her missing baby . . . and in a way, he is. If he'd just stepped in – tried harder to help – maybe the anorexia wouldn't have consumed her. Maybe she wouldn't have died.

Maybe I wouldn't be in this hellish place right now.

'And what about Anna?' he asks, his voice now low and tight. 'What should I tell her? She loves you. She wants nothing but to be with you. Are you really going to turn her away?' He touches my arm again and I jerk away. 'This isn't the same as you taking care of Margo,' he says. 'You don't need to protect Anna from this.'

For a second I feel my legs buckle – my *will* buckle. It would be so easy to go inside that coffee shop, to let myself fall into my wife's arms and drink in her warmth and love. But I can't – of course I can't

– because my father's wrong. Taking care of me – a weak man battling a deadly disease – *is* like taking care of my sister. He doesn't know that because he wasn't there. His life wasn't hijacked by the whims of disease. He didn't find Margo that morning when she'd finally given up. He doesn't know she relinquished a child – a child she loved yet seemed to have lost all hope of seeing again. He didn't have to pack up her possessions, then struggle to move on. He doesn't know the despair, the dark desolation. If he did, he wouldn't be asking me to inflict such things on my wife.

Pain flashes through me and I gulp in the diesel-scented air. Knowing that my world with Anna remained untouched by sickness and fear kept me moving through this strange and awful place. But now . . . now my father turns up, telling me they know I'm sick. They know everything, and that wonderful idyllic life we'd had – the life I left to protect – has been invaded. I swallow, seeing mould growing over it, turning it dark and damp just like Margo's rabbit.

'Tell Anna . . .' I swallow, bitterness and heartache propelling the words from my mouth. 'Tell her to forget me. Tell her to move on.' I meet my father's eyes and laugh, barely recognising the sound emerging from me. 'You should be able to advise her on that one.'

And then I rush across the street, not even caring if any cars are coming – I just need to get away. The doors of the cancer centre slide open and I race through them, my chest heaving.

This is my world now. This world of sickness, of poison, of death. I'm starting to feel like I really belong here.

CHAPTER TWENTY-SIX

Anna

I head out of the loo and back upstairs just in time to see Richard settling into his seat.

'Did you grab something to eat?' I ask, before noticing there's nothing in front of him. 'Oh, God. Don't tell me they've run out of food again. Honestly, you'd think they'd have a better stock here.' I can't count the number of times I've forced down a stale croissant because the shop 'had no delivery today'.

I slump into a chair, exhaustion ambushing me. How I wish I was home stuffing my face with pickles or whatever bizarre pregnancy craving might hit, with my feet up on our coffee table as my husband buzzes around me. *Soon*, I tell myself, straightening my spine. *Just give it a little more time.*

But Richard doesn't answer my question. Instead, he shakes his head. I raise my eyebrows, noticing his pale and stricken face. 'What happened? Is everything okay?'

He runs a hand along the table's scarred surface, as if he's trying to get a grip on his emotions. Then he looks up at me, his face carefully arranged into a neutral expression. 'I just saw Mark.'

'What?' Instantly I'm on my feet, the chair tipping over backwards and rattling on to the floor. 'Where?' I swivel left and right, my heart beating so fast now it feels like it might break out of my body. 'Where is he?'

'Anna, sit.' Richard waves a hand, motioning me downwards, but there's no way I can relax. How can I? How can I, when my husband who I've been trying to find for what feels like forever is somewhere nearby? My eyes swing wildly around the cafe. But . . . where is he now?

'He's across the street, probably getting treatment,' Richard says, and I sink into my chair. *Oh*. It's strange that Mark wouldn't wait to talk to me, but Mark does hate being late for anything – I'm the same. He always says it shows disrespect for the other person's time. And treatment is the top priority now so we can conquer this thing.

'Well, come on then.' I grab my coat and shove my arms into the sleeves, not even caring that the collar is all twisted. 'Let's go over and see him.'

'Wait.' Richard takes my arm. 'He says . . .'

'What?' I shake my head. What could he possibly say? He knows that we're aware of his illness – that we want to be there for him. No other barriers can separate us.

'He says he wants you to move on. To forget him.'

'*What?* Mark wouldn't utter those words . . . would he? My thought from just a few days ago flashes into my head: he *had* to know I'd try to find him. And now that I have, surely he can't expect me to head back home – to give up on us. If he thinks that, then he doesn't really know me at all.

I gulp, thinking of all the things I didn't know about him. I've always been open and honest with my husband, but is there a chance he never understood just how much I love him? He must not, I realise . . . not if he could say that to Richard. But I'm here now, and he's just across the street. And if ever there was a time to tell him how I feel – how we're going to be a family – then this is it.

Richard sighs. 'He doesn't want either one of us to help him, it seems. Me, I can understand. He's angry because of the past, and I can't say I blame him. But you . . . well, I—'

I don't let him finish. I grab my bag and leap to my feet. I push open the door of the cafe and head on to the street, my unfastened coat flapping behind me like broken wings. Cold air sears my lungs and skin, but I barely feel it. All I can see are the lights in front of me – the lights of the place where my husband is lying.

The doors of the cancer centre slide open and I rush over to the reception desk. 'Hello, I'm here to see my husband, Mark Lewis.' I can barely hear my words over the pounding of my heart. 'He might be having chemotherapy?'

'Go on up.' The woman nods towards the lifts. 'All our chemotherapy services are on the first floor. You can check with reception there.'

I hurry to the bank of lifts and jab at the 'Up' button. It seems to take forever, but finally the doors open. When I reach the first floor, I run over to another reception desk situated in front of a wide glass panel. Through the panel I can see a vast room. A small waiting area with treatment bays is on one side, while the rest of the space is taken up with large padded chairs, potted plants and shelves with books and magazines. It resembles more a hair salon or mall than what I'd imagined a chemotherapy centre would look like. I strain to catch a glimpse of Mark, but—

'Can I help you?' A man behind the desk appears in my line of vision.

'Um, hi. My husband is here.' I gesture to the room behind us.

'Name?'

'Mark Lewis.' *Come on, come on,* I think as the man taps so slowly on the keyboard. How on earth do you get to be a receptionist if you can't even type?

'Okay, yes, he's waiting to see the nurse. Go on through . . . oh, just a second. There's a note here.' He slides his glasses up the bridge of his nose and scans the screen, and it takes all of my willpower to hold back a scream.

'Sorry, it says here he doesn't want anyone to accompany him.' The man looks up at me.

'No, no, you don't understand.' My voice is shrill, so I take a deep breath, sensing that this is the kind of man who simply shuts down at women's hysterics. 'I'm his wife. I need to see him. *Please.* Please let me.'

But the man shakes his head. 'Sorry. We need to abide by our patients' wishes, I'm afraid. We can't—'

But I've already made a break for the door. I'm just about to grasp the handle when the man positions himself in front of me, blocking the door and any access to it. Out from behind the desk, he's much bigger than he appeared, and his bulk dwarfs me. There's no way I'm getting through him – or that door. Instead, I lunge to the left and start hammering on the glass.

'Mark!' I yell, hoping my voice is penetrating this shield. '*Mark!* It's Anna. I'm here! Please, I need to see you. I have to tell you something!' I'm almost tempted to scrabble in my bag, rip open the gift and hold up the baby T-shirt, but there's no way I'd want to do that in front of an audience.

Heads swing around, eyes wide as they meet mine, and a nurse scurries over to the door. The receptionist grasps my arm and starts pulling me away from the glass, and there's nothing for me to grip on to – nothing to prevent him from hauling me away.

'Madam, you need to stop right now or I'll have to call security,' he says, but I barely even hear him, because my eyes are locked on those of my husband, who's staring at me through the glass. I catch my breath and smile, certain that everything will be all right now that we've finally made contact. For just a moment I can see him – the man that I love, the man who will love our unborn baby with everything he has in him. Excitement courses through me as I realise I'm just seconds from telling him about our child.

But then . . . Mark blinks and turns away. My smile fades and I stare at the space his face inhabited, unable to believe what's happened. He can't have dismissed me just like that. He must be getting up from the chair, putting down his magazine – *something*.

I stare through the glass as I wait for Mark to approach the door, but there's no movement, and panic slices into me like a knife. I try to breathe – try to find the air to scream his name, to make my shout pierce the glass and reach him. But the man is dragging me further and further away until there's nothing I can do but silently stare through the glass separating me from my husband, willing Mark to face me.

To come back to me once again.

CHAPTER TWENTY-SEVEN

Anna

After the receptionist frogmarches me from the building, I cross the street in a haze of hurt and confusion. Richard is sitting in the same chair at the cafe, as if he knew I'd be returning soon. I lurch through the door like I'm staggering home from war, and he stands and holds out his arms. I fall into them, my eyes tearing up when I smell his cologne: it's the same fresh, clean scent that Mark wears. Richard tightens his grip and for a split second I feel like I'm back in my husband's arms.

But then . . . pain rips into me and my chest heaves as I struggle to hold back the emotions building inside, because all I can see is Mark's face, so pale and drawn, and his stare piercing through me, like he didn't even know me. The way he turned away, leaving me standing alone on the other side of the glass, with no chance of bridging the gap between us. I shudder, picturing his hollow cheeks and bloodshot eyes . . . an echo of how I'd imagined him in worst-case scenarios. Is that because of the chemo or because he's very ill? Will he be all right? I collapse into a chair, bile rising in my throat. For God's sake, I still don't even know what he has.

Richard brings me another coffee despite the fact that the staff are mopping the floor, keen to head home. The memory of how Mark and I met flashes into my mind, and tears spring to my eyes. Those two people seem like another couple.

'I don't understand,' I whisper, staring down into the coffee I can't contemplate drinking. 'How could he not even talk to me?' Richard sits across from me and touches my arm, his eyes full of sympathy.

A few minutes pass in silence, with each of us lost in our own tortured thoughts. Then Richard sighs heavily. 'Did Mark ever tell you how Margo died?'

I shake my head, thinking that Mark never even told me about Margo's existence, let alone how she died.

'She was anorexic, from around the age of thirteen,' he says, fingers gripping his mug so hard they turn white. 'I was a GP and I should have spotted it sooner, but I just never thought . . .' He clears his throat. 'Well, I thought it was because of all the training she was doing. She was a talented runner, and she and Mark would go on long runs for hours. Mark got her into running, actually – she idolised him, and anything he did, she wanted to do, too. They were only two years apart, and Margo was constantly trying to show him she was his equal. I was happy she was so interested in staying healthy . . . I'd seen so many obese kids who hated anything to do with exercise. But then she started eating less and less and exercising more and more, and we got worried. We'd take her to counselling, she'd get better and then it would start up again.'

I nod, but I still don't say a word, watching as the staff stack chairs around us. Neither of us move, like we're locked in this terrible time and place.

'Of course, we all begged and pleaded with her to eat,' he continues, leaning forward as if he can't get the story out fast enough. After everything that has happened tonight, his words have a sense of urgency about them. 'Sometimes she would take a few bites for Mark. And sometimes nothing we did or said would make any difference. She'd end up in hospital, then a recovery centre, and for months at a time she'd be well.' He pauses as if he wants to stop there but can't. He shifts on the chair.

'After she turned eighteen, things really went downhill. Margo refused to see any more counsellors, and of course we had no control over her or access to her treatment plan at that point. We tried everything – we talked for hours, spoke to nearly every specialist in the country . . . we even offered her money if she'd just commit to something. My wife and I practically ripped each other apart, arguing non-stop about the best thing to do.' He shakes his head. 'Nothing we said made any difference, and Margo just kept getting thinner. So . . .' He winces. 'We told her she'd need to continue getting help or she'd have to move out.'

I bite my lip, trying to imagine parents asking their child to leave – their child who's ill, who's depending on their strength. How does that happen?

'We didn't think she'd really go,' he explains quickly, as if he doesn't want me to condemn him. 'She was so weak that she rarely left the house. We thought it would jolt her into actually doing something. But I guess we underestimated her, because she *did* go – straight to Mark, who had moved out and was working on the bank's trainee scheme at that point.'

Richard sighs, then sips his coffee. 'I didn't want that burden on him, but what could we do? If we went back on what we said – if we took Margo in again without agreeing to follow a plan – we knew she would almost certainly die. She had to find her own way, without family to enable her. And I told Mark as much, the few times we spoke. It sounds harsh, I know . . . it took my wife and me years to come to that point. But we really believed it was the only way.'

He meets my eyes, and I flinch at the pain in them. 'Mark couldn't be that tough, though. Looking back, we never should have asked him to be. He became the one who lived with Margo, supported her, managed her illness and cared for her . . . until she committed suicide.'

I cover my mouth. 'Margo killed herself?'

Richard nods. 'Mark was the one who found her. Like us, he'd tried everything – he practically gave up his life to care for her. But in the end . . . well, she just couldn't fight the disease. Mark was furious we'd taken such a tough line with her. He felt we'd abandoned her. And maybe he was right.' Richard winces, as if he can hardly bear the turmoil going on inside him. 'I'm telling you this to help you understand *why* my son will do what he can to push you away – why he'll try so hard to protect you. If you know the horror of watching someone die . . .'

'*Die?*' The word leaves me as a whimper, swirling in the air in a mist of fear and panic.

'I'm not saying that Mark is going to die. But Anna . . .' Richard swallows, his face tight. 'I know it's hard to hear, but Mark does look very ill. Of course, we don't know what's wrong, but after seeing him, I'd wager that whatever he has, it's quite serious.'

'But you said . . .' I can barely hear the words over the frantic beating of my heart. 'You said you were confident the specialists could help him.'

'And they probably can.' Richard nods. 'Like I told you, there have been so many advances. But I do think you need to prepare yourself.' His face softens, and he reaches out to touch my arm again. 'It may not be an easy road ahead.'

His eyes hold mine as thoughts clog my mind. I'd hoped – of course I had – that this cancer was one you could just cut out, have a round of chemo and be done with it. And maybe it still is; Richard could be wrong. But even if it's not, what does it matter? Easy road, hard road, I don't care. All that's important is bringing Mark back to me – to us.

I push back from the table and get to my feet, swaying slightly as the room spins.

'Anna?'

'I'm fine, I'm fine.' I take in deep breaths until the world rights itself. 'I just want to go home now.' So many emotions are whirling inside of me that I can't even start to think of what to do next. I need to regroup – to gather myself and try to come up with a way to reach out to my husband. To break through the wall he's erected to protect me . . . from him.

Richard bundles me into a cab headed back to Sophie's. 'Would you like me to come with you?' he asks. 'Make sure you get back all right?'

I shake my head. 'No, that's okay. So I guess . . .' My voice trails off as I try to figure out what to say next. *See you later? Talk tomorrow?* The truth is, our mission to find Mark is what brought us together. And we've done that: we've tracked him down, and he's turned us both away. It feels like we each need to find our own way to get through to him now.

'We'll talk soon.' Richard pats my hand and tries to smile, but it barely lifts his lips. 'Goodnight.'

The cab wends its way towards north London, leaving behind the cancer centre . . . leaving behind my husband. It lurches in and out of the rush-hour traffic, but I barely even notice. Even though I'm nearing collapse, I can't keep still. My feet tap as I replay what happened over and over, my heart painfully squeezing with each loop. I was so sure that once we just saw each other the strength of our emotions would carry us through. And then the baby . . . the baby I never even got the chance to tell him about. *God.*

My head pounds and I press my fingers to my temples, trying to block out Richard's words about Mark's condition – trying to block out tonight. *I need to stay strong,* I tell myself. I can't dwell on what happened because I know that if I do, the fear and doubt will swell until I can't even move any more. And I need to keep moving, need to keep it together – to find a way to tell Mark about the baby. Because once he knows about our child, he will come back to me. Every fibre of me throbs with that certainty.

'Here we are.' The cabbie's voice breaks the silence and I blink in surprise that we've arrived already.

'Thank you.' I pay the fare, climb from the cab and stand back, watching as it turns and disappears into the black night.

Inside Sophie's, the kitchen is warm and cosy. Flora is sitting at the table, colouring in a map. Her face lights up when she sees me. 'Hey, Auntie Anna!'

'Hey, munchkin.' I shed my coat, eager to slough off everything to do with this night, then cross the room to give her a quick cuddle. She smells like felt tips, spaghetti and laundry detergent, and tears come to my eyes at the mix of familiar scents from my childhood. 'Where's your mum?' I'm desperate to sink into my sister's comforting arms, to let the pain and confusion come pouring out and to drink in her reassurance and faith in me and Mark. I need her to boost me up like never before.

For a split second, I consider telling Sophie about the baby, but I shove the thought away. I can't bear to dilute the moment by telling someone other than my husband first.

Flora tips her chin up. 'Upstairs.'

I nod, ruffle her hair and then take the stairs two at a time. I don't trust myself to say any more; emotions clamour inside me, fighting for release. I rush through the half-open bedroom door, but the sight that greets me stops me in my tracks.

It's absolute chaos. Empty drawers are scattered around the room, hangers lie like open traps on the carpet and a huge suitcase rests on the floor. It couldn't be further from its usual immaculate state. And in the midst of it all is my sister, furiously removing clothes from Asher's side of the wardrobe and throwing them on to the bed. It looks like a Ben Sherman catalogue exploded in here. 'Sophie?' I say carefully, not sure if I should be interrupting her.

Sophie spins towards me. 'Oh, hi. I didn't hear you come in,' she says, then turns away to continue her task. I watch silently as suit after suit comes flying out of the wardrobe to join the pile on the bed. I'm dying to talk, to tell her what's happened, but . . .

'Just sorting Asher's stuff from mine,' she says in an oddly chipper voice that I don't think I've heard before. 'He's rented a flat on the high street and he wants to start moving his things. The sooner, the better.' The upbeat tone becomes bitter.

My eyebrows fly up. 'That was fast! I thought you'd just talked about separating a week ago.'

'I know.' Sophie nods. 'But guess what?' she asks in that same brittle voice. I don't even try to guess – I stay quiet to let her continue. 'Turns out the reason he's so eager to move out is that he has a girlfriend.'

My mouth drops open, and I shake my head as I try to absorb the news. Asher has a *girlfriend*? It sounds so odd coming from his wife's mouth.

'But . . .' The word dribbles out.

'Yes, he moves quickly, right? But actually, he's been seeing her for almost a year now. At least according to him. Who knows how long it's really been going on.'

'Oh my God, Sophie. I'm so sorry.' I try to reel her in for a hug, but she shakes me off, continuing to empty the wardrobe as if her life depends on it.

'He wanted to tell me now because she's going to move in with him,' Sophie says, her mouth twisting. 'More fool her – she'll just become the domestic skivvy I turned into. He only wanted to live with her once I vacated the position.' Finally, she sits down on the bed, running her hands over her face.

'I feel like such an idiot,' she says. 'I was trying everything to make us better. And I guess in the back of my head, even though I meant it, part of me hoped that by telling him I wanted to separate he'd realise that he did want to be with me – that he *would* try to make it work. Instead, he ran straight to his backup – a backup I didn't even know was waiting in the wings.' She rubs her eyes furiously, as if defying them to start crying. 'I was right all those years ago. There usually *is* another woman. Why did I even bother trying? What a total fucking waste of time.' She glances up at me. 'At least you don't have to worry about that. At least you know there isn't someone else. You just need to find him . . .'

A wave of pain hits so hard I can barely stop a cry escaping my mouth. I can't believe I *did* find Mark and he wouldn't talk to me. But then . . . then I remember what Richard told me – why my husband would try so hard to push me away. It's because he loves me, I remind myself, and nothing else. I need to hold on to that.

'What happened?' She notices the look on my face.

I sit down on the bed beside her, wondering if I *should* tell her about tonight's events. It's not exactly the uplifting news she needs to hear right now. Once I explain the reason behind Mark's actions, though, I'm sure she'll understand.

'We found Mark tonight,' I say finally.

Sophie's mouth drops open. '*What?* You found him? What the hell are you doing here? Go home, or wherever he is, and be with him!' She grabs my arms and tries to lever me off the bed, but I manage to shake her off. God, she's strong.

'No, no, it's not that easy.' I stare down at the floorboards for a second, my reflection distorted in the shiny gloss. 'He, well . . . he doesn't want to come home.' My stomach twists again at the words.

Sophie's brow furrows. 'What do you mean, he doesn't want to come home? He knows that you know about his cancer, right? And that you want to be there with him?'

I nod, everything inside me aching. 'Yes, his father told him all of that – Richard was the one who saw Mark first. And then I tried to see him when he was waiting for the nurse and he wouldn't even let me in. But—'

'You're sure he saw you?' Sophie interrupts. She looks like she doesn't want to believe what happened just as much as me.

I nod again. 'Yes, definitely. He saw me and he turned away. But listen, Soph . . .' My voice trails off as she jumps to her feet, resuming her sorting.

'I'm so sorry, Anna.' *Bang.* A hanger cracks on to the floor, and I flinch. 'I really thought you two, well . . . that no matter what, you would stay together.' *Bang.* 'But you just never know, do you? You never know what's going on inside their heads. Even after years together.'

She turns towards me, fury twisting her features. 'You know what? *Fuck them!*' She slaps a suit down on the bed so hard the mattress shakes. 'Fuck them both. If they don't want to be with us, then why should we care? I'll tell you this much: don't waste your time trying to convince someone to stay with you. They either do or they don't. It's that simple.'

My mouth drops open at her outburst. I draw in a breath and try to stay calm. 'Look, I can understand why you're angry at Asher. I'm angry at him, too.' God, a *girlfriend*. Poor Sophie – no wonder she's furious. 'But Mark's not Asher. Our situation is nowhere near the same.' My husband has cancer, for goodness' sake. And then there's the baby . . . the baby Sophie doesn't know about. The baby *Mark* doesn't know about.

The baby that will change everything.

'Richard told me all about Margo and how she died,' I continue, desperate to make my sister understand – to hear her words of reassurance and support. I know she's hurting, too, but I can't even begin to reach out until I calm the storm of emotions inside me. 'And it's . . . awful.' I explain about the anorexia, her struggle to overcome the disease and how Mark found her after the suicide. 'If I'd gone through that, I might act the same way.' But even as I say the words, I know I wouldn't – couldn't – be that strong. 'Soph, Mark pushed me away to protect me, to stop me from going through everything he did. He loves me, I know he does. I just need a chance to talk to him – to sit him down face to face and really thrash this out.' I take a deep breath, thoughts flying through my head. 'We don't know when he'll be back at the cancer centre, so maybe we can focus on finding out where he's staying. He'll likely want to be nearby, given all the appointments he'll probably have. I know we've rung those places, but I think it'd work better in person. I'm going to take a picture of him door to door, to every hotel, and see if I can find him and—'

'Anna.' Sophie grips me firmly by the shoulders, looking straight into my eyes. 'You *did* find him. You – and me and Richard – put everything into tracking him down. You haven't been at work for weeks, or even in your own home. Your life is shut down, and I understand that.

Of course you'd do everything you could.' She shakes her head. 'But whatever his reasons – whether it's because of the past or something else – Mark doesn't want to be with you.' She pauses, as if wanting to impart extra emphasis to her next words. 'You need to stop now.'

I gape at her. 'Stop?' She sounds like Mark, telling me to move on. I shake my head in disbelief.

Sophie sinks on to the bed beside me. 'I know Mark's ill, but that doesn't give him the right to treat you like shit. For Christ's sake, he ran off without even giving you a reason! He must have known you'd try to find him, but he left you nothing, not even a bloody phone number. And after spending all those hours tracking him down, he flat out rejected you.' I flinch at her words, but I don't turn away. I won't let her anger and bitterness batter me down – I can't.

'People change,' Sophie says. 'Because of illness, life, other women . . .' She lets out a low laugh. 'Do you think I ever imagined the man who begged me to marry him would end up cheating?' She shakes her head. 'I thought Mark would never hurt you, but look at what he's done.' I try to interrupt, but she holds up a hand. 'It doesn't matter *why*. Life happens, illness happens, people do shitty things. We should know that – look at our own family.' She tightens her hold on me. 'You need to stop believing now that everything will be all right. Because it *won't*. Mark isn't the man you married. Not any more. And the sooner you accept that, the better. Take it from me.'

I break free from her grip, anger building inside me. Sophie was the one who always told me things would be fine – that Dad would be back; that *Mark* would be back. Why the hell is she doing this now? I don't need to hear this. I don't need to let my doubts and fears balloon. What I need is energy and drive – to be built up, not torn down.

'Things may not ever be all right in your marriage,' I say. 'But Mark and I will be fine.' I try to keep my voice steady despite the doubts now bleating in my ears. *Damn* Sophie.

'Fine.' Sophie jumps to her feet and crosses to the wardrobe, chucking shirt after shirt on to the bed. 'You continue living in la-la land. But, Anna, I'm out. I'm not going to help you any more. I can't help you find Mark, then watch as he rejects you again. Because that's exactly what will happen.' She pauses, her hand twisting the arm of a suit as if she wishes Asher was in it right now. 'And . . . did you ever think that for once I need *your* help now?'

'You need my help?' I stand and face my sister, furious at her certainty that Mark will turn me away once more. Instead of calming the storm, her words have whipped it up to an even greater ferocity. 'You were the one who asked Asher to leave, Soph. *You* put an end to your relationship. Sure, he has a girlfriend, but . . .' I take a deep breath, rage sweeping through me. Unlike my sister, I've had absolutely no say in my life these past few weeks. I've been completely powerless, and never have I felt feebler than at this moment. 'You chose to make him leave – you made that decision. So what exactly do you need help with?' The words fall from my mouth before I can stop them and – judging from the pained expression on Sophie's face – they've certainly hit home. I freeze for a second, my anger restrained by an urge to throw my arms around my sister and tell her I don't mean it – that of course I'll help her.

But then her voice rings in my head, saying that Mark will reject me, and my fury returns even fiercer. I won't stay here with her a second longer – I *can't*. She clearly doesn't grasp the strength of Mark's resolve to protect me. I'm not even sure I did, at least not until Richard's story tonight. And she doesn't know I'm pregnant, either . . . thank goodness. I shake my head, just imagining how strong her tirade against Mark would be if she did. For the first time my sister doesn't get my life at all.

But so what? I don't need her help. I'll find Mark on my own.

I rush from the bedroom before Sophie can respond to my attack, every bit of me vibrating with emotion. I grab my things from the spare room, throw them in a bag and then thump down the stairs and through the kitchen, anger tunnelling my vision as I rush towards the door. I need to get out of here. I need to go back to our flat – our home, with Mark beside me . . . once I find him – where we will be a family.

'Auntie Anna?'

Flora's voice floats through the air behind me.

I turn, pasting a smile on my face. 'Sorry, I forgot you were there!' I take a few steps back into the kitchen then lean down to give her a quick goodbye hug.

Flora pulls back from my arms. 'Is Uncle Mark okay?' She bites her lip, her eyes locked on to mine.

My heart drops, and I wonder how much Sophie has told her. 'Well, he's a bit poorly,' I say, my mind flashing back to that terrible image of Mark's hollowed cheeks. *God.*

'But he'll come back again soon, right?' she asks. 'It's just I have this new game on the tablet I want to show him, and Daddy said he would take a look, but he's really . . .' Her voice falters. 'I've been waiting ages to show Uncle Mark.' Her blue eyes search my face eagerly, as if she knows I'll say yes – as if there really isn't any other possibility.

I take a deep breath. She's right, this niece of mine. There *isn't* any other possibility.

'Yes,' I say, my resolve growing by the second. 'Yes, he'll come back again.'

'Good.' Flora grins, her little face crinkling, then she climbs back on to the chair and resumes her colouring.

I head off into the night, pausing to turn and gaze up at the house, light streaming from the bedroom where my sister is surrounded by the detritus of her marriage. I picture the pain on her face and I waver for a second, remembering how hard she's tried to find Mark . . . and how little I've done for her – how I brutally batted away her request for help. I've never spoken to my sister that way, but then she's never refused to help me.

She'll be all right, I think, anger reigniting as I recall her words. She's always been the strong one, and now I need to match that strength. The light flicks off inside the bedroom and I turn and walk away.

CHAPTER TWENTY-EIGHT

Mark

It's over a week – I think – since I returned to my B & B that night from the cancer centre, and over a week since I left my room. The doctor said it's normal to feel so tired – my body is undergoing an assault on all sides – but just hobbling to the loo seems like a major journey, never mind pounding the streets to somehow find Grace.

And it's not just my body that's being battered. Every time I close my eyes the events of that terrible night join the horror parade of memories scrolling through my head. The images tear at my heart, ripping off the protective layers I've built up to expose the soft, tender flesh inside me. Anna's cries mingle with Margo's pleas – my wife's frenzied pounding on the glass sharply contrasting with Margo's deathly stillness. The past has risen up to meet the present, colliding in a fireworks display of pain.

I still can't believe Anna and my father found out about my cancer, then discovered where I was . . . in just a few weeks. How the hell did they manage that? Was it Anna or my father who tracked me down? I can't imagine the two of them working together – they'd never even met.

I shouldn't have turned around when I heard the commotion. I knew the voice was hers. I should have just ignored it, but I couldn't stop myself. I had to see her. I wanted to glimpse her face one last time.

God, I wish I hadn't. I can't erase the memory of Anna's smile when my eyes met hers – the sound of her anguished screams as she was dragged off. I'll never forget the blind rage inside me, propelling me to twist away from her . . . anger at my cancer, anger that she somehow found me, anger at *life*. I was shaking after she left – shaking so much that the nurse asked me if I was all right. I couldn't answer. I wasn't all right. I'd just rejected my own wife . . . I'd hurt her so much.

I stare at the letter beside me – rather, the empty sheet of paper – and wonder yet again if I did the right thing. Anna knows about the cancer now; despite my best efforts, it's too late to keep the knowledge from her. And by tracking me down she's made it clear she wants to be with me. She's not my father – she never deserted me. She's done everything she can to find me. Am I really going to force her to stand on the sidelines as I go through this? Keep her at arm's length while my life fades away? Keep her away from the man she loves?

I don't know, I don't know. I let out an agonised sigh as I get out of bed, then I pad across the room to retrieve my jacket and shoes. I'll think about it more later, when my mind is clear. Right now I need to head back to the cancer centre to have the incision for my catheter checked. The wound is red and angry-looking, and the last thing I need is an infection. I can barely move as it is.

'Cleaner!' There's a rap at the door, and I run a hand over my mouth, trying to look halfway presentable. I don't know why I'm trying, though. If I haven't scared her off by now I'm not going to. She comes and goes at very random hours – I could barely rouse myself to answer her knock these past few days. She pushed inside anyway, her face a mask of efficiency, and proceeded to tidy everything as I lay there, barely moving. Given the state of the room (never mind me) I wouldn't blame her if she ran away screaming. I certainly would, if I were her.

'I bring you food and water from downstairs,' she says in her thick Eastern European accent each time she arrives. I don't argue – just nod and say thanks as she sets down several bottles of water and bowls of soft oats I can just about manage to choke down.

She pokes a head around the door. 'You're up! Feeling better?'

I nod, grateful she's seeing me on my feet for once. 'Yes. Thank you so much for bringing me the water and food.'

'No problem.' She shrugs. 'I bring you some fresh towels and more water. Do you need anything else?'

'No, I'll be fine.'

'Okay.' She shrugs again, then turns to go.

'Thanks . . . what's your name?' After everything this stranger has done for me, I feel like I should at least know something about her.

'Anna.'

The name hits me between the eyes and I slump down on to the bed, trying to suppress a low groan. *Anna.* Of course it is. Even when I try to run from her – even when I turn away – I can't escape.

'Anna,' I say, my voice hoarse. 'Thank you.'

I feel like an old man as I trudge down the street. Drizzle floats through the air, and I tip up my face to let the moisture settle on my skin – to feel something tangible other than the emptiness echoing inside me. Because in the month since I left my wife I feel just that: empty. Seeing her face was a harsh reminder of the love I have – the love I've pushed down deep just to get through the hours. I want to be with her and I know she wants to be with me, but I still don't know if I can pull her into this terrible place where I find myself now.

It's warm inside the centre and the bright lights burn my eyes. I head up to the first floor and check in, then follow the nurse to a bay and lie down. I'm exhausted already and I've only walked about one street. The sounds of the centre fill my ears, and in the bay next to me I can hear a man and a woman settle in for their treatment.

'Don't worry, I'll be fine,' the man is saying to the woman. 'Just go and get Chloe from nursery before you're late.'

'It's okay. Mum's going to collect her,' the woman responds. 'I don't want to leave you.'

'I'm not going to die right now.' I can tell he's trying his best to keep his tone light, but I can hear the tension in his voice, too. 'Give me at least another few weeks.' I hear him shuffle, groaning to get up. 'Right, well, I'm going to head to the loo before we get started. If they come, tell them I'll be back in a tick.'

'Okay,' the woman says.

I hear a rustle and the scrape of metal rings as the curtain is pulled back, and after the man has left, the woman speaks again.

'Hi, Mum. Are you on the way to get Chloe?'

There's a buzz as her mother responds on the phone, and then I hear the woman's muffled sobs.

'Oh, Mum. It's awful. I hate it here. You'd think I'd be used to it by now, but this whole place feels like a room full of dying people. And Dylan . . .' She lowers her voice. 'He just looks awful. I can't sleep at night. I'm afraid he'll die at any second. He's having problems with his breathing now, and the doctors say it will only get worse. And Chloe . . .' I hear a gulp. 'Chloe's actually scared of him. This morning she wouldn't even come into our bedroom. She asked me who he was, and where Daddy had gone.' I can barely make out the words through her crying. 'I can't bear it, Mum. I *can't*.'

My heart aches as I listen to the woman try to control her sobs. *God. At least Anna and I didn't have children,* I think. I never thought I'd be grateful for that, but I am now.

I hear footsteps returning and the rasp of the metal rings as the curtain opens again, and the man groans as he lies back down on the bed.

'Did the nurse come?' he says.

'No, not yet!' The woman's tone is bright and cheery, with no sign of her tears from just a moment earlier. If I hadn't overheard her telephone conversation, I'd believe she was coping brilliantly.

I lean back in my chair, thinking that Anna would be like that. She'd show me her strength – she'd be brave. But away from me . . . I close my eyes against the image of her breaking down, just like the woman beside me has – saying she can't bear it, can't take it any more.

And I know without a doubt that I cannot do that to my wife. I made the right choice: watching me go through this is worse than staying on the sidelines, and if distance will protect her, I'll do whatever it takes to stay as far away as possible.

CHAPTER TWENTY-NINE

Anna

I barely stop over the next week, whirling from the print shop to collect the flyers I've made up with Mark's face on them then back down to Euston. I begin my assault on hotels, B & Bs and guest houses, knocking on doors, pushing into busy receptions and interrogating staff. My cheeks and nose are red from the cold and my fingers are constantly numb despite my gloves. My feet ache, my calves strain and I'm permanently exhausted, but I won't allow myself to give up . . . not even when I sink down on to our sofa at the end of a long day with Sophie's voice creeping into my head, saying that Mark has changed – that if he could hurt me like that, he's not the man I married.

He is, I remind myself. He's doing this to protect me – because he loves me. But even as I try to keep this in mind, my brain continues asking me – over and over – if my sister could be right. Has he changed? Or is there a part of him I never really knew – a part that would push me away, no matter what I said? Mark's cold, distant stare that night he rejected me floats before my eyes, and I think of Margo and everything from his past that he never told me. Surely something so tragic had a huge impact on him . . . an impact I knew nothing about.

I just need to find him. If I can tell him about the baby, everything will be all right. I'll make everything all right with Sophie, too – she'll understand once she knows I'm pregnant. It's been a week since we've spoken, and despite our harsh words, I can't help thinking of my sister and that she might need my help. *Does* she need my support? It's hard to imagine; in all these years, she's never asked me for anything. I bite my lip as guilt curls through me. *She's strong,* I remind myself. She'll get through this . . . and so will Mark and I.

I slide a hand down to my stomach, and I'm so grateful for this child that makes me feel like I'm not alone. Without anyone around me, my world has shrunk down again: to this flat; to the streets I'm searching, which are so familiar from my years working in the area, yet now feel foreign without my job to anchor me here . . . and to the baby inside me. But the baby is all I need right now – that and Mark. To feel his arms around me, pulling me close to him. To know that, whatever lies ahead, our love can carry us through. Because this past month – God, has it been a month since he left? – amidst all the uncertainty, the fear and the confusion, I've never doubted one thing: that Mark loves me. He wouldn't have tried so hard to protect me if he didn't.

I can't wait to break the news to him that we're going to be *parents.* I smile, shaking my head. It still hasn't sunk in completely – I guess because I've kept the news to myself, waiting for the moment when I track my husband down. The tiny baby T-shirt is tucked away in my rucksack, lodged against my back as I make my way up and down the streets . . . a kind of talisman to draw him in.

It's dark as I climb the stairs of yet another guest house just a few streets from the cancer centre. The Christmas lights strewn haphazardly in the grimy windows of this B & B make it look more sad than cheerful, the garish colours illuminating the peeling paint and stubborn weeds poking through the paving slabs. The door is open and I stick my head inside. No one's around, so I pad through to reception.

'Hello?' The small, cluttered space behind the desk is vacant. I notice a bell and ring it, the noise sounding even louder in the hushed silence.

'Sorry, I was just out back.' A woman with a pen stuck in her frizzy hair appears from behind a curtain. 'How can I help?' She shoots me a distracted smile that only lifts the corners of her mouth, then looks down to read a paper on the messy desk in front of her.

'Hi, sorry to bother you, but I'm looking for this man.' I shove the printout with Mark's photo in front of her nose, hoping she'll focus on it for just a second.

Her eyes slide over it and then she shakes her head. 'No, sorry. I'm just a temp, though, so . . .' She shrugs, not even bothering to finish her sentence.

'Can I leave this here?' I put the paper on the desk, praying someone will see it before it gets buried in the avalanche of other documents arrayed there.

'Fine.' She's already halfway back through the curtain and I sigh, making a mental note to circle back here tomorrow.

'Lady?' A woman in her early twenties wearing a tabard and carrying a mop approaches me shyly. 'I have seen this man.' She nods towards Mark's photo on the stack of papers in my hands.

'You have?' My heart leaps. 'In this hotel?'

She shakes her head. 'No, not here. At another hotel I clean for – down the street, around the corner. Called Euston Stay Inn. I – N – N.' She spells this out automatically, as if she's done it a thousand times.

I grasp her arm. 'Oh, thank you, thank you.' My heart is racing and I rush to the door, eager to get down the street as fast as I can and over to the place where my husband is.

'I hope he feels better,' the cleaner says. 'Tell him Anna says hello.'

I spin towards her. 'Anna? Your name is Anna?'

She nods, and a huge jet of hope spurts up inside of me. It's a good omen that the woman who has led me to Mark has the same name as me, surely.

I run down the street, the cold night air ripping at my lungs, then turn the corner. The lights of yet another row of hotels beckon. The names flash past me as I hurry towards the Euston Stay Inn. I race up the steps and open the hotel's front door, then hurry to the desk where thankfully a receptionist is waiting.

'Hello, welcome,' he says.

'Hi,' I huff as I try to catch my breath. 'I'm here to see one of your guests. Mark Lewis?'

The man nods and checks on his computer, then shakes his head. 'No, I'm sorry, there's no one registered here by that name.'

'There must be.' I almost insist he check again, but then I remember that Mark may not have given his real name. I turn the stack of flyers in my arms towards him so he can see Mark's picture. 'This is the man here,' I say, tapping the paper.

'Ah, yes. Up the stairs, room four.'

I don't even say thank you. I just turn and rush up the stairs, struggling to breathe as my heart pounds with hope and love. I stop for a second outside the door, wipe the sweat from my face and remove the gift from my rucksack.

Then, with my smile growing bigger and bigger and excitement fluttering inside me, I lift my hand and knock.

CHAPTER THIRTY

Mark

I collapse on the bed when I return from my appointment at the cancer centre. The nurse told me I was fine – she simply changed the dressing on my incision, took my temperature and implored me to return if I feel feverish – but my insides feel like jelly. It's not just the walk that's taken it out of me, though. It's that couple – hearing the woman's sobs as her partner battles cancer. Whatever tiny, lingering hope I harboured that somehow Anna and I could get back together has been crushed. I couldn't stand to have her cry by my bedside like that woman – not like I did with Margo . . . although I never cried, I realise now. Did I? I hurt so much I practically *vibrated* with pain, as well as with guilt and regret. But crying? I couldn't. I tried to lock away all my emotions, like the memories in the storage unit. I couldn't let them overwhelm me if I wanted to move on.

But now . . . I sag on to the bed. I feel raw and exposed, and it's not from my illness. There's no barrier now between me and my past; not any more. I'm right back in that awful time with Margo – unsure which way to turn, uncertain if I should try and get my niece back or focus on making my sister better.

I shake my head as grief crashes through me. My sister died and my niece is missing. And what did I do? Tried to move on. Tried to build a life away from the horror . . . a life away from pain.

I failed at that, too.

There's a knock on the door and I glance up in surprise. The cleaner usually comes in the daytime, and it's almost six in the evening. I shrug and call out, 'Come in!' I wait to hear the key turn in the lock, but there's nothing, so I heave myself from the bed and plod to the door, thinking that maybe reception wants to talk to me. The landline in my room doesn't work (not much here does) and, if memory serves, I need to pay my rent for next week.

I swing open the door and step back, everything inside me freezing as I take in the person standing before me.

It's not the receptionist.

It's my wife.

'Mark,' she says, her voice shaking despite her smile. She makes a move as if she's going to hug me, but then drops her arms to her sides.

I stare at her. I can't look away, as much as I need to. Now that she's right in front of me I want to drink her in – every bit of her, from her red cheeks to the hair that's stuck to one side of her face. Her eyes are wide and I can tell she's nervous by the muscle twitching under her eye. I long to take her in my arms, to burrow myself into her warmth.

But then . . . then I remember my wasted body, and the sound of the woman's sobs at the cancer centre tear through my mind, my heart. I *cannot* do this to Anna. I know this with a surety that throbs in every part of me. I made a vow to put as much distance as possible between us, and now I need to keep it. I can't fail again – not this time.

I take a breath, summoning up every ounce of strength left inside me to fight this battle – a battle I need to win; a battle that will crush my wife, but ultimately save her. *I need to see her as the enemy,* I tell myself. It's the only way I can do this.

'Mark, look,' she says, the words bursting from her before I can launch my attack. 'I know you didn't want to talk to me, but we really need to. There's something I have to tell you, something I—'

'Stop,' I say, wrenching the word from inside of me. 'Anna, you need to *stop*.' My voice is so cold – so heartless – that I barely even recognise it. I can see by the way she draws back that she doesn't, either. 'There is nothing you can tell me that will change things. Do you understand? *Nothing*. You're having twins, you've discovered a cure for cancer, you're taking off to the moon. Nothing at all.' She flinches as if I've struck her, but I harden myself against her. 'I don't care what happens to you any more, and you shouldn't care about me. We are done, over, *finished*.'

'But—'

She tries to step forward but I block her way, giving her a little shove back. Surprise flickers through me at my actions, but I need to do this. I need to end this, once and for all. I marshal all my energy for a final assault, blinding myself to her anguished expression.

'I didn't want to tell you, but I was going to leave you, anyway. The cancer, well . . . it just made me do it sooner.' She gasps and covers her mouth and in that second I hate myself for what I'm doing to her – for the cruelty I'm stunned I have within me – but I force myself to continue. 'I don't know what else I can tell you. I'll send you some divorce papers, if that's what you need. Just go. Just go, and leave me alone.'

I push the door closed, desperate to force her out before the pain overwhelms me. Just before it clicks shut I notice the wrapped box in her arms. I sink backwards on to the bed, my legs collapsing beneath me.

How like her to bring me a token of love, I think, despair and grief filtering through me as I picture her in a shop, selecting a card and something she knows I'd like: chocolate, maybe, or even those cufflinks I had my eye on. I imagine her desperate to find me, knowing I'm ill, spurred on by hope and love as she trudges down endless streets. After all, if the roles were reversed, wouldn't I do the same? Wouldn't I do everything to keep us together, even *knowing* how hard it is to watch someone you love die?

But we're not the same people. We don't have the same starting point . . . not by far. Anna might be strong – perhaps stronger than I thought – but she has no idea what it's like watching disease claim someone you love. And my sister had a hope of recovery . . . in the right hands, anyway. I have none. You can be as strong as you like, but you can't hold out against death.

I listen as Anna's footsteps fade away. I hear the front door of the B & B thud closed. I've won the battle – I *haven't* failed this time – but I feel anything but victorious. Before sadness and pain overwhelm me, I pick up the pen and finally start to write my letter.

To seal my fate – our fate.

CHAPTER THIRTY-ONE

Anna

I stare at the scratched wooden panel just inches from my face. I can't breathe – can't move. I feel paralysed, like my muscles have forgotten how to work. Did Mark actually close the door on me? Did he say that he was planning to leave me, even before the cancer . . . and that *nothing* I could tell him would make a difference?

Not even having a baby?

I stand like a statue, trying to grasp on to just one emotion as my husband's words batter me over and over, like a flurry of blows to the gut. I can't make sense of anything – can't even begin to absorb that what he said is true. Mark wasn't going to leave me. It was his cancer that made him go. He left to protect me and to save me from what he went through with his sister.

We were happy. We *did* love each other. I can't have been wrong about that – about the life we built, our perfect world. Can I?

I wait for the automatic voice that always responds 'No, of course not' to pipe up, to allay my doubts and fears like it always has this past month. But it's silent now, as if it's disappeared. I've been beaten back by words, dissolved by the harsh reality of coming face to face with the man I love and being knocked down so cruelly – so *brutally* – in a way I never believed he could behave, not in a million years. In one fell swoop, he's demolished our perfect world, too – at least, the world I believed existed, regardless of what he kept hidden in his past.

Maybe Sophie was right and I was living in la-la land. Maybe that world never existed in the first place. I guess it didn't if Mark was planning to leave me. *Planning to leave me.* God.

But why . . . why would he keep trying to have a child with me if he wanted to leave? Did he not care that much – about me *or* his baby? Did he really mean that even if I told him about our child it wouldn't make a difference?

I can't believe that. I just can't. No one could be so callous, and certainly not Mark. Not that man I know.

Then Sophie's words about people changing ring in my ears so clearly it's almost as if she's right here beside me. I shake my head as the realisation sinks in that I *don't* know him – at least, not the man inside that room. Maybe he's changed, or maybe I never knew him to start with. But whatever the reason, I can't deny that the man I thought I married is gone.

I was so ready, so prepared to give him my all . . . again. To build something new – something wonderful – with him and our baby. To take on the fear and uncertainty ahead – to face why he didn't tell me about Margo – and grasp the chance to have something wonderful together.

But in the end, maybe he's right. There *is* nothing I can say – not even that I'm having his baby – if he meant those vicious words. I vowed I'd never give up, never stop trying to bring us together, never lose belief in us. But I can't chase something so elusive if one of 'us' has morphed into something unrecognisable.

Tears streak down my cheeks and I let them drop silently on to the carpet below. Doors open and close, voices shout down corridors and, out on the street, someone who's had too much to drink is trying to sing 'Jingle Bells'. I feel like every bit of me is hyper-alert, as if by tuning into the environment around me I can protect myself from the pain inside.

But finally I need to move. My legs feel numb from standing so motionless, my head is pounding and my back aches, but these are nothing compared to the agony gripping my heart. I stare at the door for one more second, willing it to open – for the Mark I know to come back again – but it stays closed. There's no noise behind it, and I know I have to go. I could stay here all night and nothing would change. Mark's certainly made that crystal clear.

I head down the stairs and shake my head when I realise I'm still holding the box containing the baby's T-shirt. 'So much for that,' I mumble, fury and pain almost lifting me off my feet as I recall my card saying that Mark will be the greatest father ever. So much for our Hallmark moment – my vision of happy families. I look around the reception for a rubbish bin, but of course there isn't one. That would be too much of a convenience. I can't bear to hold this box any longer, so I drop it on to the reception desk on top of a pile of papers. If this place is as disorganised as the last fifty B & Bs I've encountered, it will be buried under more paper by morning.

Then I walk down the steps and out into the night – away from my husband, away from my hopes and away from our future together.

CHAPTER THIRTY-TWO

Mark

I don't sleep all night after Anna leaves. I furiously scribble word after word to her, praying my explanation will make her understand how I could treat her that way . . . even though, looking back, I'm having trouble understanding it myself. I know I had to be harsh and throw whatever bricks I could, but oh, the things I said. The way I mentioned children, like we hadn't been desperately trying for our own. How I tossed out divorce, something I never – not in a million years – would have applied to our happy, secure marriage.

How I told her I was leaving anyway.

I rub my eyes, as if I can erase the image of her awful expression when I flung those words at her, but it's branded on to my eyelids. Her face crumpled and her body slumped, as if any hope inside her had suddenly deflated – like I was a stranger, not the man she'd spent the past ten years with. I feel like a stranger to myself now, too, and I don't just mean my wasted body.

Why am I doing this? I think to myself, putting down the pen. Is the pain I'm causing Anna now – the pain I'm causing myself – worth it? Maybe my wife is strong enough to be by my side. Maybe she's stronger than me, and it's my actions – not my illness – that will damage her beyond repair. My heart lurches when I picture her back home in our flat, curled up on the sofa all alone, crying like her world has fallen apart.

It has. *Our* world has, and I'm the one who destroyed it – well, me and my cancer. I had to push her away to keep her safe. I couldn't fail, and I can't cave in now. I need to keep reminding myself of that.

It's too late, anyway, I think, picking up the pen again. I've brutally rejected her, and all I can do is hope that this letter allays some of her pain once I'm gone.

I don't even know if what I'm writing makes sense, as page after page fills up with frantic words. I can barely read my scrawl at the best of times. I'll go back and make it legible later. Somehow it seems important to get it all out now. I write all night, only lifting my head when the cleaner comes in – a different one; it seems fitting that it's not Anna. She brings me food, tidies up and leaves again without a word, and still I keep working.

Finally, I have nothing left to say. I feel empty, hollowed out, with nothing left to live for – nothing except finding Grace, that is.

I stand up, blinking as the room rotates around me. I feel hot and cold at the same time, but I can't sit back down. I need to open those boxes at the storage centre and see what's inside . . . see if there's a way to find that baby before packing up my life. I don't need to protect myself from the pain of memories any longer – I can't anyway, since all of my armour is now stripped away. And after last night, I'd be amazed if I even *can* feel any more pain.

I don't have the energy to shower so instead I spray everywhere with deodorant, trying not be sick as the strong scent fills the room. I pull on my trusty padded jacket, slide the phone into my pocket and stagger down the stairs. The reception is empty as usual, so I head into the frigid air to flag down a cab. The sky is such a brilliant blue it hurts my eyes, and I squint against the light. Everything feels raw, as if sandpaper is scraping against my senses.

Thirty minutes later we pull up to the storage centre. I follow the route from a few days ago, through the reception and straight up to the second floor. The locker door opens and the light above me snaps on. The stack of boxes is there, just as I'd left it. I lift up my arms, my muscles feeling heavy and weak, and I struggle to get the boxes down.

I force myself to scrabble through one box and then the next, looking for anything that might give me a clue to Grace's whereabouts. My heart lifts as my fingers touch something that feels like a stack of papers, and I haul them out. The sheets are all stuck together, melded into a solid lump by water and time. Carefully, as if I'm performing surgery, I try to peel them apart, but it's impossible – they rip and tear, the writing lifting from the pages' surfaces, rendering each paper completely unintelligible. I try to make out what I can: a British Gas bill from what must be Ben's flat; an old pizza flyer; a reminder from the doctor's surgery of Margo's next appointment. There could be something here from social services I guess, but if there is I certainly can't decipher it.

Shit.

I lift down another box and tear it open. Thick jumpers, tops and trousers spill out, cascading on to the floor in a rainbow of colours. I can't help smiling, remembering how Margo always loved wearing bright colours. In fact, we buried her in a red dress I'd never seen on her, but I know she loved. She used to stroke the silky fabric, telling me that when she gained enough weight she was going put it on and take me out to a West End show.

My throat closes up and I force myself to shove the box aside and open the next. *More clothes,* I think, my heart dropping as I root through a jumble of trousers. Right, time for the next one – the last one. I crouch down, my pulse racing as I open the box's flaps. It looks somewhat promising, a mix of yellowed novels, magazines and . . . I scrabble around in the bottom of the box, my fingers closing around a small object that's heavy in my hand. Is that a phone?

I draw it out, examining it in the bright light. The clunky frame coated in heavy plastic is a throwback to the past when smartphones were only a figment in some computer whizz's imagination, and an image pops into my mind of Margo on the night before she died. I heard her voice so I went into her room and was surprised to see she was talking on the phone. She used to be a real chatterbox, but ever since she'd moved back in with me after Ben left I'd rarely heard her speak on the phone. I'd taken her talking as a good sign, slowly backing out of the room with a smile on my face. Oh, how wrong I was.

I turn the mobile over in my hands, wondering who she was speaking to that night. Would the call still be registered on the phone? Or could it contain a message, a phone number, a contact . . . *something* that could point me in Grace's direction? I try to turn it on, but of course the battery is long dead and – I run my hand around the empty box – there's no charger either. That would be way too easy.

I'll head down to Tottenham Court Road now, I decide, desperately wanting to lie down, but knowing I need to carry on. As the centre for all things electronic in London, someone there should be able to sell me an old charger that would work with this phone. Hopefully, it's escaped any water damage. I stand up now, hastily repacking Margo's things. Some day, after I've tracked down Grace, I'll go through her mother's possessions and pass some things on to her. And for a second, surrounded by my sister's life, it almost feels like she's right there beside me – like she's smiling down at me and is at peace for once.

'I will find Grace,' I mumble, repeating my vow from the graveyard. 'I promise.'

I ask the man at the reception to call me a cab, and a few minutes later it pulls up out front.

'Tottenham Court Road, please. The end with all the electronic shops.' There's no reason to be more specific – any cabbie worth his salt knows which end that is. I lean back in exhaustion as the cab makes its way back towards central London.

As we head through the streets the city sparkles with Christmas decorations. The festive season is approaching, and . . . I shut my eyes, realisation flooding through me that this will be my last one, and I'm spending it alone. An intense yearning judders through me – a yearning to be with Anna, holed up in our flat, surrounded by books, mugs of hot chocolate and mulled wine as the Christmas tree winks on and off in the December darkness.

On Christmas Day we always sleep in as long as possible until an excited phone call from Flora awakens us. Sophie spends Christmas at Asher's parents and Flora opens our gift there, then rings the second she discovers what it is. I have to say, I have a knack for choosing the perfect gifts for Flora. Even Sophie jokes that she can never top what I give her daughter, although she always accuses me of going overboard. And I do, I know, but deep down I guess it wasn't just Flora I was buying a gift for – it was Grace, too.

After the phone call, we lounge in bed for a bit, curled up with each other against the pesky cold draughts that poke their long fingers through our ancient sash windows. Then we have French toast, coffee and cinnamon bagels slathered with cream cheese, rubbing our bellies and groaning as we open our gifts. We always pay the price of indigestion for our gluttony, but after years of Christmas morning struggles and pleas with Margo, I suppose I wanted to just let go – to celebrate the normalcy of overeating on Christmas Day.

When we're able to move again, we wrap up warmly and pull on our wellies, then head out into the silent streets and over to the Heath for our traditional Christmas walk. No matter the weather, the Heath always seems even more magical on that day. Bare branches arch overhead, the ground is spongy with dead leaves beneath our feet, and the scent of damp earth colours the air. And I'll never forget one Christmas when we were caught out in a snow squall, tiny flakes swirling through the frigid air. I grabbed Anna and spun her around, her laugh encircling us.

I wonder what she'll do this year. A sharp pain goes through me as I picture our flat, all decked out with the decorations we've curated like an art show over the past ten years. Will she have a tree? Who will help her put it up if I'm not there? And who will remind her to turn off the Christmas lights each night before she goes to bed?

Anger stirs inside me and I shake my head so hard I get a crick in my neck. How I wish she'd never found out about my cancer. How I wish she'd simply thought I'd left her. Why couldn't she just let me go? Why the hell did she need to track me down – twice?

Did I really think she would *just let me go?* I ask myself. A few phone calls, a few messages and that's that? Did I think I could escape our relationship – the one we've poured ourselves into, the one we've moulded into something so special – by closing the door behind me? The fact that she fought for me – that she tried so hard to find me and that she succeeded – makes me even more certain that I need to protect her now. She might think she's strong, but she would lose herself in this illness. She'd give everything she had, and I can't let that happen. Anyway, after what happened last night, I think I've made my feelings more than clear now. I muffle a cry as I remember her stricken face and my awful, awful words. I hope she'll be all right.

She will be, I tell myself. She has Sophie, and her life is still intact. I know I've hurt her terribly, but she will heal.

'Tottenham Court Road.' The cabbie's voice cuts into my thoughts and I turn my head to look out the window. Buses rumble past, people push by – the world outside is alive. I hand over some cash, then try to open the door without hitting anyone on the busy pavement. The cab pulls away and I stand for a moment, then move to the side when someone swears and tries to get by me. God, I forgot about the craziness of Christmas shopping in central London. It's years since I've been down here. Anna and I always shopped online rather than brave this chaos.

After being locked in my room for the past few days, barely talking to a soul besides the cleaner – and after leaving my life behind – this place seems even crazier than usual. Lights flash from the huge theatre on the corner and the nearby Tube exit spews an endless stream of people, all laughing and shouting, high on life . . . or drunk. I lean back against a shopfront, not even sure how to penetrate the crowd.

My legs start to buckle, but I push past the people and head towards the row of shops across the street before what little energy I have deserts me. I pull open the door, explain to the man behind the counter what I'm looking for and show him the phone. He shakes his head and suggests the next store along, and I cross my fingers in the hope that I won't need to repeat this process too many times. I already feel like I'm going to pass out.

'I need a charger for this phone,' I say to the man inside the next shop. Sweat beads on my forehead and I wipe it away. Heat washes over me like a wave, and for a second I'm certain I'll be sick.

The man takes the mobile from me, turning it this way and that. 'Haven't seen one of these for a while,' he says. 'Let me check in the back.'

I manage a nod, then grip the counter with both hands and concentrate on breathing steadily.

'All right, mate?'

I jerk upright at the sound of his voice. 'Yes, fine.'

'You're in luck. I found one for you. At least, I think I did.' He holds the charger up in the air. 'Want to give it a try?'

'Sure, that would be great.' The last thing I want is to get all the way home – well, back to the B & B – only to find out the charger doesn't work . . . if the phone is still functional, that is. I'm not sure I could manage another journey back here. It's not that far, but it feels like miles.

He takes the phone from the counter then unwinds the charger and plugs it in. We both stare at the mobile, and I'm willing it to come to life.

'Have you used it lately?' the man asks, still watching the phone.

'No, not for over ten years,' I say. *Thirteen, to be exact.*

'Ten years?' The man raises his eyebrows. 'Well, the SIM card probably won't work. Mobile phone providers tend to deactivate them if they haven't been used for a certain amount of time.'

'Oh.' My heart drops. I hadn't thought of that.

'But if any information was saved on the phone – like contacts and such – you should be able to access that.'

'Okay.' I cross my fingers, hoping that Margo had saved something on there. I'm not sure how much help her contacts would be, but something is better than nothing.

The phone lights up and the man smiles. 'Bingo. It's working.'

'Oh, brilliant. Thank you.' I hand over my debit card and pay, my fingers itching to grab the mobile and see if my sister *did* save anything on the phone.

The man catches my gaze. 'Have a look.'

I pick the phone up, my heart pounding. The SIM isn't working and of course there's no signal. But maybe the contacts . . . I scroll through to 'Contacts' and click it open, sighing at the long list of names. When Margo was well she collected new friends like children collect seashells. Well, I have plenty of time to call them all.

I click through the contacts, hoping to feel a flicker of recognition, but there's nothing. Until – my father? I blink at the name, wondering why he would be on the list. Whenever I encouraged her to get in touch with our dad, Margo was adamant she'd never talk to him again. I shrug internally, thinking that perhaps she just automatically put his details in there – but then I didn't do that on my phone, and he's my dad, too.

'This is great – thank you,' I say to the man, putting the mobile down again. I can't wait to get back to my room and start calling those numbers – maybe after a brief lie down, just to regain some energy. My head is throbbing and it's all I can do to stay upright.

I watch the man unplug the phone and charger then shove them into a carrier bag. I silently will him to hurry before I collapse. I grab the bag then push open the door, forcing my muscles to move in this strange, numb state that's descending over me. The edges of my vision start to go black and I blink furiously to try to clear my sight, but the world swings around me and the darkness closes in, and the last thing I remember is the grimy grey pavement rushing up to meet me.

CHAPTER THIRTY-THREE

Anna

I sleepwalk through the next week. Days pass, one to the other, and I don't leave the flat. I hole up inside, unable to do anything but sit on the sofa and stare into space, trying to absorb the fact that Mark really is gone; that even if I had told him we are having a baby – even if I'd revealed I was having *twins*, like he said – it wouldn't have made any difference.

I still can't believe he meant those words, but then . . . then I think of his hard face saying that he would have left me anyway, even if he didn't have cancer. I remember everything he didn't tell me about Margo and his past. I think of him pushing me out of the room and the door slamming in my face.

As if I was nothing but an inconvenience to be shooed away.

As if he didn't love me.

Did he ever love me? Or is he like Asher, his emotions pulling a disappearing act over time? Anger rattles through me, and it's so intense I spring to my feet – anger at Mark, yes, but also at my sister for being right about our situation . . . for realising that Mark wasn't who he'd seemed, even before I did. Why couldn't I see it? Did his illness blind me to everything else? Was I so desperate for a happy family that I was willing to sweep everything else aside?

I gaze around the flat at all the things we held dear, an urge to smash everything swarming over me. My mind flashes back to Sophie manically clearing the bedroom of Asher's things and understanding filters through me. I don't want any reminders of my life with my husband either. Mark hasn't cheated on me, but he has betrayed me, heart and soul. Because despite what I thought was a perfect marriage, I really was in the dark. I had no idea of Mark's tragic past and its lingering effects on his present. I thought our marriage had everything I'd always wanted, but it didn't – not transparency, not trust, not strength. And in the end . . . not love.

Mark is ill. He might recover completely; he might have years left or he might have months. I'm pregnant, seemingly about to raise a baby alone. But whatever the circumstances, I can't think about him any more. I *won't*. For my own sanity, as well as for my child.

Fury rips into me and I grab the nearest object – our framed engagement picture. I lift it high then throw it hard against the floorboards. The glass makes a satisfying shattering sound before splintering into a million different shards that will be impossible to clean up, but I don't care. I grab the photos from the wall and smash them, too, then sweep my hands along the bookshelves, upending all the knick-knacks we've collected through the years and the books we've read together. I've never been a violent person and part of me can't believe I'm actually doing this, but it feels way too good to stop.

A few minutes later I'm standing in the middle of the room and there's nothing left to dismantle. I stare at the mess in disbelief: cushions on the floor, lampshades askew, broken glass everywhere. It looks like I've been burgled and, actually, I feel like I have. I just never thought my husband would be the thief.

I pause for a minute to catch my breath, then head into the bathroom. I sink down on the toilet and rest my elbows on my knees, trying to get a grip on my whirling anger. But instead of my pulse calming, it quickens when I catch sight of crimson blood staining my knickers.

Oh my God. There's not much, but it's more than a drop . . . and I can hear it dripping into the toilet, too.

Panic and fear rush through me as I wonder what this means. I know it's still early in this pregnancy . . . eight weeks or so, if my calculations are correct. And I know miscarriages are common, but I never even thought about the possibility of losing this child. I suppose I was too focused on finding Mark to really consider anything else.

Please don't go, I silently beg my baby. I may want to pack up everything to do with my former world, but I don't want to lose this child who's been with me through the horror of the past month, a silent partner in my quest to reunite our family. And even if bringing our family back together may not happen – even if it *won't* happen, I remind myself – it feels like my baby and I are a pair now, melded not just by blood, but by love. Love . . . and hope for whatever future we might build together. 'Please don't go,' I say aloud now fervently hoping that somehow my baby can hear me.

I stay frozen on the toilet for what feels like forever, the tiles chilly beneath my feet and the light burning my tired eyes. My thighs turn purple with cold as time ticks by until I finally dare to move. I ease off the toilet seat, holding my breath as I glance down at the toilet bowl. Ribbons of blood curl through the water, but there's not nearly as much as I'd feared. Everything seems all right down below – no stabbing pain; no wrenching ache – and the bleeding appears to have stopped, thank God.

I bite my lip as I hobble back to the lounge, afraid to move in case the bleeding starts up again. It's too late to go to the GP now . . . should I head to hospital? Will they do anything for me since it's so early in the pregnancy? Anger grips me that I'm going through this all alone and I take deep breaths to beat it back. I can't let it ambush me again, not like that.

Sophie would know what to do, I think, gingerly lowering myself on to the sofa. Back when she was pregnant with Flora she used to regale me with endless horror stories about labour and birth. She'd studied the baby books so much she could have given the midwife a run for her money.

But it's not just her encyclopaedic knowledge I need – it's *her*. It's been two weeks since we've spoken – the longest we've ever gone – and I've missed her desperately. She's always been there as a protective presence in my life. Can I really fault her for wanting to prevent me from being hurt? Now that I understand the pain she was feeling after Asher's betrayal, I can hardly blame her for her actions. I cringe, guilt filtering through me when I remember how Sophie asked me for help and I just ran off, completely shutting her out.

I grab my mobile and dial her number, crossing my fingers in the hope that she picks up. God, I hope she's all right.

'Hello.' Her voice is cooler than usual, but at least she's answered.

'Soph . . .' I pause, wondering where to start. I don't have time to waste though, so I launch straight in. 'I need your help. I'm pregnant, and I started bleeding.'

Her breath catches and I wait for the torrent of questions, but thankfully she snaps into emergency mode. 'How many weeks are you? What colour is the blood? And how heavy is it?'

I answer everything as quickly as I can, so grateful for my efficient older sister. I don't know how I've got through the past couple of weeks without her. 'Do you think I should go to hospital?' I ask.

'Probably not,' she answers. 'Not if there wasn't much blood, and the bleeding has stopped anyway. I had a bit of bleeding with Flora . . . it's quite normal, and it doesn't necessarily mean you're having a miscarriage. You should go to the GP tomorrow though, just to get checked out and make sure everything is all right.'

'Okay.' I let out my breath slowly, my muscles relaxing for the first time since spotting the blood.

'Anna . . .' Her voice is hesitant. 'You're pregnant? *Shit.* I mean, well . . . When did you find out?'

'A few weeks ago,' I say. 'I didn't tell you because I wanted to let Mark know first.'

'I can understand that.' Silence falls on the line between us, and then she says: 'Is that why you were so desperate to find Mark again? Because you wanted to let him know about the baby?'

I nod, then realise she can't see me. 'Yes.' My voice is hoarse and I wrap my arms around myself as my mind replays the horrible scene when I *did* find him again.

'God, I'm sorry, Anna. I wish I'd known – I would have kept helping you. I was just . . . so angry – at Asher and at Mark – at how they'd treated us, you know?'

'I know.' I rub my eyes. 'And I'm sorry, Soph. I'm sorry I left like that when you needed me, too. I just couldn't think of anything else – anything but getting through to Mark.' I sigh, shaking my head. 'But actually, you were right about Mark, and how he's changed.'

Sophie draws in a breath. 'You spoke to him?'

'Yes. And it was . . . terrible.' His words are still freshly branded on my heart, stinging every time I remember them. 'He was like someone else, Soph. He literally pushed me away.' A tear streaks down my cheek and I swipe it away.

'But did you tell him about the pregnancy?' Sophie asks. 'I know I said he's changed and all, but it *is* his baby.'

'I tried,' I say, drawing a blanket up around me, as if it can keep me and my child safe. 'But he wouldn't even let me talk. He said . . .' I breathe in, trying not to let emotions swamp me. 'He said he was planning to leave me anyway, even before the cancer – that nothing I said would make any difference, not even having a baby. And then he slammed the door in my face.'

'Holy shit.' Sophie's voice is low, as if even she can't quite believe how cruel my husband has been. 'Holy *fucking* shit. What an absolute bastard.'

'Yeah. That's one way of putting it.' I shake my head, incredulity running through me that those words really do apply to Mark . . . to the man I married.

'God, Anna. I can't believe you've been going through this on your own! Why the hell didn't you call? I mean, I know we had a bit of an argument, but still.' She pauses. 'You're not going to try to contact him again, are you?' she asks in a cautious tone.

'No.' My voice is firm and I mean it. Whatever Mark and I had – however our lives intersected – it is over. 'I need to focus on my baby now and try to get through this on my own.'

'You know you're not alone,' Sophie says. 'I'm here for you . . . and the baby, too. I can't believe you're pregnant.' I can just imagine her shaking her head. 'Tell you what – why don't you come stay with me and Flora again, at least until Christmas is over? I've really missed you, and Flora has, too. You can't knock around that flat by yourself over the holidays.'

'Okay,' I say, without even having to think about it. This place isn't a home any longer and I can't wait to get out of here.

We say goodbye and I put my hand on my soft and yielding stomach. Mark may never be a part of our baby's life, but I know – with a determination so fierce it echoes in every cell of me – that I will do everything possible for this child. Stay strong for it, take care of it, be its world.

I glance around the smashed-up flat then throw off the blanket and slowly stand. It's time to get on with my life – a new life I never imagined I'd be leading, but a life I need to build for myself . . . and for my baby.

CHAPTER THIRTY-FOUR

Mark

I toss and turn, lost in a grey haze. Machines beep, needles prick my arm and I feel the tight pull of an IV line packed with drugs to yank me from this dangerous place – caused by an infection, apparently. A silly infection that threatened my life because of my weakened immunity. Cool hands, dry hands, hands that are brisk and efficient come and go at all hours. Through my closed eyelids I see the lights above me morphing from a fluorescent brightness to a dim yellow as the days slide into nights.

Darkness crouches over me and I try to stop myself from sinking into it . . . into the parade of grotesque masks that invade my sleep, if you can call a tangled, twisted spate of unconsciousness 'sleep'. Anna's agonised face, then Margo's stiff and waxy skin, then Grace, her visage blank and unformed . . . I'd cry out if my throat was working, if something inside me functioned right now. But everything seems dull and blunted – everything except the desire to find Grace, although even that feels far away, a blazing sun swathed in fog.

And one day – at least I think it's day as those bright lights are on – someone new grips my hand. Someone who lingers, not like the nurses who come and go at the speed of light. Fingers curl around mine with strength, as if they're anchoring me here, like they don't want to let go. I drift in and out of consciousness and they're still there, a solid presence to soften the blows of my subconscious assault. I can't help grasping them, a lifesaver in this ocean of sickness.

I lift my eyelids now, my mind clear for the first time in days. I'm still clutching the hand, and my eyes move upwards to see . . . my father.

'*Dad?*'

My father smiles and reaches out to touch my arm. I'm tempted to pull away, to let him see that if I'd known the hand belonged to him I wouldn't have latched on to his strength. But he's holding my fingers too tightly and I don't have the power to fight.

'What are you doing here?' I struggle to sit up, an impossible mission in these stupid beds. 'How did you find me? And does Anna know where I am?'

'Relax,' my dad says, pressing me back down again. 'I've been calling the hospital every day just to check if you'd been admitted. I knew you might be at some point. That's just the nature of this disease . . . and no, Anna doesn't know you're here.' He sighs. 'Although she certainly deserves to, I think,' he continues in a gentle tone. 'I didn't want to cause her any more pain though. She was in pieces after she left the cancer centre that night.'

I wince and swivel my head away from him, unable to bear the sympathetic expression on his face – sympathy for my wife, the woman I hurt, even if it was for the best. And my father doesn't even know the worst of it. Shutting the door in her face took everything I had, turning me into a person I didn't know existed. I thank God that that's the end of it and I won't need to do it again.

'I know you told me to stay away from you, and I understand why. But I can't. I won't – not this time.' His voice cracks, and he clears his throat. 'Please, as soon as you're well enough, come home with me. Let Jude and me take care of you, help you get well. Let us be your family again.'

His words curl around me with the seductive warmth of a fuzzy blanket and, for an instant, I long to say yes – to be a part of a family once more, the family that Margo's disease broke apart. To lean on their collective strength and let them buoy me up.

But how can I? How can I do that when my sister is dead – dead because of the failure of our family? Because of my father – because of *me*?

'I . . . I can't,' I say, looking up at the ceiling. A jolt of emotion – regret, longing? – jars my heart, but I ignore it. 'Just . . . just leave me. Please.' I want to sound strong, but instead my voice emerges thready and weak. I'm so, so tired now, my battery utterly drained. *How many times will I have to keep doing this?* I wonder. How many times will I need to keep pushing people away?

'All right.' My father stares down at me, but I don't meet his eyes. 'Well, I'll be back to check on you tomorrow. Call if you need anything. Do you have your phone with you?'

The phone. Oh God, Margo's phone. I close my eyes as the memories scurry through my brain: leaving the shop with the carrier bag in my hand, then the blackness swamping me. Where is that bag now? I sweep my eyes around the tiny confines of the bay, but there's nothing.

'Have you seen a carrier bag anywhere?' I ask, my heart beating fast. I can't have lost that phone. I can't. It was my very last link to Margo, to the people in her life – to someone who might know where Grace is.

My father's brow furrows. 'A carrier bag? No, I haven't seen anything.'

My heart plummets. *Shit.* Without the phone, I have nothing. I strain to recall the names in her contact list, my eyes widening when I remember seeing my father's number.

'Dad.' My gaze locks on to his. 'Margo had your number on her phone. Did you . . . were you two in touch before she died?' I know it's highly unlikely, but I might as well ask. I've got nothing else to go on.

'Yes,' he says, and surprise judders through me. 'We were.' An expression I can't decipher crosses his face, and then he clears his throat. 'She wanted me to help her with the baby.'

My jaw drops and I cast about for something to say, but nothing emerges. My mind races as I try to process his words. He knew Margo had a baby? Why didn't he say anything to me? And *did* he help – or did he deny Margo that, too? Is that why she overdosed?

'I spoke with her that last night – the night before she died,' he continues. 'She rang me up and told me everything: about the baby and how the child had been taken away.' He pauses, swallowing hard. 'And she asked me to help . . . not to get her baby back, but to make sure Grace ended up with a good family – a family that would love her and take care of her the way she couldn't. She didn't want me to tell you she'd called – she didn't want you to feel guilty that you couldn't help. Of course, I said I'd do whatever she needed me to. I'd no idea she was planning to take her own life. I thought it was a good thing she was looking to the future – I thought she was starting to reclaim her life again. And I was so pleased that I *could* finally help.'

I stare at my father, the resentment inside me shifting slightly as his words sink in. So he did help . . . finally. At least in the very end he didn't turn Margo away. It might not make up for abandoning us, but it's something.

'I was stunned she'd gone through all of that – that *you'd* gone through all of that with her. Her pregnancy, the relapse, social services . . . Christ.' My father shakes his head. 'Stunned – and so sorry I wasn't there. I told her that, too, but she said it didn't matter. That she had "the best brother ever", and that you'd done everything you could, and more. She loved you so much.'

I blink, my eyes stinging with unshed tears as a tiny bit of relief works its way through the cloak of self-loathing I've worn since her death. Because even though I let my sister down – even though I couldn't help with Grace – somehow she still believed in me. She still saw me as her big brother, not the useless failure I'd thought I was.

'Do you know where Grace is?' I can barely bring myself to say the words.

My father nods. 'I do.'

'Where?' The word bursts out of me, my heart beating fast. I'm more awake and alert than I've been in days.

He smiles. 'I adopted her, Mark. Grace is at home.'

My mouth opens and closes as I try to grasp on to his words. My father adopted her? Grace has been living with him all this time?

'Why the hell didn't you tell me?' I ask him when I'm finally able to speak.

'I tried,' he replies, then he sighs. 'That time . . . that time after Margo died . . . well, it wasn't easy, was it?' I shake my head, both of us knowing that's an understatement. I can barely even remember the days afterwards.

'In the first few days, I rang up and got in touch with the council – Margo had given me the name and number of her social worker. I hadn't thought of taking the baby myself. Jude and I had only just married and I wasn't sure I could thrust a new baby on her. I was just going to make sure, if I could, that the couple who adopted the child were people I would have chosen. The social worker showed me a few profiles, and they seemed . . . okay. I'm sure the council vetted everyone, but something about letting this baby go to strangers didn't sit well with me. Maybe the social worker saw that – I don't know. But she asked me if I'd ever thought about adopting the baby.' He shifts in the chair, the plastic creaking beneath him.

'I went home, my mind spinning. I'd already raised two children – and made so many mistakes.' He grimaces. 'I wasn't sure I was ready to take on another responsibility like that, to pour all my love, emotion, everything into raising another child.'

'So what made you change your mind?' I ask.

'Jude did.' My father smiles. 'When I explained what was happening and that I just wasn't sure I was ready to throw myself into parenthood again – that I wasn't sure I'd ever recover from the mistakes I'd made the first time around – she told me that no matter what happened in the past, trying to shield yourself from any future hurt and pain by cutting off love is just damaging to yourself . . . and those around you. So you might as well take that risk, because life will happen, whether you want it to or not.'

He's silent for a minute, and his words expand to fill the room before settling on my chest, pressing down on the very heart of me. Is that what I've done? Have I cut off Anna to save *myself* the pain of having to watch her suffer as I fade away? I shake my head, remembering yet again the woman sobbing in the bay next to me. No, whatever I've done, I've done it for her. When she reads my letter she'll understand that.

'And so I told the social worker I'd adopt Grace,' my father continues. 'It took a while for all the checks and the paperwork to go through, but finally she was mine. I tried to tell you – I don't know how many times I called, how many emails I sent – but you'd made it clear you wanted to move on.'

I nod, regret seeping through me. I did want to move on. I tried so desperately hard that I didn't even tell my wife, the person closest to me. Fleetingly I wonder what Anna would have said if I *had* told her? Would she have been horrified at how I'd failed my sister? Or would she have come to Margo's grave with me, holding my hand and maybe helping me heal?

But Jude is right: if I'd only talked to my father – if I'd only let a tiny slice of my past in – I wouldn't have missed out on all these years of Grace growing up. I wouldn't have tried so hard, maybe, to block out that terrible time. I would have known that even if I'd failed my sister, her daughter was safe . . . and that Margo still believed in me.

And maybe . . . maybe I could have forgiven my father. Because even if he was too late to step in and save Margo, he stepped in to save Grace. A huge chunk of the bitterness I'd been holding on to ever since Margo showed up at my door falls away.

'I'm sorry,' I say. 'I'm sorry I didn't talk to you. I . . . I couldn't.' How do I explain that rekindling our connection would have felt like betraying my sister? Not to mention my anger at how he left me to deal with her illness all alone.

But my father nods as if he understands. 'I'm sorry, too. If I could go back, I'd do things so differently. But you can't, can you? You can only affect what's happening now.' He gazes down at me, his face softer than I've ever seen it. 'I've lost one child already – and I lost you for way too long. Now that I've found you . . .' His eyes fill with tears, and he looks away and coughs. 'I can understand if you don't want to come stay with us when you get out of hospital,' he says, turning back again. 'But come and visit, all right? Meet everyone. Meet Grace.'

I nod slowly, thoughts flying through my head. Our family made mistakes – tragic ones with tragic consequences. But time and life, like Jude said, has eroded and reshaped it into something else – something that saved Grace. I don't know how long I have left, but maybe I can become a part of the fabric of this new family while I'm still able.

'Actually . . . if the offer is still open, I'd love to stay,' I say. 'On one condition.' I swallow. 'I don't want to talk about Anna. I *can't*.' That chapter of my life is closed and it needs to stay that way. One way or another I've damaged her enough.

My father sighs and shakes his head, but he doesn't argue. 'All right,' he says simply, grasping my arm. And this time I don't want to move away.

CHAPTER THIRTY-FIVE

Anna

In the days that follow, I make a start at re-entering the world . . . a world without my husband. I visit the doctor, who tells me all is fine with the baby – there's been no more bleeding, thank goodness – but that I should avoid any stress wherever possible. I go back to the university, happy to have something to anchor me and structure my days, despite the endless piles of marking. And I move into Sophie's spare bedroom again, throwing myself into their family in an attempt to fill the gap left by Asher.

I can't, of course, and these weeks before Christmas are the worst time possible to highlight someone's absence. No matter how cheerful Sophie pretends to be, I can see that she's hurting. From the pinched look in her eyes as we put up the Christmas decorations together to the creak of the floorboards I hear at 2 a.m., I know it's not easy. I'm beyond happy to be out of the flat I shared with Mark – away from the memories of all our Christmases there. I haven't been back since the night I smashed things up, but Sophie went over to tidy things and pack away our favourite possessions. One day, when I'm ready, I'll fill our place – my place – with my own treasures.

'I wish I didn't still care,' Sophie says to me one night, gulping her drink. 'I was the one who told him to leave, after all. Granted, I didn't know about his affair, but . . .'

'I know,' I say, plopping down into what is now my seat at the kitchen table. 'But you were together for years. You can't just forget all that.' As soon as the words leave my mouth though, I begin to doubt them. *Can* you forget all that? Mark seems to have done so . . . if those years ever meant anything to him in the first place. Sometimes I wonder if I simply imagined our happy times together, my blinkers firmly in place. How could I not see the man who lay beneath the loving exterior? How could I just carry on so happy and secure in something that didn't exist?

I sip my sparkling water and remember one Christmas when I'd really wanted to go to Lapland. I'd stacked up the brochures, researched hotels and bought the tour books. But Mark, well . . . he hadn't wanted to spend the money, and of course I didn't push. On Christmas morning I'd padded out from the bedroom, rubbing my eyes. It was still dark and it felt like the middle of the night. Then I wondered if I was dreaming – candles glowed on every surface and the whole place was covered in white . . . creating a winter wonderland within our very own flat.

I'd laughed as I spun around the room, landing in Mark's arms with a giggle. He couldn't give me Lapland, he'd said, but wasn't this much better? And even though his creation was glorious – despite the fact that we were picking 'snow' off the floor for the next six months – actually, I would have preferred Lapland. At the time, though, I'd shoved down that thought, grinning as he hugged me tightly.

Looking back, the glow of that memory feels like it's laced with black. I loved our warm, cosy Christmases; I loved *us* . . . or, at least, the 'us' I thought we were. But now that he's gone I can finally let myself see that there were things about my husband I was happy to let lie, being too scared to delve into whatever darkness might have lain dormant there. All those times he disappeared into himself, shutting off me and the world. The way we always stayed in, whether just for dinner or to avoid a bigger trip, like to Lapland. How I never drove, how over the top his protectiveness of me was and how he never wanted to talk about anything that upset me – or him.

I always told myself I never minded any of it, but I wonder now what would have happened if I had tried to push Mark – push us – from our comfort zone. Would he have cracked, showing the terrible side I'd glimpsed since he left? Or could we have adjusted? Did we only last so long in such harmony because we were both unwilling to face any negativity?

I guess we'll never know.

Sadness pushes down on me and I shove away these thoughts, telling myself to focus on the future. This time next year I'll have a five-month-old baby by my side cooing and trying to reach its chubby fists up to grab the tinsel. My life will be changed beyond imagining, although Sophie is doing her best to tell me way more than I wanted to know.

That child will be my world, and everything else – all the horror and pain of the past few months – will fade away . . . along with those ten years Mark and I spent together, I guess.

Maybe love is easier to forget when it never really existed in the first place.

CHAPTER THIRTY-SIX

Mark

After all this time I've found Grace – the baby I abandoned, the baby who haunted my thoughts for years. I held off seeing her while I was in hospital, not wanting our first conversation to take place amidst the chaos here. But finally, after completing my second round of chemo, the doctors released me, sending me home with strict instructions to rest. And I *can* rest now just knowing that my niece is all right . . . that she's lived these past thirteen years in such a loving family (surrounded by brothers and a sister I still can't believe exist!). I'll never forgive myself for what happened with Margo, but at least Grace is okay. No matter how much time I have left – whether it's two months or ten, it won't be clear until I have that scan – I'll know that much.

After paying my bill and retrieving my things from the B & B (thank goodness my stuff was still there; I probably have the cleaner to thank for neatly packing them and storing them away) my father and I began the journey to his home in Berkhamsted. I was so full of nerves I could barely speak. Dad told me Grace knew only that her mother had been ill and had died of disease, but I feared that somehow she'd see that I'd failed Margo – that I'd ignored her cries to be reunited with her child. Despite the cold of the day I was a sweaty mess by the time the car pulled up to a large house that sparkled with white Christmas lights.

'Welcome to the jungle,' my father said, nodding towards the children whose noses were rammed up against the glass. 'I have to run this gauntlet every time I come back from somewhere.' He shook his head, but even in the dim light I could see his eyes shining.

We climbed from the car, leaving the boxes in the boot, then walked slowly up the driveway towards the house. Despite it looming over us, something about the structure made it seem welcoming and cosy – a true home. My heart lurched as I thought of my place with Anna and all the things I'd left behind.

My dad opened the door and instantly a wall of children knocked him sideways, wrapping their limbs around him. I stood back silently, keeping an eye out for Grace. It was so strange to see my father with a family – with a *young* family. For years I'd pictured him living the privileged life of a wealthy, retired doctor, complete with a trophy wife. It's hard to reconcile that image with this man who tied himself down with even more responsibility . . . especially after I was so sure he'd dodged the burden of caring for Margo.

'This is Mark,' my father said, after he'd managed to extricate himself from the hurricane of hugs. 'Come and say hello.'

Instantly the children morphed from wild to shy, clinging to his legs.

'Hi,' I said, squatting down until I was eye level with them. 'Is it okay if I stay here for a bit?'

They all nodded, eyes wide.

'This is Peter.' My father put a hand on the tallest one's sandy head. 'He's ten. And then Oliver, who's seven. And finally, this is Isla. She's three.' He raised his eyebrows. 'Not exactly planned,' he says in a low voice. 'But then, what in life is?' He glanced around him. 'Where's Grace?' he asked. 'Peter, have you seen Grace?'

'I'm here,' came a voice from behind us, and we all swung around. Standing in front of me was a teen who was almost the spitting image of her mother at that age: same ginger hair, same freckled skin. It was like Margo's ghost had joined us, and a shiver went up my spine.

I stood there, frozen, as my mind transported me backwards in time: Margo running beside me, a cheeky grin on her face as she chatted away. The moment she really did beat me on a training run and I had to feign an injury to stop the endless teasing. Her glowing face when she crossed the finish line in first place during a school cross-country meet, then ran straight to me and gave me a huge, sweaty hug. Suddenly, a swathe of happy memories washed over me, as if by finally meeting Grace I'd lifted the veil of darkness that had blocked me from seeing them.

'Hi.' I tried to smile, but my muscles wouldn't obey. 'I'm Mark.'

'I know.' Grace grinned, and this time I did smile back. Her smile was like Margo's, too, the same wonky grin that her mother hated. But while Margo was all sparky energy – at least before the disease had her in its grip – I could already tell that there was something much calmer about her daughter. My niece.

When Grace narrated the family photos for me later that evening, I flinched as she cheerily pointed to a framed picture of Margo, readying myself for tears, blame, *something*. Instead Grace just moved on to tell me about the surrounding snapshots of her with her brothers and sister. I watched her happy face and felt something shift inside. Losing her mother wasn't a tragedy for her – she was too young to even remember her. And while I will always feel guilty that I didn't do more to help her return to Margo, Grace has a wonderful life – a life I'm grateful to be a part of.

I can hardly believe I've finally found her, right here in the heart of my father's family. The place is a madhouse, with constant noise and chaos, but it's a madhouse filled with love. I couldn't think of a better place for Grace to grow up, and my father and Jude are doing a fantastic job. My father's happy to have Ben, Grace's biological father, come out for a visit, too, if that's what Grace wants.

My first impressions of Grace were right: she's a quiet, thoughtful girl who'd prefer to curl up in her room with a novel or her sketchbook . . . more like me than her mother, who used to talk so much we always threatened to put in earplugs.

When I'm having a low-energy day, Grace creeps into my room and reads aloud for me, her voice carrying me off to the worlds of her favourite books like *Jane Eyre* and *Wuthering Heights* – she's very into the Brontës at the moment, thanks to my recommendation. Grace's high, lilting voice reminds me of Flora, and I often wonder how my other niece is doing. Does she know I'm ill, or is she looking forward to our annual play-day on New Year's Day, when we spend hours together testing out her Christmas haul? Apart from Christmas, it's one of my favourite days of the year – hers, too, I think. I wince, guilt flooding into me when I remember promising her we'd play games on the new tablet she wanted. I knew it would be hard to cut Anna from my life, but I never realised how difficult it would be to shut out others, too.

Grace's visits are the highlights of the days when all I can do is breathe in and out – when the pain threatens to swamp me; pain from my cancer, yes, but also pain from the past. Because even though my life with Anna *is* in the past, and no matter how much I try to block it out, I just can't. I still dream of her every night – still ache when I think of the awful things I said. I still miss her with every part of me.

And now, waking up on Christmas morning, she feels closer than ever, like I could reach across the time and space of the past two months and pull her up against me.

As I watch the kids tear open their gifts with gleeful expressions, I think about the family we tried to have – the family we never will have. *I did the right thing letting her go,* I tell myself yet again, *so she can go off and make another life*. And I'll make sure that, when I'm gone, Jude sends her the letter I wrote in what feels like forever ago. Hopefully that will help her understand.

The day passes in a haze of turkey, mince pies and the excited cries of children who've consumed too much chocolate. I head up to bed early, drowsy on my half-glass of wine and wanting to be alone with my thoughts . . . alone with my memories of Anna. I wonder what she's doing right now. Is she thinking of me, too?

I change into my pyjamas and get into bed with my book for company.

'Uncle Mark?'

Grace's voice comes through the door and I set down my book.

'Come in!' I call.

Grace pokes her head inside the room. 'Hi!' She's decked out in a garish Christmas jumper with stripy leggings. With her hair in bunches and chocolate smeared around her mouth, she looks about five rather than thirteen.

'I just wanted to give you this,' she says shyly, handing over the package in her hands almost reluctantly, as if she's not sure she wants to part with it.

'Oh! Thank you,' I say, raising my eyebrows. 'I thought I'd got all my presents already.'

She ducks her head down, her cheeks colouring. 'I wanted to give you this on my own.'

I smile to put her at ease and gingerly remove the tissue, trying not to rip what looks to be some kind of drawing or sketch. I slide out a canvas, my heart filling up as I stare at the painting: it's our family, with Dad and Jude standing smack in the middle and the three little ones in front of them. Grace is sitting in a chair to the side, and above her . . . I squint at my image, swallowing hard as emotions rush in, then glance up to meet Grace's eyes watching me eagerly.

'It's wonderful,' I say, putting an arm around her. 'But how—'

'I asked everyone to pose for a photo,' she explains, 'and then I did the painting from that. You were a bit trickier, but I managed to get you in there!' She grins. 'Do you like it?'

'Like it?' I shake my head. 'I *love* it. It's brilliant. You're very talented.'

Her cheeks go even redder, but I can tell she's pleased. 'I hope it's okay that I haven't put your wife in there,' she says, her voice tentative. 'I asked Mum, but she wasn't sure . . . she said it might be best to leave her out for now.'

I draw in a breath as my gut squeezes. 'Yes, maybe it is for the best,' I manage to say. Grace has never asked about Anna; I wasn't even sure she knew I was married. Automatically I twist the heavy ring on my finger – the ring I still haven't taken off. I suppose that it's a bit of a giveaway.

'Mark?'

'Yes?' I brace myself for whatever she might ask.

'Where *is* your wife?'

'Well . . .' I meet her inquisitive gaze. 'We're not together just now,' I say, trying to be as vague as possible.

'Why not?' She fixes me with a laser-like stare, and I pull up the duvet like a shield.

'Things are a bit complicated,' I say, knowing that's such a cop-out, but unsure of what to say. How can I explain what really happened to a teen?

'Do you want to be together?' she asks.

'Yes.' The answer comes to me instantly. Despite what I kept from my wife, we did have a wonderful marriage. I want us to be together – I always have, throughout all of this. It was never a question of wanting to or not. It was a question of stopping her from having to go through what I did.

'Well, you should be, then,' she says, like she's made a final verdict. 'Right, more Christmas pudding?' She rubs her tummy, and despite all the emotions tumbling through me, I laugh. 'Come on, let's go and get some!'

I groan. 'I don't know how you have any room left in there! I'm stuffed!' Secretly, I'm pleased that she doesn't seem to have inherited any of her mother's food aversions. I don't know if it *is* inherited, but I can't help but worry . . . and I notice Dad and Jude watching carefully, too. I give her another hug. 'Thank you so much for this,' I say, gesturing to the painting.

She smiles and closes the door behind her, and my eyes return to her present. After so long I'm finally part of the family – my family, the family I'd pushed into my past. But I can't take my eyes off the space beside me in the painting, the space where Anna would be if none of this had happened.

Then again, if none of this had happened I wouldn't have found Grace . . . nor forgiven my father and met Jude and the kids. I close my eyes now, picturing the quiet cocoon of our marriage miles away from this crazy house. It was safe, yes, and I'd thought that was what I wanted – protected from the past; protected from the pain. But the pain was inside of me, and no matter how much I tried to shield myself from it, I couldn't. I'm only seeing that now that my soul is starting to heal.

I catch my breath, wondering if Anna is starting to heal, too – starting to make a new life. Is she spending tonight with Sophie's family, surrounded by people who care? Raising her glass in a toast to good health and cheer? Or . . . I squeeze my eyes shut against the image of her eyes glistening with tears, staring at the empty space beside her as my terrible words continue to tear through her.

I hope she's all right, but there's nothing I can do now . . . nothing except wait for time to pass. Next Christmas, life will have moved on. I'll be gone, and this nightmare for us both will be over.

CHAPTER THIRTY-SEVEN

Anna

Christmas Day passes in a haze of food, presents and sleep. Thankfully it couldn't be more different from the quiet ones I'd spent with Mark. Sophie blares out Christmas carols and the three of us hold a dance contest. A huge turkey with all the trimmings emerges from the oven with military precision and Flora's mountain of presents has taken over the lounge. It's noisy, it's chaotic and I'm loving it. It's such a whirlwind that when the silence descends after Asher picks up Flora the house seems empty and sad. Sophie plucks the whisky from the kitchen cupboard and throws back slug after slug while I sink towards sleep. I guess you can only maintain the noise for so long before memories work their way in, and I can see the sadness pulling at my sister's face.

As for me, well . . . I'm still waiting for the past to fade, for Mark's painful words to lessen their grip on me. I'm getting through the days all right – filling Flora's time with trips to the zoo, pantos and skating at the ice rinks dotted around the city – but the nights, when the lights fade and the darkness comes in, are sheer torture. I have stopped trying to find Mark and I *will* make a new life, but still my mind keeps working, struggling to find the man I thought I knew, endlessly sifting through memories and desperately trying to latch on to something positive.

It's New Year's Eve and Flora and I are watching cheesy films on the sofa as rain batters the windows. Sophie's determined to hit the South Bank to watch the fireworks and she's gone off to buy us ponchos.

'Auntie Anna?' Flora turns towards me.

'Yes, munchkin?' I smile as she curls up against my side, thinking that if my child is even one-tenth as cute as Flora is, I'll be happy.

'I know you said Uncle Mark was a little poorly, but he'll be okay for tomorrow, right?'

Oh, shit. Sophie still hasn't told her about Mark – at least, not the full story. 'Tomorrow?' I ask.

'Yes, our play-day. Uncle Mark promised he'd be here like always.' Flora shakes her head at me like I should have remembered and my heart sinks.

Of course, the annual play-day. I *should* have remembered. Every New Year's Day Mark and I make the trek across the Heath to spend the day with Sophie's family. I'm not quite sure when that visit turned into a play-day, but soon Mark was spending the whole day with Flora, playing board games, combing Barbie's hair or – more recently – playing games on her collection of electronic gadgets. Sophie, Asher and I would sit back and relax, listening to the two of them laugh and yell as the day unfurled. I think Mark looked forward to it just as much as she did.

I thought he did, anyway. Did he really enjoy it, or was it all an act? How could he promise a *child* something, then completely renege on it? A child he loved almost as if she was his own?

But then . . . this is a man who told me he didn't even care if I was carrying his child. Surely I can't be so surprised he's abandoning his niece?

'I'm sorry, Flora,' I say, putting an arm around her. I don't want to hurt her, but it would be even worse for her to wait in hope. I know what that's like. 'Mark won't be able to do that this year.' Or the next, or the next . . . Anger floods through me as tears streak down Flora's cheeks and her chin trembles. 'But I'll play with you!' I say, wiping her tears with my fingers. 'I'll play with you as much as you want.'

She jumps off the sofa, her features bunched. 'I don't want to play with you! Uncle Mark promised. He promised! I know he'll be here. He will!' She stares at me defiantly and I sigh, slowly shaking my head back and forth.

'I'm afraid he won't, Flora.' God, I wish I was wrong, but I know I'm not. Mark is gone from all our lives.

'I hate him!' she cries, then she runs up the stairs before I can even grab her for a hug. I hear the bang of her door slamming shut and I sink back on to the sofa, flicking off the telly as my restless mind finally stops working. It doesn't matter if I saw the real Mark that day or if he was just pretending. He's gone, like I told Flora, and that is that. I may never fully understand what happened in our marriage because it wasn't just up to me, but I can control myself now – I can do what makes me happy and start to heal.

And for the first time I know I'll be okay.

CHAPTER THIRTY-EIGHT

Mark

The house has returned to normal after the chaos of Christmas, thank goodness. The older kids have gone back to school and the younger ones rotate between Jude, the nanny and nursery. I love the silence during the day, but I also love the way the house comes to life at around three when they're all home again. I lie in bed listening to the chatter and clatter as they canter around, and I drink in their energy.

I haven't much energy myself these days. I'm due for my third and final chemo cycle next week, but I don't think the treatment is helping: my pain is increasing, appetite has become a distant memory and my muscles feel more uncertain every day. The doctor has booked a scan in for a few weeks' time, so I'll know for sure how I'm doing then.

I'm lying in bed one afternoon when there's a knock on the door. 'Come in!'

Jude pokes her head around the door. 'You okay? I found something for you.' She's holding a package in her hands. 'Another Christmas gift, I think.'

'A Christmas gift?' My brow furrows as I wonder what she's talking about. I reach out to take the slim box wrapped in blue and pink tissue.

'Sorry, I forgot to put it under the tree – I found it ages ago when I unpacked your things from the B & B.'

The B & B? I jerk as a memory flies at me: Anna standing at the door with this box in her hands. But . . . how did it end up amongst my things? I flinch remembering how I shoved her away before she even had a chance to speak.

'Well, are you going to open it?' Jude is standing there, watching me.

I shake my head. 'No, not now. Maybe later tonight.' Truthfully I'm dying to open the gift for a momentary connection to my wife, even if it is just a bar of chocolate. But I want to unwrap it alone. I want to savour the moment.

'All right.'

I wait until the door clicks closed and then I tear the tissue from the box, setting the card aside for later. The cardboard is plain, giving nothing away. I jemmy under the tape on one end and slide out . . . a tiny T-shirt?

The fabric is soft under my fingers and I carefully unfold it to reveal the words 'Mummy + Daddy = Me'. I stare at the lettering, trying to make sense of it. Anna wouldn't give me something like this unless . . . she's *pregnant*? I grab the card and skim the words inside, my heart squeezing inside my chest.

Oh my God. She is. She's having a baby – *our* baby. I gulp. And I told her that nothing she could say would make a difference – not even having twins – then shoved her away.

What have I done?

My chest starts heaving as questions fly through my mind. How many months along is the baby? Is everything okay with Anna and the child? Anna's been through so much, and then my rejection . . . My heart misses a beat as a thought enters my mind. She wouldn't get rid of it, would she?

No. I shake my head with absolute certainty. Whatever I've done to her – however difficult life has been – I know she is strong . . . strong enough to be there for this child.

And I need to be strong, too.

I ease myself into an upright position. It's not about protecting Anna. Not any more. It's about being *there* for her – being there for our child. Love and tenderness swell inside, and for the first time in weeks, energy courses through my muscles. I may only have limited time left. I may never even meet my child. But it's time to focus not on pain and tragedy, but on hope.

I'll go to the flat right now, I decide, excitement building inside me. It's late afternoon and Anna should be back from work by the time I get to our home. I can't wait to see my wife – to put my arms around her while I'm still able and to tell her that I'm sorry. The words are feeble, I know, but I need to say them. I need to explain everything: that I thought I was protecting her and that I *do* want to be with her – to let her play a part in deciding our future. And I need to play a part in the life of our child, too.

I slide from the bed and pull on my jeans and a proper shirt instead of the battered old T-shirt I've been living in. *It's been wonderful living here,* I think, running a brush through my thinning hair. I've had a chance to really get to know the kids, Grace, Jude – and to rekindle my relationship with my father. But suddenly I'm itching to get home again, to be surrounded by all our treasured possessions that formed the foundation of my life with Anna . . . and to start adding new things to our life, too.

There's a knock on my door and Jude sticks her head in. 'Sorry, just seeing if you want a little snack . . . Oh. Where are you off to?' she asks, looking at me in surprise.

'Well . . .' I draw out the word, anticipating her happy response. 'I'm going to see Anna.'

She throws her hands up in the air. 'Oh, thank God. It's about time! I know you didn't want me and Richard to say anything – well, you know how we feel about it anyway – but seriously!' She crosses the room and gives me a quick hug. 'Good luck. You're doing the right thing.' She pulls back. 'But maybe . . . maybe you should shave first?'

I run a hand over my face. I'd almost forgotten my beard was even there. 'No.' I shake my head. 'This is part of me now. I kind of like it.'

'Okay.' Jude shrugs. 'Want a ride to the station? I can get your father to run you over in a few minutes.' She glances at her watch. 'If memory serves from back in the day when I actually had a life and went places, there's a train in half an hour. Come down and have something to eat, and then I'll get Richard to take you.' She eyes me closely. 'Are you all right to make it into London on your own?'

I nod, knowing I look like death warmed up. 'I'll be fine. Thank you.'

Half an hour later I wave Dad off and head towards the platform where the train is pulling in. My breath makes clouds in the air as I hurry down the packed platform and on to the train. Luckily I manage to find a seat and I collapse into it, watching as we zip past fields and trees, winter-bare branches gleaming in the setting sun. I left Anna in the dark . . . the dark of the night, the dark of my soul. And despite the evening closing in, it feels like I'm returning to my wife in brightness, no matter what the future holds.

The train pulls into Euston and I make my way to the Northern Line. My legs jiggle as the carriage travels northwards, my excitement and happiness growing until I can't sit still any longer. I'm dying to get off the train and throw my arms around Anna – to draw both her and our baby close to me. I want to start over – to put the whole of myself into our world and give as much as I can while I'm able.

Is this what Anna felt like when she finally tracked me down? Was she eager to build a new world together . . . to form a family? Pain ricochets through me as I picture my wife, high on hope, buying that T-shirt and writing that card, even when she didn't know where I was. Her elation as she discovered my B & B and climbed the stairs . . . And then having the door slammed in her face.

I pray she doesn't do the same to me. *She won't,* I tell myself, hope lifting me up. Not with our baby inside of her. Not if we have a chance to be a family.

After what feels like forever the train arrives at Highgate station. I get off, my chest heaving as I climb the escalator steps – probably not a great idea given the state of my health, but I don't care – and then I lurch up the steep pathway towards our road. I can hardly believe that I'm back in such a familiar place . . . *our* place.

I retrace my path in reverse from the night I left, my heart pounding as I get closer and closer to our flat. *She will say yes, I know she will. She will say yes, I know she will.* The jogging rhythm of this thought propels me forwards, faster and faster, until I'm through the front gate and standing in front of the door. I use my key to enter, then climb the stairs to our flat. I pause for a second, take a deep breath and knock.

I hear nothing except for the whoosh of my pulse in my eardrums. I knock again, louder this time, telling myself that she must be home by now; she never stays late at work – or she never used to, anyway.

I pound on the door once more, and our neighbour Jens across the hallway opens his door.

'Jesus Christ, mate,' he says. 'Can you keep it down? I'm trying to get some rest before the night shift tonight.'

'Sorry.' I jab a thumb towards our flat. 'Do you know where Anna's gone?' We weren't close to our neighbours – only stopping to chat if we saw them on the landing. But still, Jens might have some idea of Anna's whereabouts . . . more than I do anyway.

'Mark?' Jens peers at me and his eyebrows rise. 'I didn't recognise you for a second there.'

'Yeah.' I rub a hand over my beard, suddenly feeling a little self-conscious about my changed appearance. And it isn't just the facial hair, I know. I've lost weight, and my face looks long and lean.

'Long time no see.' Jens pauses, as if waiting for me to explain matters, then shrugs. 'Well, no. I haven't seen anyone there for ages, actually. It's been really quiet.'

'Okay, thanks.' I push out the words, disappointment swirling inside me as Jens nods and closes his door. Perhaps I was a little naive to think I could suddenly turn up and my wife would be here waiting. But where could she have gone? I punch her number from memory into my phone, praying that she picks up, but it goes straight to voicemail. I click off. There's no way I'm going to have our first contact after all this time be over voicemail.

I stand still for a minute, my foot tapping on the floor. Maybe Sophie would know where she is? Anna and she were always so close, sharing everything. I envied their relationship – it made me miss Margo that much more, made me wish I could talk to Anna about things that bothered her, too. But I couldn't – just hearing about anything that made her upset, anything I couldn't protect her from, stirred up such anger and worry inside of me that eventually she stopped talking about them.

My heart sinks when I realise I don't have Sophie's number on the new phone I'd bought after leaving my old one behind when I left. *Shit.* I eye the door to our flat in front of me, thinking of the list of emergency numbers I always made sure to keep in the drawer by the kitchen sink. I know the number is there.

Before I can stop myself I've fitted the key in the lock and swung the door open. I won't stay long. I just need to find that number—

I freeze, my eyes widening as I take in the room in front of me. It's the same place – the same furniture and bookshelves – but it feels like I'm staring at it through a different lens. All the novels we enjoyed together are gone, the walls have been stripped of our photos and even the blanket we used to curl up in is missing. It feels like the world we built – the life we lived here – has been erased.

I swallow hard, trying not to think of what this means. Of course Anna would be angry. Of course she'd be upset. Can I blame her? She tried for weeks to find me, only to have me push her away – push her and our baby away. Those missing possessions mean nothing anyway. It's her I want to be with – to have a family in the time I have left. Determination courses through me as I picture us in this lounge with a child crawling about and cooing, and I draw in a breath. First things first: I need to talk to my wife.

I head to the kitchen and pull out the list of numbers. I slide my mobile from my pocket then punch Sophie's number into it, praying that she answers.

'Hello?'

'Sophie, it's Mark.'

'Mark?' Sophie's voice is incredulous and I swallow back the nerves jumping in my stomach. God, I hope she knows where Anna is. I can go to her work tomorrow, I guess, but I really want to talk to her tonight.

'Yes. Listen . . . I need to talk to Anna – in person. Do you know where she is?'

I hear Sophie draw in a breath and I steel myself for her response. She won't be happy with how I've treated her sister, I know. If anything, Sophie is just as protective of Anna as I am.

'You want to talk to Anna now? After all this time?'

'Yes, I do.' Desire swells inside me, and it's so strong it almost lifts me off my feet. 'Do you know where she is?'

'I'm sure as hell not going to tell you. You've fucked up her life enough, don't you think? I trusted you not to hurt her, and you hurt her terribly. . . worse than anything I could have imagined. Do you really think I'd tell you where she is now?'

'I only just found out about the baby,' I say quickly, desperate to get the words out before she hangs up on me. 'When she came to see me the last time I didn't know.'

'Oh, so you think that makes it okay?' Sophie asks, her tone brittle. 'Listen, Mark. Anna's doing all right, but she doesn't need any more upset, any more emotional strain. It's still early days for the baby and she's had a bit of bleeding. Everything is okay, but . . .'

I draw in a breath at her words. *Bleeding?* My heart thuds in my chest. She has to be all right. The baby has to be all right. I couldn't bear it if they weren't.

'Just leave her be, okay?' Sophie's voice is strong and firm. 'She doesn't need you. She doesn't *want* you. Listen, I hope you're okay. I hope you shake off the cancer. But don't call again.'

The line goes dead. I lean back against the kitchen counter with Sophie's words ringing in my ears. I know miscarriages happen – Margo was terrified of them, always talking about making it into the safe zone at three months. If Anna got pregnant in the weeks before I left, the baby would be . . . just about at the three-month mark? So when did the bleeding happen? Is it a recent thing? Have there been any more complications? Or is everything fine now?

I let out a cry of frustration and run a hand over my face. God, this is torture. This is my child and my wife and I don't even know the barest of details. My body jerks as I realise that Anna must have felt like this, too – times a thousand. She still doesn't know I'm dying, and I haven't just shut her out. I've obliterated her from my life.

I push off from the counter, my shoulders lifting in a sigh. I don't want to put Anna or our child at risk. I might be very ill, but I'm not going to drop dead in the next few weeks. Maybe I'll wait a bit – until the pregnancy progresses, until everything is okay.

And then . . . then I'll come find her – her and our child.

CHAPTER THIRTY-NINE

Anna

'Guess what?' Sophie bursts into the bedroom and my eyes fly open. Thank God it's Saturday, because despite sleeping for ten hours, I'm absolutely exhausted. I thought the second trimester was when you start to glow, but the only thing I'm radiating is fatigue . . . despite following Sophie's litany of advice on eating properly, getting lots of rest and even going to prenatal yoga. It's beyond me how I'm supposed to be super-bendy when my internal organs are rearranging themselves, but the baby doesn't seem to mind my lack of flexibility. I've not bled again since that horrific night, thank goodness, and my doctor has assured me that everything is wonderfully normal.

'What?' I ask, swinging my legs over the side of the bed and sitting up.

'The builder finally sent through his quote for the en suite in here, and I think I can swing it. I know sharing a bathroom with Flora and her sparkly bathtub probably hasn't been the best experience.' Sophie makes a face and I smile. For all her cuteness, Flora makes an unholy mess, the likes of which I've never seen. Last night she decided to cut her Barbie's hair in the washbasin, trailing bits of doll hair across the floor.

I shake my head. 'Sophie, I've told you, don't do this for me! I have to go back to the flat soon.' I've stayed way longer than I meant to – partly because I wanted to, but also because it's good to be here for

Sophie and Flora. But I need to move on now, away from this world of sparkly bathtubs. This time has been invaluable, giving me both physical space and headspace from my marriage . . . a start at a recovery. And I'm ready to expand that even more – to begin to create a home for me and my baby.

I even bought my first piece of baby kit: a gorgeous stripy blanket made from the softest fabric I've ever touched. I can just imagine my baby wrapped up in it, so peaceful and cosy, as I swing the Moses basket. I take a deep breath, preparing for the usual rush of sadness and anger that sweep over me whenever I picture my future alone. But when it comes this time, it's tempered with growing excitement at meeting my child. I still have a long way to go, but I hope by the time this child is born that my happiness outweighs the pain.

'Well, I am doing it for you a bit, because I want you to stay! But mostly I'm doing it because it will add value to the house, and I still don't know what's going on in that area.' She makes a face. 'Asher keeps making noises about selling, so we'll have to see.'

'As long as you're not doing it *just* for me,' I say. 'Speaking of the flat, I should get over there and pick up the post.' I shield my eyes as I peer out the window. It's a lovely late-January day, perfect for a walk across the Heath.

'Want me to come with you?'

'No, that's okay.' I still haven't been back since the night I started bleeding and I need to do this on my own. I squint at my sister, noticing she's more dressed up than usual. 'Where are you off to today?' Flora is at Asher's for the weekend, so Sophie's living a child-free life for once.

'Is this top all right?' She plucks at a light blue silk shirt.

'It's gorgeous,' I say, eyebrows rising as I note that she's dodged the question. 'So . . . where are you going?'

'Well . . .' Sophie's cheeks colour and she ducks her head. My mouth falls open.

'Well, *what*? Don't tell me you're going on a date!' My voice rises to a screech.

'Well, sort of. I mean, it's just coffee. Not really a date.'

'That's a date, Soph.' I shake my head, unable to believe my ears. 'How did you meet him?' I can't work out when my sister has had time to meet someone – maybe she's been using Tinder, though the idea of Sophie using a dating app is a difficult one to swallow. And part of me can't believe Sophie is moving on so quickly either. Just the thought of dating again makes me shudder. I may be getting ready to make a new world, but that new world is for me and my child. I can't imagine including someone else in that right now.

'Tim is the dad of one of Flora's friends at school. We've known each other for ages, but we were both with someone else. And now we're not.' She shrugs. 'It's probably never going to be serious, and Flora doesn't know a thing about it, but it is nice to feel . . .' She pauses, as if searching for the right word. '*Appreciated*, I guess. Excited, even. Like someone is actually looking forward to spending time with you, not just taking for granted that you'll always be there.'

I nod like I understand, but truthfully Mark and I never had that problem. I always felt valued, like he couldn't wait to get home to me, and whenever we were together I was his top priority. I don't know if that was real or not, but it did make me happy. Whoever he really was, I loved the man he showed me – until the end, that is. I can't change those feelings, no matter the pain and anger he's caused me. And I hope he'll be all right – that he'll get through this illness. But I've truly accepted now that, whatever happens, Mark will be without me.

I get dressed, then throw on my wellies and coat. At the last minute, I grab the bag with my baby's blanket, thinking it will be a good first step towards reclaiming the flat – at making it mine after so many years of sharing. Although the air is cool the Heath is packed with people taking in the sunshine. A kite swoops in the sky, its bright colours sharply contrasting with the deep blue sky behind it. My muscles work as I climb a hill, and I stand for a second, a smile lifting my lips as the wind whips my cheeks.

When I arrive at the flat I fit the key into the lock and swing open the door, stepping back when I see the space in front of me. In my mind it was still chock full of our treasures – the cocoon we'd comfortably lined. Now the bookshelves are barren and the walls where pictures once hung are naked and forlorn. The once-neat pillows and blankets on the sofa are dishevelled, and dust dances in the sunlight streaming in through the windows.

I throw open those windows to let in fresh air then stare around the room. This is the place where we built our life, but now it's stripped bare of all those things that formed our world. In a way it echoes the state we're in now: our defences dropped, our barriers down, revealing the skeleton of our marriage . . . the skeleton whose bones have crumbled.

I sweep my eyes around the space again as if I'm saying a final goodbye to the life we had here – to the couple I thought we were. Then I cross the creaky floorboards and spread the baby blanket on the sofa – a token of my future. My wedding band shines in the sun and I glance down at it, remembering the moment when Mark slid it on my finger, his eyes full of tenderness and love.

My heart twists, and I realise I can't keep wearing this ring. The love and commitment it represents don't reflect what we had – not now, and maybe not ever. It couldn't keep our marriage safe and protected any more than this room could. The only people who could do that were *us*.

Slowly I slide the band off my finger. It feels right that I'm doing this here, in the flat where our marriage played out – in the place where Mark left me. In the place where, next time I'm here, I'll be embarking on a new life with my baby.

I shut the windows and scoop up the post. Then I close the door behind me and head back out into the streaming sun.

CHAPTER FORTY

Mark

Even though I told myself I'd plenty of time left to get in touch with Anna, I can feel my body gradually slowing, like a wind-up toy whose battery's draining. As the days pass and January morphs into February, every movement is more laboured, every breath more ragged. My arms and legs grow thinner while my stomach has started to swell. Jude and Dad pepper me with constant 'suggestions' to reach out to my wife again, unable to understand my hesitation. I still tell myself to wait a little longer until the baby is well into the second trimester and whatever risk has completely passed. It's driving me crazy not being there for them, but I'll do what I need to for the safety of my family.

I'm meeting with my doctor today for the results of an MRI, which will show if the chemo is slowing the cancer's progress. I'd be lying if I said I wasn't anxious, but whatever the results I know now that you can't let your fears force you to flee from the people who love you most. They are the ones that will gather you in and lift you up when you need them. They are the ones who will act as a safety net when life drops you in it . . . if you give them a chance.

'Ready to go?' Dad knocks on the door and I lever myself from the bed, feeling my body creak and groan.

A couple of hours later I'm sitting in front of the doctor, trying to focus on her words. Chemo not working . . . tumours still growing . . . spread to other places in my body. I'm not surprised – I could tell by the carefully controlled expression on her face that the news would not be good.

Dad reaches out to touch my arm and I nod my head. Terms like 'palliative care' and 'pain management' drift over me and I shift in my chair. None of this matters. I'm going to die – sooner rather than later, it seems – and there's only one thing I need to do: find Anna. I don't have time to waste, and the foetus should be at four months now . . . if all has gone well. For the first time I'm grateful for the centre's close proximity to Anna's workplace. I'm just a few streets from the university and she'll be at work for another few hours yet.

I turn to my father. 'Dad . . . I need to go see Anna. I'll meet you back at home.' I barely have the energy to make it down the stairs and I don't know how I'll drag myself over to the university, but narrowing the distance between Anna and me seems like something I need to do on my own. I love having people around me now, but no one can bring us together but *us*.

Dad meets my eyes. His face is pale and grim in the aftermath of our meeting and he puts an arm around me. 'Good,' he says, tightening his grip. 'I'm glad. She needs to know what's happening. I'll wait here for a bit, just in case you need me. Call if you do, okay?'

I nod and force my muscles to propel me down the street. Every step feels like a marathon in itself and my breath tears at my lungs. Sweat coats my face and I have to pause every few metres to stop from collapsing. But I'll get there. I'll get to Anna – to our baby.

Finally, I reach her building. I sink down on a bench inside, remembering how I came here all those years ago to hear a lecture on Hardy and how I walked away with my future wife. I pray that this time will be the same.

I close my eyes, almost hearing Anna's voice in my head. There's a loud bang as a door opens and closes and I sit up straight. Wait a second – that *is* Anna's voice. I get to my feet, nerves flooding through me as I trudge the few steps towards the lecture room where her voice is coming from.

My heart swells when I see her at the front of the class, nodding as she focuses intently on something a student is saying. She's wearing a pink jumper – I remember its softness up against my skin. Her cheeks are red and her hair is pushed behind her ears like it usually is. She laughs and nods at whatever the boy is saying, and the class laughs, too, a burst of happiness echoing around me. I can't see any signs of pregnancy, but she is only four months along . . . and that jumper was too big to begin with. She looks healthy, alive, in a place she loves.

I catch sight of my reflection in the window and I draw back. My face is hollow and my eyes are sunken. I know it's a trick of the light, but I look transparent and ghostly next to Anna's solid presence. I move my eyes back and forth – from my wife to me, from my wife to me – and a memory of the woman sobbing in the bay next to me rips into my head.

Can I really do this? Can I reinsert myself into Anna's world – a world she doesn't want me in any more . . . if Sophie is to be believed, that is? And even if she *does* want me, will the upset of my death – because I am going to die, and soon if the doctor is right – be too much for her and the baby?

I stand at the door, frozen, unsure which way to move. And then my eyes catch sight of her hand as she scrawls something on the white-board and my heart drops.

Anna's finger is bare. She's taken off her wedding ring.

I turn slowly from the window, her voice fading as I walk down the hallway. I've finally come to find her, but it's too late. Too late to start over . . . too late to even be there for her in my remaining few weeks. Sophie was right: Anna really has moved on – made a start at that new life I forced her to have.

I've ripped apart my wife's world once and I can't do it again.

CHAPTER FORTY-ONE

Anna

It's been one of those rare warm days today – a day when you can almost smell spring in the air, even though it's still only February. The air was soft, the sun shining, and I actually cracked open the window in my office. I sit back in my chair, trying to picture this time next year. *I'll have a baby*, I think, shaking my head at the thought. It's still hard to believe, even though I've actually seen my child on the ultrasound now. Sophie went with me and we burst out laughing when the consultant assumed we were partners.

In a way, we *are* partners – albeit not like the consultant meant. Sophie's helped me move back into the flat, visiting shop after shop with me in my quest for the perfect new mattress and sending me endless emails about the best baby gear. I've watched Flora when Sophie goes out with Tim (who she continues to deny she's dating) and I've helped Sophie dissect her wardrobe and analyse Tim's behaviour. It feels like we're both on the path to new lives now.

I'm scanning a student's almost completely unintelligible essay when my office phone rings. Eager to escape the rambling on the page in front of me, I grab the receiver.

'Hello?'

'Um, hi.' A female voice comes through the phone and I sigh, thinking it's a student from the tedious first-year class I've taken on for this semester. It's always so depressing when you see that some students can barely form a paragraph, and the last thing I want to do right now is explain the meaning of 'thesis' yet again.

'Is this Anna?' the voice says, and I glance at the clock, hoping the call won't take long. I want to finish this paper and make a break for the door.

'Yes, it is. Can I help?'

'This is Grace Lewis,' the voice says. The name sounds familiar – I run my mind's eye over the class list, then shake my head. I haven't a hope in hell of remembering which section she's in.

'I'm sorry,' I say. 'Can you tell me your class?'

'No, no, sorry. I'm not in a class of yours.'

'Oh.' I'm stopped short at that one. 'Well, can you tell me why you're calling?'

'I'm Mark's niece,' she says.

My heart stops beating and everything inside me freezes. Oh my God. *Grace Lewis.* I don't know why I didn't twig at the surname. I guess it's because Mark feels so far removed from me – so far from my life now. And . . . since when does Mark have a *niece*?

'Grace,' I say, as my mind furiously scrabbles to produce anything to say. 'Hi.' I take a breath and try to control my heart rate, which seems to have gone into overdrive. I don't know what to do – I don't know what to say. Has Mark asked her to call? Is he okay? What does he want? And why might he want to get in touch now after everything he's put me through? A million questions flash through my head, but I'm not sure I want to ask any of them. I'm not sure I want to know the answers.

'Can you come and see Mark?' she asks, cutting through the silence.

'Has he *asked* you to call me?' My pen taps furiously on the paper in front of me as my head spins.

The line goes quiet and I let out my breath as I realise he hasn't. I guess it's easy enough to find me if you know my name. One Google search will bring up where I work, and from there you can track me down quickly.

'No,' she says, then she pauses. 'But, Anna . . . well, the chemo isn't working, and . . .' Her voice shakes. 'He only has a little time left. Please, just come and see him. *Please.*'

A little time left? My chest tightens, like someone has clamped a band around it, and the corners of my vision darken as if my world is closing in. Mark is . . . dying? His pale, drawn face flashes into my mind, along with Richard's words that, whatever he has, it must be serious. I knew there was a chance Richard was right, of course, but I didn't want to think about it. I couldn't think about it.

But now . . . now I know. Mark won't live, with or without me. In another few months – maybe this time next year – Mark won't be here. I try to breathe through the sadness and pain hammering at my heart, questions flying through my mind. Should I tell him about our child? Would he want to know before he dies? I wince at the word, hardly able to get my head around it. Or would he want me to leave him alone now, once and for all?

Can I leave him alone, knowing I'll never see him again – knowing I'll never see my husband alive? My gut twists and I swallow back the bile that's building in my throat.

'It's not that easy,' I answer, pain slicing through me as I remember Mark saying that he was going to leave me anyway. Would I go there only to be pushed away again? 'It's—'

'Complicated?' she fills in before I can continue. 'Mark said that, too.'

I let out a low laugh and shake my head. After all this time – after everything – we're actually on the same page.

'I don't know, Grace,' I say finally. 'I just . . . don't know.' I pause for a second, wanting to explain, but I don't even know where to begin.

'Well, he's at his dad's house in Berkhamsted,' she says, and I nod, surprised but relieved that he's there and not alone. 'Come soon, okay? They . . . they don't know how long he has. I'd better go.' And then the phone goes dead before I can say another word.

I sit in my office until the cleaner starts sweeping the hallway outside. I can't move – can't propel myself from this moment in time. My husband – because he *is* still my husband, no matter how far away he feels – is dying. *Will* die, in a matter of days or weeks, if what Grace says is true. I knew it was a possibility, but now that it's a certainty it's shaken me to my core. So many questions still lie between us – so many things are still unexplained. Like did he ever love me . . . ? And, of course, there's the baby, *our* baby. I've tried so hard to push all of that down and get on with living, but am I really going to let him go without a chance to talk? Will he *give* me a chance to talk this time?

The questions hammer my skull as I take the Tube back home and interrupt my sleep all night. I'm plagued by visions of Mark calling for me, of me reaching out to him, then him turning away. In the morning there are bags under my eyes, and I trudge through the following day like a zombie.

'What the hell is up with you?' Sophie asks as I slump over her kitchen table that evening. I'm on babysitting duty and she's getting ready for yet another non-date with Tim.

I jerk up and wipe my face. I think I actually drifted off for a bit there. 'Oh, sorry.' I don't think I slept more than a couple of hours last night. 'Well . . .' I sit upright in the chair, willing my eyes to stay open. I know what Sophie thinks about Mark – she couldn't have been clearer on that point – but I need to get this out, as if saying the words will help give me the same clarity. 'I got a phone call yesterday afternoon,' I say. 'From Grace Lewis, Mark's niece.'

'Who?' Sophie raises an eyebrow. 'Mark has a niece?'

'Margo must have had a baby at some point,' I say, realising yet again that there's still so much I don't know. Will I ever find out? Do I *want* to? 'Grace asked me to come and see Mark. Apparently he hasn't much time left.' I shake my head, still unable to believe it.

'*Wow*,' Sophie says, reaching out to touch my hand. 'And so . . . what did you say?'

'I told her I don't know.' I press my hands to my head, trying in vain to reduce the pounding. 'I know what you think, but Mark is dying. Things are over between us, but this . . . this really is the end.' I swallow hard against the emotions rising in me and glance up at my sister. 'But then it's not like he asked me to come, you know? If he really wanted to see me he would have called me himself. And I just don't know if I can take him rejecting me again.'

Sophie's eyes slide away from me and she bites her lip. 'Actually, Anna . . . Mark did try to see you.'

My breath catches in my throat. 'What do you mean?'

'He rang me up a few weeks ago. He was at the flat and you weren't there. He wanted to know if you were with me or where he could find you.' She swallows. 'He said he'd only just learned about the baby.'

I stare at her, my mouth falling open. Mark came by the flat? But why? And how on earth did he learn about the baby?

'So what did you say?' I ask slowly.

'Well . . .' Sophie's face tightens and her leg starts jiggling. 'I told him that you were happy and that the baby was fine, although you'd had some bleeding, but that he shouldn't upset you. And he shouldn't get in touch again.' She winces. 'I'd no idea he was so ill – he never said. I'm sorry, Anna. I guess I should have told you, but I couldn't bear to watch you go through any more with him.'

I nod, trying to absorb her words. Mark came to find me, after all – after leaving me, after slamming the door in my face, after throwing such terrible words at me. He *did* care that I was having our baby, so much that he stayed away to make sure we were safe . . . even though he was dying.

'It's all right,' I say to Sophie, who's watching me anxiously. 'I know you were trying to protect me. But you don't need to any more. No one does.' I take a deep breath. 'I need to see him.' After everything that's happened, I don't know what's left between us – if there even is an 'us' any more. But I do know our journey together isn't over – not yet. I need to tell him about our baby face to face and to let him know we're all right. At the very least he deserves that much . . . and so do I. That horrific night at the B & B can't be the last time I see him. I won't let it be my final memory of him.

Sophie nods, reaching out to take my hand. I almost expect her to dissuade me, but instead she tells me to go now – she'll stay in tonight – and to call if I need her.

I feel almost numb as I pull on the baggy coat I bought to cover my growing bump. I make my way to the Tube, then on to the train at Euston. For the first time since he left I know exactly where my husband is, but I'm not sure who I'll find when I see him. A guarded, silent man holding on to his secrets to the end and still unable to let me in? Or the man who reached out to me and his child, who took a step towards us . . . towards life?

Berkhamsted station is buzzing when I arrive, packed with commuters hurrying home. I step off the train and follow the route that's burned into my memory towards Richard's house. I picture all of the kids piled on the sofa watching night-time telly, their giggles and shrieks echoing through the house, with Mark pride of place in the centre of the chaos. He would love that . . . or would he? I sigh as doubt pricks me yet again. I should be used to that now, but I lived our whole marriage in such certainty that sometimes the doubt still surprises me.

The large house comes into view and I slow my pace. I stare up at the windows, every muscle tight with tension. My husband is inside this building . . . my husband who has done everything possible to cut me off. I think of the time he blanked me at the cancer centre and how he shoved me away at the B & B. Am I totally crazy to come here now? To open myself up to more hurt and pain after I've managed to pull myself together again?

No, I tell myself. Because this time I'm not doing it just for him. I'm doing it for me, too – for me, and for my baby . . . to have a chance at peace in our lives, at resolution. And whatever lies in front of me, I'm strong enough now to face it.

I walk up the pathway and bang the knocker on the door, trying my best to breathe and stay calm.

'Anna!' Jude swings open the door and I almost take a step backwards. Her friendly face is drawn with dark circles under her eyes. 'What are you doing here? Did Mark call you?' She beckons me inside.

I shake my head. 'No,' I say, stepping gingerly into the warm house in case Mark senses my presence and chucks me out. 'Grace did.' In the background I can hear the drone of the telly and the chatter of voices.

'*Grace?*' Jude raises her eyebrows.

'Yes. She told me . . .' I gulp in air. 'She told me that Mark might not have long. Is that true?'

Jude heaves a sigh and runs a hand across her face. 'Yes. It is. He's really been declining these past few days. Richard was debating whether or not to call you, I think. He didn't want to cause you more pain, but he thought you should know.'

I nod, brushing aside her words. I did wonder why Richard never got in touch after that night at the cancer centre, but then I never called him either. Anyway, it's not important now. 'Is Mark here? Can I see him?' I bite my lip, wondering if Jude will tell me he's banned me from visiting.

Jude nods and beckons me up the stairs. 'He might still be sleeping – he does a lot of that lately. But you can sit with him until he wakes up.'

'Should you . . . ?' I swallow. 'Do you want to check if he's okay with seeing me?' If he really is that ill, then the last thing I want to do is upset him.

Jude puts a hand on my arm and smiles. 'Anna, I don't know everything that's happened between you two – why you've been apart until now. But I do know one thing: Mark loves you. Come on.'

My eyes tear up as I follow her up the stairs and down a corridor. Is she right? Does he love me – still? Is it even possible for us to come together now after so much pain?

The door is half shut and a soft glow comes from inside the room. I can hear a girl's voice reading something aloud and I instantly recognise it as Grace's. I smile as the words from *Jane Eyre*, our favourite Brontë book, drift towards me.

'I think he's just gone to sleep,' Grace whispers as Jude nudges open the door. She slides off a chair in the corner and comes out into the corridor. Even in the dim light her resemblance to Mark is striking, despite the ginger hair and freckles. She catches sight of me and breaks out into a grin. 'Are you Anna?'

'Yes.' I can't help returning the smile in spite of the emotions swirling inside me.

'I knew you'd come,' she says, throwing her arms around me. 'Mark's going to be so happy.'

I return her hug, fervently hoping she's right. 'Thank you for calling me, Grace.' If it hadn't been for her . . . I shudder, thinking that I may never have seen my husband again.

Mark stirs in the bed and Jude takes Grace's arm. 'Let's let them have some time together, okay? Anna, you are more than welcome to spend the night . . . or however long you want to stay, actually. You're family, too.'

I nod, my heart swelling at her kindness. 'Thank you.'

The door closes and I make my way across the room and shrug off my jacket, sinking on to a chair. Mark's eyes are closed and his head is tipped towards the light. I catch my breath, a tear streaking down my cheek as I take him in. His skin is chalky white and air wheezes in and out of his lungs. A ragged beard covers his chin and his hair is thin and wispy. He looks like he's aged about ten years in the few months since he left me and I swallow back the sobs clamouring to escape.

I reach out to take his limp hand and my heart squeezes as I notice something glinting on his finger.

My husband is still wearing his wedding ring.

Maybe it doesn't mean anything – maybe he forgot to take it off, or maybe it's stuck on there – but I can't help feeling that it's there for a reason, and that whatever he said, he hasn't abandoned me – abandoned us – after all. My eyes sink closed and I wait for my husband to wake up.

To open his eyes and to talk.

CHAPTER FORTY-TWO

Mark

The house is quiet when I awaken, but I can sense someone beside me. I hope it's not Grace; it's way too late for her to be up on a school night and lately she's got in the habit of falling asleep by my bed, as if she's afraid I might not be here in the morning. Jude and I do everything we can to shoo her off and into her own room. I have to admit I enjoy the company, though.

I turn towards the chair and my eyes pop as surprise jolts me. It's Anna, right there in front of me, her eyes closed and her chest rising and falling in deep sleep. For a second I think I'm dreaming . . . I've been dreaming about my wife so much lately, as if my subconscious is dying to spend more time with her before shutting down. Have I conjured her up here somehow? I don't want to move in case she disappears, so I just stare: dark lashes against her cheeks, the puff of air lifting those flyaway strands from the fringe she's forever pushing away, her breasts moving up and down with every breath.

Slowly I reach out to touch her – to feel her. I can only reach her leg, which radiates warmth beneath my fingers. Her eyelids flutter open.

'Hi,' I say, smiling as she blinks awake in the way I know so well. Love swells through me and I long to feel her in my arms.

'Hi.' Her fingers clasp mine and she meets my gaze. Silence swirls around us, filled with so many unasked questions. How did she find me here? Why did she come? Is the baby all right? And there's so much I want to say, too, like I'm sorry. I'm sorry for the awful words I threw at her, turning away as she crumbled – that even though I was trying to protect her, I was wrong. I'm not the cruel, harsh man I forced myself to become out of love . . . and fear. Fear of damaging her – damaging me. And although I did try to piece us back together, I should have tried sooner.

It's so very tempting to stay silent, in the middle of the night with no one else here but us; to remain suspended in this moment where nothing can touch us – no problems, no troubles, no past. But I can't, because even if I wasn't ill, I don't want anything to come between us.

I try to sit up, to move closer to my wife, but my muscles fail me and I have to lie back down again. The chair creaks as Anna gets up and I open my mouth to tell her not to go. But before I can she sits down next to me on the bed. I meet her eyes and reach out to take her hands, knowing that now I need to tell her everything. I don't know where to start but, for once, I'm desperate to talk.

'Anna, I'm sorry.' Three simple words leave my mouth – words that will never be enough for the pain I've caused. Guilt and regret wash over me as I meet my wife's eyes. I thought I was saving her – saving us – from a world of pain. Instead I tore us apart so brutally it's a wonder we're still breathing.

It's too late to go back and change all that. She's removed her wedding ring – her finger is still bare – but it's not too late to make her understand. I draw in a breath, struggling to fill my lungs. Damn this disease.

She catches me looking at her bare ring finger and shakes her head.

'I had to take it off,' Anna says. 'I had to try to move on – to make a new life, for our baby as much as for me.' She meets my eyes. 'And I was so, so angry. Angry that you never told me about your past when I thought I knew everything. Angry that you just took *off*. And all those things you said . . .' A tear slips down her cheek and my heart shatters into a million pieces as guilt grips me once again. 'They were just awful.'

'I'm sorry,' I say again. 'You know I didn't mean them, right?' I stare hard at her, as if I can show her just how much those words weren't true. 'I was just . . . trying to stop you from witnessing *this*.' I gesture to my swollen body, my old-man face, even the bedpan in the corner. This is my reality, and I need to share it with her now – to bring her into my world.

'And I did try to find you,' I say, anxious for her to know that I tried to set us on the right path – that I recognised how wrong I was. 'I went to the flat as soon as I found out about the baby, but you weren't there. I called Sophie and she told me you had some bleeding and it was best I stayed away. I didn't want to do anything to jeopardise our child, so I planned to wait until the pregnancy was further along.' I eye her belly, thinking that even underneath her heavy sweater I can just about make out a bump. 'So . . . *is* everything okay . . . with you and the baby?' I glance up at her, holding my breath as she slowly nods her head.

'Yes,' she says, and I can feel a smile growing on my face. 'Yes, everything is fine.'

Happiness bursts inside of me . . . happiness mixed with an incredibly sharp sadness, because I know I won't be there to see this child. I won't be around to make sure the baby is okay – I won't be able to protect it from the world. But I know I'm not abandoning him or her, unlike how I felt with Grace. This time the baby will be surrounded by a wonderful family, with the best mother ever – the *strongest* mother ever.

Silence falls, and I reach out and take my wife's hand, praying she doesn't move away from me. I curl my fingers around hers, with hope building as she squeezes back. I take a deep breath, knowing that if I want my wife to fully understand why I left, I need to start from the beginning – to tell her everything from my past, no matter how painful. I don't know if it will bring her back to me for whatever of my future remains or if it will push her away, but I need to let her into that darkest part of me.

'I need to tell you about Margo – my sister.' My voice cracks. 'And I need to tell you about Grace.'

And as the night turns into day, with my family around me, the words spill from my mouth. I can't change what has happened between us, but from this moment on, my soul is laid bare – my past exposed, my heart open.

Ready for my wife, if she still wants me.

CHAPTER FORTY-THREE

Anna

When I open my eyes the next morning I'm not sure where I am. All I can feel is Mark's arms wrapped around me; all I can hear is the rasp of his breath in my ear. Am I back home, in our old flat? I stare up at the ceiling as children's voices pierce the air, and the knowledge filters in: I'm at Richard's house after Grace's call from the day before yesterday.

My eyelids sink closed as Mark's words float through my mind, words about Margo . . . Grace . . . and trying to find her again. I knew about Margo, of course, but I'd no idea that Margo had had a child, or that Richard had adopted her. Mark hadn't known about the adoption either, and I suppose that's why Richard never said anything to me about it.

I'll always wish Mark had told me about his past earlier – that he'd shared it with me from the start. Perhaps I could have helped him; perhaps we'd have had the strength to make it through the past few months without Mark tearing us apart. I realise now how much it hurt him, too, and my eyes fill with tears of pain and regret for us both.

Mark's eyes slowly open and he smiles over at me. I reach over and touch his forehead, smoothing out those wrinkles once again. Then I run my fingers through the wiry bristles of his beard.

'Do you like it?' he asks, laughing when I say it would look better on a grizzly bear. He takes my hand and draws me in closer, until I'm right up against the heat of his body. I can feel his bones through the thin fabric of his pyjamas, but he's as warm as ever. It radiates through to the very core of me . . . right to our child.

Mark's hand slides down to my bump, his fingers cupping the taut skin. 'I still can't believe you're having a baby. *We're* having a baby.' He shakes his head, his eyes filled with wonder and tenderness. Then his face tightens, and his arms pull me in even closer, as if he's trying to burrow into the heart of me. 'Anna . . .' My name emerges from his lips in an anguished sigh. 'I wish I could be there for you when this baby is born – to see you become a mother, and for us to be a family. I can't tell you how much. I couldn't even *begin* to tell you how much.' Tears fill his eyes, spilling over and tracing a path down his thin cheeks and disappearing into his bristles. He lets them fall with no shame or embarrassment, holding my gaze without turning away.

A sob tears at my chest and I rest my head in the crook of his arm, reaching up to wipe away his tears. I've never seen Mark cry – not once in our ten years together. My husband may have struggled with his sorrow, but there was also a lot of happiness and joy between us. Now, after all this time, it really does feel like we've nothing to hide. Not fear, not pain, not sadness.

'Me, too,' I say, my own eyes starting to fill. 'You really would be the greatest father ever.' Grief pulls at me so strongly I can barely stand it.

Mark smiles through the tears still streaking down his cheeks. 'I'd like to think I would be. I've certainly got the skills down pat. Okay, maybe I'm not the world's best footballer' – I nod, remembering the time Flora asked Mark to teach her how to play and he ended up on his arse – 'but I could learn. And I've got styling Barbie's hair down to a fine art.'

'Well, there you go,' I say, grinning despite the pain inside. God, I've missed our bedtime chats. I roll away from him slightly so I can see his face better. 'But Mark . . . there's still a chance you might make it, right? Just another few months?' I can't help asking, even though I know that chance is very slim.

'Anything is possible.' Mark's face is serious. 'But I probably have weeks, not months.' He draws in a raggedy breath. 'No matter what, though, I hope you know that I love you. I love you *both*.' He shakes his head. 'I wish I hadn't wasted time, leaving you like that. I wish—'

I put a finger over his mouth and nestle against him again. He's right: we've squandered enough time, and I don't want to waste any more lingering on regrets.

What matters now is that we do have a chance, however long it may be, to be together – in a marriage that's been battered and bruised, but is still together . . . still together because of love. That's what brought us back to each other in the end.

And that's what will keep us strong through the difficult days ahead.

CHAPTER FORTY-FOUR

Mark
One month later

My physical world has shrunk to the four walls of this bedroom. I know every inch of the ceiling – I can trace every crack in the plaster with my eyes closed. I haven't left the room in weeks . . . and I know I may not again. Because with each day that passes, my body is protesting the struggle to live. Despite hardly eating, my belly is swollen, like *I'm* the pregnant one, while my limbs have shrunk. I haven't looked in a mirror, but my skin feels papery and thin, my cheekbones hard. When Anna washes me, it feels like the sponge will rub straight through my skin.

And the pain. Oh, the pain, it wraps itself around my mind, my body like a vice, squeezing and twisting and making me call out. Thank God for morphine. Thank God for drugs.

But while my physical world has shrunk, inside I feel like I've expanded. There are people around me, people I love. My father and his family, Grace and, of course, Anna and my son.

Because we know now that we're having a son. My father used his medical connections to bring a mobile ultrasound here – along with a sonographer – since I'm in no state to leave the house. Just seeing my child bobbing happily in his mother's stomach brought tears to my eyes, even more so when the sonographer happily informed us we were having a boy. I didn't care either way, and I don't think Anna did either, but just knowing makes me feel closer to this child . . . this child I'll never see.

A knock on the door interrupts my thoughts. 'Come in!'

Grace enters the room holding a pen and paper. 'Ready for some more?' she asks.

I nod, and she sinks on to the chair beside the bed. Anna's gone off for her daily afternoon walk around the town to get some much-needed fresh air, and Grace and I have been using this time to write letters: two letters, to be precise. One to my son, telling him all about me and how much I love him.

And another to my wife.

But this time the letter to Anna isn't trying to explain why I had to leave her, driven by a mad urge to make her see that I'm not that terrible man. This time it's a love letter – to her, to us and to the strength I see in her every day . . . from going to her antenatal appointments alone to sitting by my side for hours. The strength I don't understand how I missed and the strength that will get her through everything after I'm gone. I know she'll have plenty of people around her, from Sophie to my father, but I also know that she'll be fine on her own, too.

It's getting harder and harder to find the right words – my brain is foggy and unclear. But Grace sits patiently as I form the sentences, craft the thoughts that will embrace my wife when I can't. And then, when we get to the end – when there's nothing more to say – I ask my niece to sign off with 'love, Mark', and I close my eyes.

I'm not seeing darkness though.

I'm seeing light.

CHAPTER FORTY-FIVE

Anna
One year later

Sunlight streams from the sky and the spicy scent of cut grass floats through the air as I make my way up the steep hill in Hampstead Heath. Thanks to my daily walks through the park I've managed to shed any lingering baby weight and get fit again – I'm not even puffing when I reach the top, despite the chubby eight-month-old in my arms.

I pause to kiss the fuzzy top of my son's head, breathing in his fresh, clean scent. It's been a difficult year since Mark died, a year full of conflicting emotions that I still don't know how to reconcile. Watching my husband fade – seeing him so very ill – was incredibly painful, and those memories will stay with me forever. But above all that, what I'll remember is not grief or despair, but love: how he squeezed my hand, and the tender way he looked at me when even clutching my fingers took too much energy. We didn't need words; we didn't need actions. We had each other and that was enough.

In those last few weeks the two of us were cocooned together, but it was a different kind of isolation from what we'd had during our marriage. This time we weren't trying to protect our relationship, as if one false move would hijack our happiness. This time we were fully aware of what might lie ahead: the harsh reality of life . . . and death. We talked for hours when Mark still could about the future and my fear of raising a child alone – about how I would cope without my husband. We cried together, too . . . at what our child will miss, what we would miss. And, of course, Mark told me more about Margo. He told me so much that I feel like I know her now as well.

When I let go of his hand on the day his life ended, I knew I'd always be grateful for the extra time we had – even if I did wish it had been longer. For after all our years together, Mark and I finally had a real relationship, the kind that can exist only when you are brave enough to embrace the darkness as well as light. A love that will persevere – that *can* persevere, despite everything. Through us, and through our son.

Matthew has brought me so much joy – brought Richard and his family so much joy – when the sadness and pain in the aftermath of Mark's death threatened to overwhelm us. When I went into labour during one of the wettest Julys on record, Richard was the second person I called after Sophie, and he and the whole family braved the flooded roads to wait at the hospital in Hampstead. I'll never forget the look of tenderness and awe on Richard's face when I placed the baby in his arms.

He and Jude, as well as Sophie, have been by my side ever since Matthew was born, and Grace and Flora are itching to babysit. Even my parents have taken up residence at a caravan site just outside London, popping by to visit their grandson frequently. Mark would have loved to see how this baby has drawn us all together.

I sink on to the grass and set Matthew down, smiling as he tries so hard to crawl over to a dandelion and fails, falling over on to his side. I set him upright again then reach into my pocket and draw out a letter . . . a letter Mark gave me, to be opened after he died. When he first passed away I wanted to rip it open then and there, desperate for anything to connect us. But something told me to wait until the pain had dulled, until I could really savour the words . . . and until I felt strong enough to face them without dissolving into grief – to match the strength he had at the end.

And now, after a year has passed, I tear open the envelope and slide out the pages. I recognise Grace's wide and loopy handwriting instantly, and I smile just picturing the two of them working together on this. The fact that Mark was so open and willing to share his feelings makes this letter even more special.

> *Dear Anna,*
> *This isn't a letter to say goodbye; a letter to leave you. I've done enough leaving these past few months.*

Tears fill my eyes as I picture the two of us seeking each other out then turning away again. Mark was right: we'd both done more than enough leaving to last us a lifetime. *Our* lifetime. Sadness twists inside me that it's over now.

> *When I die, I won't be gone. It's simply my body that's stopped working, but the part of me that's important – my love for you and our son; our hopes and dreams for the future – will always be there. That can't be taken away, can't be changed, no matter what happens to me. That will bind us together, forever.*

Tears drip down my cheeks as I scan the rest of the words that are full of love and joy, of admiration for my own strength. I reach out to take our son in my arms, hugging his warm, chubby body close to mine. My world is now a messy mix of joy and pain, but that's what real life is, I guess. Nothing exists in a vacuum – no emotion, no marriage. Life *is* complicated, like we both said so long ago. But it's also easy, too . . . when you open yourself up to it.

I get to my feet and gather up my son, both of us gazing at the city spread out beneath us.

'Come on,' I say, not sure if I'm talking to myself or to him. 'Let's get going.' Then I head down the hill and into the world below.

ACKNOWLEDGMENTS

A big thank you to everyone at Amazon Publishing for their continued support: Emilie Marneur, Sammia Hamer, Sana Chebaro and Bekah Graham have all been wonderful throughout the past few years. I couldn't ask for a better team of people to have around me! I owe huge thanks to my agent, Madeleine Milburn, who has read multiple drafts of this project, and to my editor, Sophie Wilson, whose encouragement and thoughtful input have been instrumental in shaping this into a book I'm proud of.

And, as always, to my husband: thank you – for being there and for bringing coffee. And to my son: thanks for sitting on my lap and providing lots of cuddles in the early morning and at night. I love you both.

ABOUT THE AUTHOR

Leah Mercer was born in Halifax, Nova Scotia, on the east coast of Canada. By the age of thirteen, she'd finished her first novel and received very encouraging rejections from publishers.

Leah put writing on hold to focus on athletics, achieving provincial records and becoming a Canadian university champion in the 4 × 400-metre relay. After getting her BA, she turned to writing again, earning a masters in journalism. A few years later she left Canada and settled in London, where she now lives with her husband and their young son.

Leah also writes under the name Talli Roland, and her books have been shortlisted at the UK's Festival of Romance.